Beyond Misty Mountain

by

Stephen Howard

Contents

Prologue

Light years from our own Milky Way there is another galaxy, a tiny and unambitious one in comparison, with only one planet.

This planet is called Torvacane.

Torvacane is peculiar. It has four criss-crossing rings that are visible only at night, radiating an ethereal silver light, clear against the opaque night sky. They are the kind of natural phenomenon that philosophers and scientists alike speculate over without ever coming to any sound conclusion, simply tossing about the word *theory* in an almost reckless fashion.

Torvacane is a somewhat aggressive planet that roams its galaxy patrolling the edges in order to remain alone, the singular planet in its minute star system. Torvacane could do with a girlfriend.

There are infinite galaxies in the universe – it's something to do with oscillating – and they all co-exist side by side; or on top of each other; perhaps below each other. It's a confusing family out there, but if there was to be a proverbial black sheep, it would be Torvacane.

It was created by its one and only god and He is called Son. He created the planet with its four vivid rings in order to travel the universe. Son, having grown bored of other gods' creations, put His own twist on zoology, geology, and pretty much any *ology* He could get His hands on during Torvacane's gestation. All this tinkering with the accepted templates left Torvacane unruly and unstable, so Son had to confine it to its own small star system which, as previously mentioned, it patrols malevolently.

You should consider Torvacane less a planet and more a badly behaved puppy.

It has its own small sun and moon which orbit the planet, attempting to supervise it, but generally failing miserably. It is difficult enough to maintain orbit around a planet with the attention span of a rabbit on fire, let alone teach it any manners.

Gods, as in popular mythology, live atop impressive mountains that break through the cloudbank, stretching toward the stars. Son wasn't much of a traditionalist. He felt it was rather too much effort climbing up and down a giant mountain, so He lives atop a hill. Val Hilla sits amongst the waves of a malicious whirlpool in a remote part of the Asthmatic Ocean, unreachable to none but the pure of heart, or so the legends say. Son doesn't often get visitors, yet somehow His post arrives every morning. There are some things that escape even deities.

There are many territories, (un)discovered continents, arid deserts and murky rainforests on Torvacane. It can be a dangerous place to be unless you're handy with a sword, a mace, a knife, or at least have a good turn of pace.

There is a continent named Seven Cities which, unsurprisingly, contains Seven Cities, and it exists in fragile peace. Peace is often fragile, such is the human tendency for self-destruction, and there is a hand hovering over the metaphorical big red button of Torvacane once more.

Seven Cities was once magnificent but vast areas were decimated during the last great war. Desolate swathes of land fill the map and city centres remain undeveloped. The scaffolding business has been booming. The rebuilding has been a long and slow process in some cases, petty squabbling grinding it down to the point of inertia. Yet for others it has moved on smoothly enough.

The war remains fresh in the minds of the people of Seven Cities, its scars plain upon the face of the land. Half a century on lessons that were learned have been quickly forgotten. Peace occupies the gap between inevitable conflict.

History doesn't repeat itself. At least, it doesn't repeat itself on purpose. It's just forgetful sometimes.

The Seven Cities are named Broth Zolust, Slotopia, Gredavia, Rathendy, Vertenve, Totulgny and Athea Hubris. Athea Hubris is the traditional head of Seven Cities and is the only city with a leader who may call himself king. Naturally, the title alone is enough to inflate the self-importance of its incumbent. Each other city is headed by a steward. The difference is essentially semantic, but tradition is tradition, and tradition is often silly.

This world isn't prepared for another catastrophe. It cannot cope. The spirit of its people has suffered enough and they're getting quite sick of being miserable. They aren't all lead singers.

Beyond Misty Mountain

The city of Broth Zolust is a bit of a hole, a cesspit of debauchery. But to the people of Broth Zolust, it's their hole, their cesspit. The unscrupulous nature of business activity within the city is a point of pride for many of its denizens. It would be wiser to strike a deal with the devil than enter into an agreement with Alcap Noe around the back of The Flying Mace. They are usually the kind of agreement you enter but never exit.

The city paving is stained black and brown, the houses all battered wooden beams and loosely tiled roofs. The streets splinter into dark alleys like gaping jaws ready to snap. Some of them audibly snarl.

One of the few landmarks of note is the market. Row upon row of stalls with makeshift roofs owned by vendors selling you items that they probably stole from you in the first place. Each morning the air is littered with cries from shifty entrepreneurs advertising whatever they got their hands on the previous evening.

And all the time the air is musty, a pungent aroma creeping up and down the streets like a beleaguered sentry. The bin men have been on strike ever since they learned about unions. Sadly, they'd never learned the art of negotiation.

There is a deplorably lascivious mile of road running through the centre of the city that accounts for the majority of its custom and it is called he Boulevard. Each establishment along the Boulevard is the embodiment of depravation which, naturally, makes it a popular tourist attraction.

Toward the end of the strip, within sight of the city limits (a poorly constructed fence designed to keep out small horses and assorted insects), is an unassuming little pub with a wonky door called the Parallelogram. A strange name for a pub, you might think, but you don't get too many rowdy sorts drinking in places they can't pronounce. That's solid Zolustian logic right there.

The Parallelogram was a bit hazy. Most of its regular clientele were heavy smokers, so you couldn't really see the ceiling for the thick mushroom cloud hovering below it. It was much like someone had nuked one of the tables.

It was a small pub with framed landscape paintings adorning the walls. The bar was set into an alcove to the right side and was surrounded by rickety stools. It looked like someone had tried really hard to make the interior look friendly and warm, probably to detract from the toxicity of the air and the savage charm of its inhabitants.

Behind the bar stood a man with a face that resembled a raisin. Dark-skinned and slightly crumpled looking, he was the proprietor of the Parallelogram. Responsible for contriving to make the place look respectable and distributing the strong, cloudy, and appropriately named ale called Grog (which came from the one tap connected to the one, admittedly large, barrel in the cellar), his name was Largo.

Largo enjoyed a good rapport with his customers because he didn't ask too many questions and wasn't choosy about who he let in. This particular pub was a favourite haunt for the type of man who once led an extravagant adventuring lifestyle, but was now a bit too old and grey to travel long distances without aggravating a hip or trick knee.

If you want to hear a good story, you buy anyone in the Parallelogram a drink. They own a lot of t-shirts.

The upside of this was trouble rarely found Largo's quaint little pub. If it did then its occupants would exercise their fondness for swinging blunt and/or sharp instruments in a carefree yet unerringly accurate manner.

To annoy such people would be like pinching an old lion. Sure, it's old, but it's still a lion.

Sat at the bar was a man much younger than most in the Parallelogram, barely old enough to be referred to as a man, and he was vociferously telling a story of heroic deeds and great treasures to two older men who appeared not in the least bit interested.

"It was an ogre when he came at me, but it was a cyclops when I was through with him." Drago came to the end of what he felt was an impressive sounding anecdote and took a deep swig from his glass. The spluttering and streaming eyes that followed seemed less impressive. The insipid expressions on the faces of Caine and Korin remained unchanged.

They were used to Drago's stories. They were also accustomed to hearing the same stories with the details skewed, exacerbated to the point where everything is bigger and has more eyes and tentacles. They daren't encourage him by feigning any sort of interest.

"I'd wager ya've never even lifted that there sword of yours above ya 'ead sonny." Caine had always been like that, direct and to the point. And it was your lucky day if it was only his words he was pointing at you.

"I bloody well have," Drago half said, half hiccupped as he slid a little on his stool.

"Two glasses and 'e's slumped. If 'e single-'andedly looted the vampire town of Dara'koola I'll buy meself an 'at and eat it." Caine would often judge a man's character on the strength of his stomach and the number of empty glasses on his table. Drago had failed spectacularly on both fronts.

"Well you will insist on popping a drop of fire whisky into his drink when he starts jumping around pretending to fight goblins," retorted Korin, hardly trying to disguise his amusement. The younger man had now settled his head onto a pillow of spilled Grog on the bar.

Turning disdainfully from the slumped Drago, Caine became serious, once more seeking an answer to his proposition.

"Well?" Caine said leaning forward, an expectant gaze fixed upon an uneasy Korin. He knew instantly what the new topic was. This was a topic Caine had pestered him about for a few days now. And Caine wasn't one for letting things go. He'd rather hold onto them until they went rotten and started to smell.

Korin exhaled slowly and deliberately.

"I just want to get this straight before committing to a definite answer," said Korin, uncomfortable in the knowledge he would swiftly concede. Korin hated when things started to smell.

"Hundreds of miles with untold horrors between us and our quarry, thousands of soldiers within the city, not to mention any other means they've used to protect it. And your plan is to march on in there and steal all of it?"

"Well, not all of it. Jus' most of it."

"And you're going to go whether I say yes or not?"

"Yep."

"Guess I don't have much of a choice then, do I?"

"Nope, 'twas inevitable." The hint of relief in Caine's voice said otherwise. But he now broke out into what would have been a toothy grin if it weren't for spacious gaps between his few remaining teeth.

Korin looked a little more contemplative. They were going to need a plan, and a very good one too, otherwise they'd be killed instantly. Or more likely slowly and painfully by the king's torturers. Korin hated torturers, they were just so earnest.

Alternatively, he also knew it was futile to plan anything at all as Caine always contrived to drive them hopelessly off course. Anyway, he was bored, so this seemed like a reasonable source of fun. It had been quite some time since they'd ventured outside Broth Zolust or, as it happened, the pub. They needed to stretch their legs, take in the mountain air, and build up a new Grog fund.

Korin had never considered it a difficult line of work. Dismiss a grave warning and tread foolishly here, blaspheme a little there, and occasionally punch a holy man in the face and steal his sceptre. And also remember to carry an extra looting bag around with you in case you were feeling spontaneous.

Whilst Caine and Korin had reached an agreement, Drago had drifted off, muttering something about it being three glasses of ale and not two. Despite being prostrate along the bar he'd overheard enough to know they were readying for an adventure. At least, Drago would remember this the following morning.

This was the sort of caper Drago bragged about having but never really had. He could only dream and wonder whether he'd ever do anything daring or brave or utterly daft.

Well, possibly the latter.

***

The wind howled as the gate slammed against its hinges at the foot of a garden path. This garden path lead to what was once a picturesque cottage, but now the grass and rose bushes were overgrown and the cottage worn. Moss crawled up the white walls like grasping hands. Perched on a cliff overlooking the River Sticks, the plot looked lonely.

Marching up the path was a young woman holding a cloak tightly against her body, recalcitrant against a gale that appeared to be localised within the garden itself.

Golden hair whipped against her face as she continued on until she reached the front door, only to be confronted by an ugly brass door knocker, which she hastily used to rap on the door. The girl retreated when the face on the door knocker became animate and shouted: "Oi, that hurt!"

She steadied herself admirably and knocked again.

The ageing door looked as though it may collapse simply from the force of her knock, but it held firm and then swung open. Standing in the doorway was a lanky man dressed in pale blue pyjamas holding a candle. "I must apologise for the rudeness. Boris is rather unused to people these days."

"Boris?" replied the girl.

"My door knocker," he said as though it were the most natural thing in the world. "Come in."

The girl walked in gratefully and pulled down her

hood to reveal pale but beautiful skin and shoulder-length golden blonde hair that had soaked through at the ends her hood had failed to protect. She strolled through to the room at the end of the plain hallway, a lounge of sorts, and collapsed into a large scarlet armchair.

Quite unperturbed and with the air of someone in the know, the man who had answered the door appeared in the lounge holding a steaming teapot and two mugs.

"Milk and sugar?" he enquired of the dripping wet and tired looking person now occupying his favourite chair. She simply nodded. He poured the drinks and left the room a moment before reappearing holding a towel. What use was a cup of tea if it was diluted by rainwater within five minutes? The girl accepted it and dried her hair and face.

"I've been expecting a visitor, though I was not sure who it would be. My foresight is somewhat limited I am afraid, very rarely anything of importance. The occasional pigeon destined to fly into my window normally, though I sense this visit may be different. I imagine you already know who I am, but I shall introduce myself anyway. I am Vectoracle Sama – you may call me Vector – and I am a wizard. What is your name?" Vector smiled warmly, pleased to have some company that didn't appear to be lost. The person sat across from him may actually have intended to reach him.

The girl was clutching her cup of tea like a mother holds her new-born. She was taking short sips, her eyes darting around the room.

Although not literally. That would be disgusting. Vector tried to refocus.

"I am Amelia, daughter of Emilius Kaio. An old friend of yours, I believe?" She was still shaking from the cold but looked up to gauge his reaction. There was an aura of intensity to her, like she was holding to some disturbed truth. Or perhaps it was the cold. Or both.

Vector observed carefully. He felt he was a good judge of character. At least, he did these days. This was no ordinary girl. You don't travel the distance she has without having strong resolve. And a cause.

He settled himself into his second favourite armchair. This felt like one of those times when a person should be seated. Ideally in one's favourite chair, but we can't have everything in life. He had not heard from Emil in a long time and with good reason. They had been companions and fought together during the war many years ago, but they were dark times, times they had tried to forget. He had most definitely not been expecting his old friend's daughter to arrive. Furthermore, he did not know why.

For the first time in a while, Vector was vexed.

"I am most curious, my dear, what is it that has brought you all this way? Last I knew of Emil he was living by Misty Mountain, just past Vertenve. A hundred miles, I would guess, from here." Attention engrossed in their conversation, Vector failed to notice the tip of his beard sinking into his tea.

A ruined cup of tea is a great waste in a wizard's eyes. All one's greatest thinking is done whilst sipping a nice warm cup of tea.

"I have not seen my father in over three months. He has been kidnapped by the king of Athea Hubris, Edirp."

The wind continued to whirl outside, bustling about like a little old woman with a shopping trolley, unconcerned about anything in its way. The roof sounded like it was rattling.

"My father is old, his magic is no longer strong, but his

knowledge is vast. I fear he is being held captive for something he knows, but it is unlikely he will tell them anything."

Vector found himself staring at the top of a blonde head. He thought he heard a sniffle.

A sadness came over Vector's face too, but also an anger that projected outwards to darken the shadows, to enrage the candle flames to flicker violently (it's a wizard thing).

He had suspected for some time that Athea Hubris may become an issue, a threat to the already unstable relationships between the Seven Cities. Edirp seemed to possess similarities in character to those of an active volcano. In addition to a right earned by the simple nature of his birth and the character flaws this often breeds, there was a history of what was often referred to as 'madness' in his family. Edirp was an accident waiting to happen.

"Yes, sadly I suspect you may be right. Edirp has been present in my thoughts for a while now. I have my spies and they report unusual activity in regards to the rebuilding process, too much time spent on battlements and arms and little investment in the city. Not to mention the mysterious goings on in regard to Misty Mountain. The rumours about significant gold reserves appear now to be completely true."

He felt it best not to mention a further facet to this already sordid business. A man linked to several successful coup attempts beyond the Asthmatic Ocean was now chief adviser to the king. There were so many flies in the ointment it had overflowed and spilled on the carpet.

"Please, Amelia, tell me all you know."

Amelia had risen from her chair, wiped her eyes with the sleeve of her coat and launched into the story of how she came to be in Vector's lounge. She told of how an armed guard had stolen in one night whilst she was away hiking. Her father had often encouraged her to go out and see parts of the surrounding lands, to 'live and learn', he always said.

When she returned their home had been ransacked, windows were broken, cupboards emptied onto the floor. It was a mess. A note, however, had drifted from the ceiling to land in her lap as she sat distraught on the floor of her bedroom. It explained her father's kidnap and who had sent the armed guard. It also urged her to seek out Vectoracle Sama, who lived up on a cliff overlooking the River Sticks, and that it was vital Amelia reach him no matter what. "It said one more thing that I didn't understand," Amelia added. "It said to tell Vector the 'old ways hadn't died out as we'd thought'. The note said nothing more."

Upon hearing this Vector's usual serenity broke. He gasped and spilled his tea. Another serious crime for any wizard, the spilling of tea.

Almost anything to do with tea that didn't involve drinking it was a crime for a wizard.

"But what does that mean?" Amelia attempted to hold Vector's gaze, but the large yawn she let out broke her concentration. Tired as she was from her journey physically, reliving the story of her father's kidnap had drained her mentally too.

"Rest for now, I shall explain tomorrow. I have thinking to do and I expect your journey was most rigorous and tiring." Vector ushered the exhausted but protesting Amelia out of his chair, down the hall, and showed her to the guest bedroom.

"Sleep here my dear. You must rest up and recover your energies. I fear we have many long days ahead of us." At this he blew out all but two of the candles mounted on the walls of the small square room, turned, and left. Amelia thought of arguing, but her journey had indeed been arduous and the bed looked so appealing she felt like proposing instantly. She had barely removed her cloak, jacket and boots before she collapsed onto it and escaped into the welcoming arms of sleep.

Vector lit another candle and settled back into his favourite chair. It was wet with rainwater, but this didn't concern him.

It was impossible, he thought. They were extinct, all destroyed during the war. He leant forward and poured a fresh cup of tea from a teapot that he had levitated across the room, terrifying a spider that had unwittingly crawled onto the handle.

He would often drift off to sleep in his armchair, yet his thoughts were rarely so morose. Tonight, it would be memories that flashed across his rather impressive mind. The memories would be of his youth, a youth marred by recklessness and the war. War was a tame word for the massacres left in the wake of those magnificent, terrifying beasts. He was sure they were extinct though. Reasonably sure at least. He still felt the shame of being party to it, it was why he and Emil had parted ways and drifted into the pages of history. If it were true, and King Edirp truly sought the knowledge of how to utilise them, it could mean the dawn of a new age of fear. They were probably extinct, thought Vector… They could only hope Emil was wrong, that a Dragon Lord had not survived.

***

Morning broke amongst the contours of Broth Zolust's erratic skyline.

The caterwauling of a gang of armed alley cats woke Drago far too early. This initial feeling of irritation soon dissipated once Drago realised the cats had him surrounded and he was lying amongst a pile of bin bags. The circumference of the alley cats' circle decreased and they closed in menacingly on him. Drago's mind could turn surprisingly quickly when dangerous situations (of a sort) arose.

"BARK, WOOF, WOOF. GRRR, BARK, BARK!!"

The cats were caught off guard more than frightened, but at this hesitation Drago leapt up and sprinted down the alley and out into the crowded street. Behind him the leader of the cat gang waved a sharpened carrot around and remonstrated angrily with his charges.

That was a close one, thought Drago, could have sustained some serious cuts and bruises there. Those cats were probably highly skilled in the art of clawing and close quarters combat. Drago slid through gaps amongst the bustling people in Broth Zolust's market street. Cries from street vendors provided the background noise to a typical day in the run-down city.

Despite being intoxicated and groggy (the name truly Grog was apt) for its duration, he'd been listening in on Caine and Korin's conversation. A fire had lit in his gut.

Not the sizeable sort of fire that could burn down a forest, but the sort that could easily light a cigarette. Maybe even a cigar.

An adventure, a quest with danger, heroic deeds, maidens to be saved perhaps, treasures to be relinquished of their ownership. All under the trusty, proficient and capable hands of two veterans, Caine and Korin. What could be safer?

With hindsight Drago would come to realise the answer to this question was 'almost anything'.

This part of the day was often reserved for piecing together the jigsaw of flashbacks that had led to his sleeping amongst the bin bags again. For now, there were more important matters at hand.

Walking home would do him good. The pungent aromas of Broth Zolust were a remarkable hangover cure. There was a rumour that bar owners down the Boulevard prayed to Son asking that he coat the air with headache cures to ensure the people would hit the bars earlier and for longer.

It was a totally unfounded and preposterous rumour, which probably meant it was true.

Drago was an amiable sort with an amiable face. Features ever so slightly too rounded to say he was traditionally handsome, his unkempt hair and brown eyes gave him a boyish look. And he still seemed to be filling out a little. Mixed messages in his brain meant he'd kept shooting up but forgotten to grow out.

This didn't quite add up to grizzled, daring adventurer, nor did a nervous disposition that only faded with the addition of alcohol.

Drago's expectations of the journey he wished to partake in were addled. He had always been quite venturesome, at least as a youthful wanderer, but he'd never felt there was a good time to go and explore the world beyond the reaches of what he already knew (or rather his mother hadn't). Broth Zolust had been his own little bubble of civil unrest.

Drago could saunter down the streets of Broth Zolust with relative ease. He displayed an ability to slip and slide deftly amongst the peoples. The shiny sword swinging by his waist helped too. Around these parts, even the overzealous pickpockets had brains enough to respect a sword sharp enough to remove chest hair at a stroke.

Their respect may have wavered, however, had they ever seen Drago use it.

Resolving to seek out Caine and Korin once he'd packed a few provisions in his satchel, he made for home.

He hurried down a side road between a crumbling old theatre (Now Showing: Closed For Repairs) and the decrepit post office (In Rain Or Sleet On Gloomy Nights, Don't Expect Any Mail). This side road opened up onto a street with two terraces running parallel towards a gruesome building that looked like it had been carved from coal. Drago thought a vampire lived there, although he'd never seen him in the flesh. Not the only one believing this, the muffled aroma of garlic clung to the air. One house had laid a 5oz rump steak upon its welcome mat. It's possible they misheard the neighbourhood watch advice.

Broth Zolust was home to some uncommon creatures as well as people. On Torvacane there were many myths that had forgotten they were not supposed to exist.

And it took a brave person to tell them otherwise.

Drago ran up the road and turned into his house, a rectangular strip cut against the grey terrace masquerading as a home. It was a breezeblock with windows.

Inside there was a staircase to the right of a small claustrophobic hall with coat hooks along the wall. Straight ahead was the kitchen and the lounge to the left. The decor was drab and unimaginative. The walls were painted beige, the floors carpeted beige, and that was about it. There seemed little in the place to make it a home, which explained Drago's tendency to drift off into dreamworld. His reality was as dull as any number of shades of grey.

"That you, Graeme?"

A voice limped from the living room to the hallway carrying these words. The voice belonged to his mother. She was a squat woman, dressed mostly in bright shawls. She looked like she had been vandalised. Drago could never quite understand why their house was so bland, yet his mother dressed as if she were obsessed with rainbows and had a penchant for taking hallucinogenic drugs.

"Er, yes mother. Actually, I've got something to tell you," replied Drago, sounding much more like a Graeme when faced with his dear old mum. He shuffled into the living room where his mother sat.

Sybill wasn't an intimidating woman. She was one of those people who prattled on day after day set in a simple routine, blissfully unaware of anything uninvolved in the routine. If a herd of disgruntled zebra were charging through the market creating a racket she'd still be nonchalantly examining her melons.

She loved watermelon.

"Yes dear?" Sybill said, looking at her son over her speedily slipping spectacles and wearing a curious expression.

Drago hesitated, he couldn't help but watch his mother's glasses gradual venture south.

"Um... I'm going to be away for a few weeks, I'm going... camping... with friends." He exhaled loudly. A more spurious version of his plans was his impromptu choice of story.

"Oh how lovely Graeme! Make sure you pack properly, you'll need your toothbrush, spare underwear, socks…" Apparently his mother approved of him getting away for a while. Currently, she was rattling through just about everything he owned (which wasn't much) and declaring it as a requirement for a camping trip. Drago didn't know how to feel about his mother's fervent acceptance of his upcoming absence.

Under the impression this was a brief sojourn just beyond the city limits to roast sausages around a campfire and sing old and mildly offensive folk songs, his mother hadn't provided him with a great deal of suitable equipment. This trip would be less carousing, more killing and not being killed. Drago's tendency to drift toward hyperbole had, for a change, led him nearer the truth. Still, there were a few useful items she'd dug out of the cupboard he wouldn't be exchanging for bronze knoblets at the nearest pawn shop. Items like the portable brass cooking set and the hunting dagger he'd been surprised his passive mum owned; the only thing she hunted was her spectacles in the morning. There was also an old map she'd had to dust off which Drago thought would prove particularly helpful. Not that he didn't trust Caine and Korin to know where they were going.

It's just that he didn't trust Caine and Korin to know where they were going.

It took longer than Drago had hoped to leave the house. His mother was one of those people that time didn't apply to. Having finally bid her farewell he set off toward the market, Fischer's Pawn Shop his next destination.

***

Caine had the unusual ability to spring the most eccentric questions on a person, questions that are entirely unrelated to the current topic of conversation.

"'ave you ever ridden an elephant?"

Caine and Korin were huddled around a small circular table in the corner of the Parallelogram, unseen by anyone more than five yards away. Its smoke cloud was in a particularly viscous mood.

Korin drank a little more from his tankard and analysed his friend's face. It flashed that familiar grin that, over the years, had become less and less occupied.

Clarity came down like an iron fist. Or some other metallic appendage.

The steward of Broth Zolust, In Seish Abel, prized above all his wondrous and not so wondrous treasures a herd of battle elephants fifty strong in number. Korin wasn't certain they'd make good travel companions.

"I fear that may be a little ambitious," said Korin reproachfully, aware that now the idea had taken root in Caine's mind, the only way he was leaving the city was on elephant back.

"Ah, ya see I thought that meself, which is why I liked the idea in the first place. S'only a few dozen guards surrounding the paddock, and the walls are only ten, fifteen feet tops. Jumping distance that is," said Caine. Leaning back in his chair and stretching, he looked very much like a man who had it all figured out. This was rarely the case. "And, as it 'appens, the city sewer runs right underneath the outbuildings where the guards stay."

"These things always involve bloody sewers," Korin grumbled, "I've lost too many good pairs of boots to your plans." Caine, wearing the same old battered pair of boots he'd always worn, continued to grin at his companion. Sewers were an adventurer's friend. People never guard sewers.

"Okay, hypothetically, you've gotten us in. But how do we sneak a couple of elephants out without being noticed, and over a fifteen-foot wall?" Korin asked.

A scuffle seemed to have broken out between a couple of irregulars near the entrance. No one stirred or removed their attention from their drinks. The unwritten rule of the bar amongst the regulars was 'whoever's nearest is responsible'. A muffled *yelp* and a *thud* signalled the end of the episode.

Conversations continued as if nothing had happened.

"In a crowd," replied Caine. Korin's puzzled look served to spur him on, like a firm yet encouraging kick up the backside. "We sneak the two out that we'll be takin' in amongst the stampedin' forty-eight others. A fifteen foot wall ain't nothin' to an 'erd that size." He leant back in his chair and winked.

It was intended to be a friendly wink. To anyone but Korin, it might have been perceived as a threat.

"Have I ever told you you're insane, Caine?" Korin was gazing in a kind of horrorstruck awe at Caine. "But I must be just as crazy to go along with it, as per bleedin' usual. Guess we best load up then, prepare for the journey." At this, Caine nodded and picked his sword up from the table. Korin followed suit.

"Ya ready?"

"Yep," replied Korin.

"Off we go then."

***

It was dusk. The rings cast an effortless glow upon the city. It might have been beautiful if it weren't Broth Zolust.

The grid shone silver in the ringlight as Caine tossed it aside none-too-subtly, much to the dismay of Korin. The sewers were as you'd expect a neglected sewer to be; damp, dark, piled with dung and home to a lot of great big filthy rats. Even Caine would struggle to refer to it as homely.

They navigated their way through the maze of passages, each one no different from the last, with the occasional echo of city life carrying down to the stagnant gloom of the sewer. A cart trundling along the uneven paving; a group of rowdy men between bars; wives dragging husbands home by the ear.

In Seish Abel's castle was situated to the north. When the sun reached the right place in the sky it imparted a great shadow upon the city. It kind of loomed.

Its castellated walls were more for show than defence. A triumph of ostentatiousness over practicality. It had turrets in three corners and a bell tower in the southwest corner. The main body of the castle looked like a grey-stoned circus big top. Beside this indulgence there was a mason's idea of a conservatory, home to fifty cramped battle elephants. Caine had been correct, the walls were thin, a herd of rampaging elephants could bring it crashing down with ease. When building walls, it rarely occurs to the builder to elephant-proof them.

It was inside this area of the castle where four guards, who'd been playing poker by candlelight in the barracks, heard a light but distinct crash from the latrines, and a faint cry of 'bugger'.

Edgily, they lifted their swords and sought to check out the banging. They were non-plussed when they discovered two old men dripping wet and shaking their boots out.

One of the men was shorter, stockier than the other with greying, straggly hair, a prominent jaw and a scar stretching down his left cheek. The second man was taller and thinner and was clearly once quite handsome before age had caught up with him. His hair was shoulder length and retained some darkness. He had grey eyes and an earring with a large curved fang embedded in it.

The shorter man had still been emptying his boot when the guards had burst in. He threw said boot with unerring accuracy into the private area of the first guard, who crumpled to the ground. Another was toppled by a flying frying pan.

The remaining two guards, not being the brightest, charged at the old men, swords swinging above their heads. A regrettable error, their torsos too good an opportunity to pass up. A swift bosh with a sword hilt and a bump on the noggin later, Caine and Korin had four guards to tie up and gag.

"Nice to get a warm-up," said Caine as he pulled his boot back on. "Upstairs should open up inta the courtyard, the elephant paddock should be right there."

"You know, you always run through the plan once we've gotten started, and everything seems fine. Then we open a door and there's hundreds more guards than you've anticipated," said Korin in expectation.

They climbed the spiral staircase hastily and Caine opened the door for a quick look out. The elephants were near the back saddled up, recently returned from some trip, Caine figured. There was one minor problem.

"I 'ate it when ya right," muttered Caine.

Korin squeezed past Caine and had a look for himself, closed the door, and turned back to Caine with a look of resignation on his face. "We're still going to steal a couple, aren't we?"

"Of course," said Caine, "did King Lionlung of the Garta and his men turn back when faced with the huge armies of Lord In Plorse Abel?"

"No, he didn't. But King Lionlung and his men were all killed."

"Beside the point," grumbled Caine, who was unused to making historical references.

"Also…" said Korin, "I don't know if you noticed but, erm, the elephants, did they look a bit ill to you? A little pale, maybe?" Korin examined the blank face of Caine.

"You might want to get your eyes tested after we get back… from raiding an entire city… and you with failing eyesight…"

Caine spat toward a bucket in the corner.

It *dinged*.

He peered out once more, closed the door behind him again and turned to Korin.

"They're bloody white!"

Caine was unaware the elephants were the rare white breed. You spend enough time in the Parallelogram and a lot of the world passes you by. However, his determination to commandeer one had elevated to a dangerously manic level. And with this he had what may pass for a brilliant idea.

"Let's head back to the sewer to mull things over."

Korin groaned.

***

After a brief visit to Fischer's Pawn Shop in which he'd convinced poor Bobby that a set of steel cocktail sticks were ornamental wind chimes, Drago set off looking for Caine and Korin, but with little luck. According to Largo, he'd just missed them at the Parallelogram. His search zipped past desperate and settled in despondent.

Drago returned to the Parallelogram and slumped into a chair, knocking a glass of ale over in the process. Stuck in an abyss of despair beyond what the inconvenience merited, he just had to hope they returned here before leaving. Drago had been so ready to plunge into worlds unknown, to slay dragons and rescue damsels in distress. Particularly the damsels bit.

"That wer ma drink!" said an angry and exceedingly large man who now occupied the space immediately between Drago and the door. This, he felt, was a problem.

"I'm sorry friend, how about another?" Drago asked in a higher pitch than usual. His new friend was, at best guess, part troll. The size and strength of a rhinoceros and the shortness of temper to match. Actually, he might be part rhinoceros, thought Drago. Not daring to consider how that genealogy could come about, he returned to the conversation.

"How about it, friend, another ale?"

This is often a tactic that works. If you refer to someone as 'friend' or 'buddy' enough times, psychologically, they soften and grow docile. It's a language trick that can help to forge the reciprocal bonds of friendship dear to so many.

Drago deftly dived aside as a battleaxe cleaved his

table in two, sending splinter missiles in all directions.

***

The sun had now set and the ringlight doused the courtyard in silver shadow. Two guards were shifting awkwardly around the edge of the courtyard wearing heavy looking armour and helms several sizes too big. One carried a frayed hessian sack over his shoulder that seemed to be moving. And squeaking.

In the middle of the courtyard was a pen, fencing in the animals. Around three sides of the pen, men and women in indulgent, baroque armour snoozed. Broth Zolust's steward, In Seish Abel, ordered the fancy armour for those with the honour of maintaining his prized elephants. The fortunate men and women assigned to this task felt lucky. Nice armour, easy task, the job is a good one, they often said.

That was about to change.

The two shuffling figures in the older battle armour reached the northern wall and proceeded to remove the helmets and Zolustian battle armour.

"No wonder we comfortably dealt with those guards earlier, I can hardly move in this stuff," said one, uncomfortable and sweaty.

"Well, it got us round t'back, din't it?" exclaimed the other.

There were no guards on this side of the pen as it was furthest from the entrance. Most of the sentries who remained awake were watching the elephants with hazy disinterest. This disinterest would be their downfall as two old men stormed the elephant pen. With an unexpected fleetness of foot and briskness of movement, one gave the other, who was still holding the writhing sack, a leg up which he used to propel his leaping self over the fence.

Touching down, he pulled the sack open and threw it towards the elephants.

The ensuing uproar of trumpeting and squeals and whole scale stampeding was a sight to behold under the ringlight. Fifty white elephants crashed through the feeble southern wall, terrified of the irritated black sewer rats zipping about in all directions.

Guards dived to and fro attempting to avoid heavy white legs, only to be confronted with nasty black rats nipping them and crawling up their trouser legs. The combination of nipping and crawling adventurously up trouser legs was enough to make any grown man queasy.

Two older men threw themselves at a couple of the still saddled battle elephants at the rear of the swiftly escaping herd. Leaving a trail of stone slabs, mortar and guards behind them, the white elephants began their assault on the unprepared and unaware city.

***

Drago came crashing through the door of the Parallelogram a little dazed, followed by an enormous, misshapen man wielding a substantial battleaxe. To Drago's warrior credit the man had several cuts on his arms and a particularly nasty one on his cheek. This hadn't improved his mood.

As the rhinoceros man emerged, ducking out of the door, he made to advance on Drago. He hesitated, however, when the ground began to shake. A faint rumbling noise splintered by robust trumpeting could now be heard above the sounds of city nightlife.

Drago looked up and was confronted by an unusual sight, even for Torvacane. Colossal white elephants charging down the streets, not caring for what was in their path, bearing down on him. He felt like crying. At the front, he swore he could make out two figures steering the elephants they were perched on. He could hear an oddly familiar insane laughter drifting down the street amongst the general sounds of destruction.

"Oi, Korin," exclaimed Caine excitedly, "is that Drago?" Korin craned forward and squinted.

"You know, I think it is. Why on Torvacane is he not moving out of the way!?"

The elephants were now clattering down the Boulevard like, well, a herd of elephants. The cat gang screeched and darted down an alley. Today has not been my day, thought the cat gang leader.

Drago stood his ground. He saw his target hanging halfway down the side of Korin's elephant, Drago's life dangling by its stomach. He began sprinting away from the elephants, frequently glancing over his shoulder.

His troll-like friend had deserted him unexpectedly.

"Daft sod's lost 'is mind," shouted Caine above the hubbub, feeling a little worried for the lad. Drago wasn't a bad sort, after all.

"On the contrary," said Korin quietly to himself, "I think he's seeing clearer than ever."

The stampede were snapping at Drago's heels and about to overtake him by literally going over him. As the lead elephant drew level, Drago leapt up and flailed at the loose rope attachment hanging from the saddle.

Caine and Korin departed Broth Zolust roaring with laughter, content with how things had turned out. Drago left Broth Zolust petrified, trailing by the side of Korin's elephant, clinging on for dear life, but laughing all the same.

***

As the morning broke across Seven Cities, a hermit living out on Concordia Plains began questioning the effect years of solitude had had on his mind. He could have sworn he observed several white elephants padding past around dawn.

***

Amelia awoke early to find a cup of tea perched on her bedside table. A fluffy purple dressing gown hung from a hook on the door. The unmistakeable smell of bacon teased her out of bed and out of the bedroom.

Of course, it wasn't simply breakfast that motivated her. She was also intent on making Vector tell her everything he knew today, especially as she'd told him everything she knew. Granted, this probably wasn't a good deal in the grand scheme of things. She suspected it wouldn't be a fair trade at all, but ignorance gnawed at her with persistence. She threw on the dressing gown and followed the sizzling sound.

"Good morning," said Vector cheerfully as Amelia trooped into the kitchen and sat down. "I felt a good fry-up and a cup of tea may be in order to get spirits up. Plus, I'm out of whisky," he tutted wistfully. "We'll need the energy anyway. We have a long journey ahead of us."

"We're setting out today?" Amelia asked as she tucked heartily into a plate stacked with eggs, bacon, sausage and beans. She hadn't expected they'd leave so soon but she was thankful for it. Patience was not a quality with which she was blessed.

"Yes, I see no reason to delay. We can decide how's best to rescue your father on the way. Though I have a few ideas I think it's best to get a fuller understanding of the situation," stated Vector. "And, I believe, I promised a further explanation as to what I suspect Edirp wants with your father?"

Despite the importance of this, and Amelia's desire to know, she could only nod enthusiastically. The risk of dribbling beans down a borrowed garment was very real.

Vector pulled himself up to his full height, looking impressive in robes of deep purple and sky blue trimmings that he usually saved for occasions of excessive grandeur (he hadn't worn them in a while).

"Well," Vector paused for effect, "as you know, many years ago the Seven Cities were ravaged by war, and much of what once was was destroyed. What people prefer not to dwell on, however, is exactly how man alone could cause so much destruction. Even we wizards were not robust enough in number to precipitate such chaos. It was the beasts under our control, using the term control loosely, that caused it."

Vector paced up and down, fidgeting with his pockets. He stared out of the window at a pleasant day. He'd felt the storm could do with a rest.

"Your father and I were two of many who were able to speak directly into the minds of the Dragon Lords. Magnificent creatures in a way, but volatile and dangerous. They could launch huge, visceral waves of fire, or simply charge through solid stone battlements. However, they were unruly and far too powerful. In the end, those that weren't slain during the fighting killed each other. We believed the last of them fell during the final battle, fought at the foot of the Misty Mountains by Athea Hubris." Vector shifted again under the watchful, fascinated gaze of Amelia.

"We believed we could change the world for the better," said Vector as he sank into his chair.

"So Edirp wants my father to help him find a Dragon Lord?" Amelia questioned Vector, still unsure of how her father fitted into things. His involvement in the affairs of others had ended years ago. They lived alone; Amelia's mother died when she was young.

Amelia had visited Vertenve often. Usually, she would go by herself. Her father was often guarded as to why he wouldn't accompany her, using weak excuses to avoid any trips to the city.

"No," answered Vector, "I believe Edirp has a Dragon Lord that he cannot control. I can't see the logic in it if he hasn't somehow acquired one of the beasts. He sought your father in order to learn how to tame it. The problem is that, at our advanced age, it would probably kill us to attempt to control one. If it gets loose then it would cause a level of destruction that could set Seven Cities back years, even decades."

Amelia's breathing was heavy, her muscles tense. How could anything be so mindlessly destructive? She refused to be hijacked by thoughts of despair. She rose to her feet. People always rise to their feet when they're being stoic.

"Then we must stop Edirp and slay this beast if it does exist," she said. She was not afraid. At least, she wasn't afraid yet. Fear has an annoying tendency to creep up on you.

She possesses many of her father's qualities, thought Vector. Determined and strong-willed. Although perhaps lacking Emil's sarcastic nature, he saw enough to know he was looking forward to getting to know her.

But they could not do this alone. Overnight, interesting news had reached Vector through the medium of an impressive golden eagle named Terry. Three men had set out from Broth Zolust on a quest to Athea Hubris. For what, he was not certain, though he had a strong suspicion it was in pursuit of something valuable and shiny. Regardless, he knew of two of the threes' exploits and felt they may prove quite useful if it came to a fight. And this sort of thing always does.

"Yes, there's no other option," came Vector's delayed response to Amelia's brave words, her eyes still watching his face carefully. He began to suspect he had dribbled beans down his beard. Orange shows up something terrible against white.

Vector disguised his apprehension from Amelia. After all, who needs impending doom hanging over their head? If Edirp really had a Dragon Lord and they had to face it, they'd probably only need a thimble to bury their remains in.

And that's enough to bring anyone down. Time for one last cup of tea, thought Vector.

***

It's amazing how often the fate of the world, whichever world it may be, falls into the hands of the plainly unqualified and, somewhat miraculously, they have risen to the challenge. Then again, there aren't many schools who offer a diploma in world saving. They just can't afford the apparatus.

***

The Concordia Plains were not as vast as they appeared against the horizon. A forest rose up the low mountain in the pale distance. Two days ride as the wind blows, travelling by elephant that is. There wasn't actually much wind. Not in front of the elephants, anyway...

The plains were flat and sparse, interspersed by clumps of chalky red rocks, practically alive with hissing and humming. Korin made a mental note to not camp too close to one of these deadly hives. Rattlesnakes are a highly evolved species around these parts, they even have a parliament with a chequered and sordid hiss-tory. It's amazing how much backstabbing goes on amongst species without hands.

And it's not just rattlesnakes that are overly organised on Torvacane. It's a commonly held opinion amongst adventurers that it helps to have studied a little zoology at some point because the animal kingdom is a lot more familiar with military tactics and criminal injustice than one might think. Korin and Caine had once come across a small village a long way down the River Sticks being looted by a gang of orang-utan militia. Naturally, they joined in the looting.

Despite the amusement garnered from allowing Drago to continue clinging to his elephant's saddle, Korin had finally heeded his pleas and stopped to allow him to clamber up onto its back.

Caine would more likely have sped up.

And zig-zagged.

Once they were clear of the city and the last remaining

white battle elephant was out of sight, they settled down, set up camp and made lunch. The elephants were well trained and stayed where they were told to, or near enough. Busily investigating the dusty plain for any lingering signs of water, of which there were none, they were content. It seemed rats were their only weakness.

The fire crackled just below the sausages roasting upon the grill that they could thank Drago's mother for.

"May as well eat up," said Caine wistfully, "the meat won't keep f'long. It's veggie soup from then on, 'less we find some good 'unting."

Drago's face dropped. It took a gargantuan effort from his mother to get him to eat his vegetables and no one else was capable of forcing them upon him.

Despite this grave injustice on the horizon there was something else occupying his mind. Drago stared into the fire, watching the flames dance like drunken sailors. He finally stirred from his reverie.

"What is it we're stealing then?" he said, grinning nervously at his companions. Caine and Korin looked at each other and nodded; may as well let him know, they thought simultaneously.

"Gold," they declared in unison. "And lots of it," added Caine, smiling his not so toothy grin.

This made sense, thought Drago. Gold is exactly the kind of thing adventurers would steal. Then they become legends, songs are written about them, kids play games pretending to be them, and they become pub names. And, of course, they get the girl. Currently, there wasn't a girl to get, but it was only day one. It occurred to Drago that Broth Zolust, on the whole, looked like a place that was short of gold. It was short of a lot of things, to be frank. A decent level of hygiene, for example. So who were they stealing from?

Korin studied the quizzical look on Drago's face. He looked like he was trying to do some really hard maths. Best to elaborate a little before the poor lad pulled a muscle.

"King Edirp of Athea Hubris has been mining the Misty Mountains for quite a while now, against the advice of many of his recently deceased advisers. He's been using expensive dwarf contractors, but apparently they struck gold…"

"Not all 'e found either, if what I 'eard's true," interrupted Caine.

"Humph," responded Korin nonchalantly, "that's nought but rumour, so pipe down." Noticing, but ignoring, Drago's now worried look, Korin continued. "The gold mine has untold, limitless levels of gold, so the rumours go, and our sources aren't the type to pass on information without being sure of it. So we figure, as Edirp has so much gold, he won't mind us borrowing a little…"

"About 'alf of it," chuckled Caine, mostly to himself.

"So that, Drago, is our aim, our purpose. Nip into Athea Hubris, bash a few guards on the head, but only if necessary of course, steal a smidgeon of gold, then find ourselves a little place in the sun and retire."

"With concubines," noted Caine, staring longingly at the cloud-filled sky.

"Yes," agreed Korin fervently, "concubines. Not too much to ask, we feel."

Things could have been worse, but they could also be significantly better too. Drago stared at the two suicidal seniors, upset by their distinct lack of a cohesive plan. To be completely accurate, there was no plan at all. What

Caine and Korin had was the bit that happened after a plan was successful.

Drago sensed that one day when he looked back on this journey the overriding memory would be a sort of chronic feeling of fear and exasperation.

Still, he thought, concubines sounded quite appealing.

He made a mental note to read up on what they were at a later date.

***

As the afternoon drew to a close and the planet's rings traced a fine line across the gradually darkening sky, the three prospective gold thieves packed up and set off across the plains on elephant back, kicking up a mean trail of dust. They were heading in the direction of the Wooden Forest, named thusly by the explorer Bumbo Clar, famed as much for his intrepid exploration as he was his lack of imagination.

He saw a forest.

And he saw wood.

Together, this equalled the Wooden Forest. Bumbo Clar was also a tall, robustly built man, which is probably why nobody questioned his naming of the forest. Or his cat, Cat, nor his horse, Horse.

Drago had always thought that the world beyond Broth Zolust's borders would be full of splendour and excitement, but he was already beginning to miss the middens of the Boulevard, the sharp edges of the market stalls and the ubiquitous smell of garlic. He remembered Broth Zolust's border. The formerly rickety and recently shattered fence. Trekking across this arid landscape, memories of home appeared grander, glazed in a fondness with which these bare and broken surroundings couldn't compare. Here, even the horizon looked poorly constructed.

The plains had once been an agricultural dream, luscious and fertile, a rich environment. But now they were dry and hard. Late in the evening they ran past the ruin of a temple to Son, God of Torvacane. All that remained was half a wall and a pile of crumbled bricks. It reminded Caine of his sixtieth birthday. As far as Caine was concerned it wasn't a good party unless something was reduced to rubble at some point.

The elephants really did cover ground at speed, pounding relentlessly across the plains. Signs of tiredness were creeping in though; they'd been running from tusk 'til dawn. By the end of the second day of constant travel the trio had reached the edge of the forest and set up camp for the night, ready to explore in the morning.

The morning brought with it an unpleasant surprise.

What hadn't occurred to Caine, Korin or Drago, none of whom had ever owned a pet, let alone a pet elephant, was that they would require water after a hard day of running. After two solid days of hard running across parched plains, sun beating down upon their grey backs, they would be gagging. By the third morning, they would most likely have keeled over and died of dehydration.

Which they had.

"Prob'ly should 'ave thought the elephant part through a little," said Caine expertly, aiming a little kick at his elephant's stomach to double check it was definitely dead.

Caine's version of an autopsy was shorter than the official procedure. "Aye, dead," he grunted, satisfied with his diagnosis.

Sitting down on a rock, Drago looked worried. And he

was aware of this fact. He considered whether his face would eventually just set this way and look worried forever. This worried him further.

"Erm, if we actually steal some gold, how do we transport it back without the elephants?"

He could hear Caine's response playing in his head before it came in his grizzled tone. Drago knew that if he wanted Caine or Korin to consider the possibility that they might be a tad underprepared, he had to try harder than this.

"Oh, summat will come up once we're there," said Caine.

"It always does," added Korin.

The air was colder at the foot of the forest. More than just a playful nibble, it was biting. Drago stood up and stared into the forest. The further in he saw, the thicker the trees became, closing up into a mouth full of razor-sharp teeth. Perhaps his imagination was running wild but the blackness of the forest seemed infinite. Despite the sun beating down upon it, the thickness of the trees blocked it out like a dastardly canopy. There was no indication of life, which is usually a sign that it's sat watching and waiting from the shadows.

Caine and Korin trooped off into the heart of the forest. They preferred to deal with things that might jump out at you after they'd actually done the jumping out. Lagging behind a few steps, Drago readjusted his satchel full of kitchen utensils and the map.

The cartographer responsible for the map, Drago had decided, was a useless fool. The plains hadn't been marked on it, and neither had the forest. In fact, large areas of it were blank. So Drago had begun filling it in himself in the hope that one day some other poor man who'd mistakenly volunteered for a quest toward certain death with two old windbags would at least know where he was when he died.

The trail was littered with wayward roots. A small amount of sunlight filtered through the occasional gap amongst the trees but hardly illuminated the way. Each tree had a mind of its own and was deviously attempting to trip the travellers up. Trees get very bored.

Drago certainly couldn't say much for the ambience of the place. A shade threatening for his tastes. There was the fluttering of wings, the rustling of leaves above and the odd howl or high-pitched tweet vandalising the muted scene. Worse still, the noises had them surrounded, or so it seemed.

The light kept shifting with the breeze, the gaps between the branches always moving with it as if hypnotised.

Captivated by his internal commentary on the mood, ambling along, Drago failed to notice Caine and Korin had stopped a little short of a break in the trees. This led to him receiving a furtive kick to the shin.

"Ow, what the…" Drago stopped suddenly, hushed by the seriousness of the expressions of his companions. He'd seen this look before – the last time the pumps had run dry in the Parallelogram – and it indicated something serious was happening. Or about to happen. Caine and Korin had a tendency to happen to people.

They signalled to use the trees as cover while they peeked around, trying to see something moving amongst the shadows. At first, Drago thought their astigmatism was playing up simultaneously, but then he saw a flash of red that alarmed him somewhat. Then came a horrific howling noise, cut off mid-howl, that alarmed him further. Something stumbled into the light and collapsed in a bloody heap.

The clearing was a perfect circle of glistening green grass surrounded by towering, broad oaks. It was the type of place that would be lovely for a picnic on a sweet summer day. Ideally without the mangled animal corpse.

On the opposite side of the circle a young girl stepped out. She was wearing a blue summer dress and a bold red cloak and hood. She crouched over the body of what was up until recently a wolf.

"Cute, eh?" whispered Caine, winking at Drago who shuffled sideways while keeping his back to the tree.

"Don't scare the lad Caine, she is holding a blood-soaked axe," added Korin.

Oblivious to the hushed conversation taking places yards away the girl pulled her hood down to reveal long, glistening auburn hair. It was at this moment Drago took the opportunity to stand on a twig. The crack echoed around the clearing.

Axe raised, hood up, the girl called out.

"Who goes there? Answer me now. I dare you to steal my kill." This sounded more like an invitation than a threat, said with such relish Drago felt it would have been as wise a course of action as testing out a mousetrap with his tongue.

It was Korin who spoke. He stepped out of the shadows and into the opening. Light percolated the network of branches overhead. In it, his fanged earring glinted. Korin held his hands out to the sides as a sign they meant no harm, but the girl didn't appear to understand this universally accepted symbol of non-violence. Gripping her axe tightly she remained in a crouched position, ready to spring like a tiger.

"We are three travellers passing through these woods. We mean you no harm."

Caine coughed sharply behind Korin.

"And we don't want your kill either," Korin added reassuringly.

They waited as the girl made up her mind about how trustworthy these so-called 'travellers' might be. These were her woods, her home. Her mind didn't so much tick over as grind. Following a quizzical glare, she straightened up and her demeanour shifted to a more pleasant and open one. A rapid, full-body transformation.

"Okay chaps, wotcha doin' round here?"

One minute someone is ready to put an axe through you, the next they're saying things like 'wotcha'. Torvacane could be a baffling place.

"I am Korin, my friends are Caine and Drago. We are headed toward the River Stick's mountain pass. We must cross it on our way to Vertenve to visit family," said Korin. Over the years he'd found deception to be a wiser choice. You should stick to what you're comfortable with, what comes naturally. If that happens to be lying, then lie like you've always lied before. In this case, he was opting for a more wholesome reason for their journey than theft.

For some reason people seemed to object to theft.

"Ah okay, well that's right past my village, I'll show you the way," she said cheerfully, lowering her hood once more. Close up they could see she had a pretty face with rounded, rosy cheeks and a carefree expression. One feature stood out.

What pretty eyes she has, thought Drago.

The girl bounced over to the three friendly trespassers in her wood. "My name's Red, pleased to meet you," she said, holding out her hand. Korin took it, relieved there would be no axe-related malfeasance today.

There was little Korin disliked more intensely than axe-related malfeasance.

Red was beaming now, skipping along, happy for the company, even if it was a bit scruffy and lacking a few teeth.

"It's getting late, per'aps you should stay the night? I've plenty of space."

They agreed unanimously. Night had stumbled and fallen and the cold had settled in. There was only thick cloud cover concealing the emergence of the full moon.

As they progressed through the Wooden Forest they gained a little insight into the life, times and mind of Red. The girl could talk for Gredavia and she was coming across as a distinctly odd individual. A particular highlight was her description of the wolf she'd near cleaved in half as a 'sumptuous find'.

Never before has an adjective felt so abused.

They soon discovered that her life had been blighted by werewolves. Her grandmother had been eaten by one, a tragedy that Red hadn't fully comprehended because she was young when it happened. In her late teens, she'd dated a werewolf, but it hadn't worked out because he was emotionally unavailable.

"I loved him and hated him," she'd said.

Drago could sense his eyes failing him. By the time the trees had thinned out and their destination was in sight he felt like her weary biographer.

During the conversation or, to be exact, Red's monologue, what hadn't escaped the three travellers' astute eyes were the peculiar and at times vicious markings on many of the trees. There were deep, angry scratch marks on tree trunks made by someone or something with as much talent for whittling wood as Caine had for interpretive dance.

It was eerily quiet. Too quiet, thought Korin. They couldn't get the birds to shut up a short way back. The word foreboding sprung to mind and the individual letters did a little jig.

They had been walking uphill for some time, steadily steeper as they left the unwelcoming forest behind and headed toward the ghastly little village they found themselves calling home for the night. Sweat slid gently down Drago's back but it wasn't a hot evening. He'd read far too many books about monsters.

The area was more of a steep hill than a mountain, but crossing the steep hill pass isn't as dramatic or epic. The lane they strode up was fenced along either side with fields for grazing animals, yet they were empty, a few patches of what looked to be wool aside.

They trudged on toward the houses.

The village was small, barely twenty buildings built untidily yet sturdily from red brick. So they wouldn't be blown over, according to Red. It had a sensation of being unlived in which was unsettling. There was no litter anywhere. Despite night having drawn in they expected at least some indication there were people other than themselves in the vicinity.

The houses were situated around a central point in the village, a wide town square with a couple of desolate stands to the side. In the middle was a raised platform upon which a grotesque statue stood. Caine and Korin had seen their fair share of odd sights but this wasn't one they'd forget in a hurry.

A stone statue of a long-limbed wolf, stood on its hind legs, towered over them all despite its hunched appearance. Unclean and grimy, illumination by ringlight offered it a nightmarish hue.

"I don't think it would be wise to stay here after all," Drago whispered to Caine. Korin was currently entertaining Red with a story of how he had once been betrothed to a princess, but he left her because she kept peeing the bed. His tone remained even but the presence of an eight-foot-tall stone wolf hadn't escaped him. It was one of those things that one cannot help but notice. Like the elephant in the room, but not actually in a room, and not an elephant.

"We'll be right f'one night. Ne'er say no to a warm bed and 'ot food, that's what I say," Caine muttered unconvincingly, his gaze still fixed on the statue. Their unusual host combined with the general aura of the place had even the unflappable Caine flapped. "Jus' be on ya guard," he added. Caine wasn't about to be eaten by any great hairy wolf or, worse yet, be forcefed wolf stew. He'd tasted wolf once before, instantly spat it out, and then spent the following two weeks being chased by lycanthropic cultists.

They were a determined bunch, cultists. Put an idea in their heads and they really stick with it. Like a wolf with a bone.

Red eventually stopped at a house in the furthest corner of the village. From here they could see the path they would take the following day just ahead of them, spiralling upward and out of sight flanked by ever more towering rock faces. The faces were grimacing.

There wasn't much choice but to take that path from here. It loomed over them fiendishly like a hornets' nest in a strong wind.

Red's house was untidy. Everything was moth eaten

and old, the sofas were worn and a fine coating of hair covered them and the carpets too. The wallpaper peeled in the corners like a tatty banana. It was as if she'd raided a tip for some useful items and stumbled across an entire house someone had thrown out.

But they were guests.

"You have a lovely home," said Drago, because his mother would have expected him to say it. Red seemed pleased.

A fire burned brightly in the fireplace, but that aside it didn't feel homely at all. There was a thick, musty smell in the air, like when your dog jumps in every puddle while out for a walk and then rolls around on the carpet at home.

"There isn't much in the cupboards at the moment," said Red as she rummaged around, fussing noisily but not tidying as she went along. Instead she just continued to talk and cause the odd clattering noise until it faded into the background for the others.

Red was one of those people that you didn't hold a conversation with, you just waited for her to come up for air.

"I'm going to head out now to pick some bits up then we'll get this bad boy cooking." She lifted the wolf up by its tail and grinned at the three awkwardly smiling and nodding men stood in her front room. "There are beds upstairs. Go and make yourselves at home, rest up if you like, food will be a little while yet anyway." She walked through into her kitchen and proceeded to make further clanging noises. Drago guessed she was either the clumsiest person in the world or, and he hoped this suspicion was off target, she was deliberately pretending to sound busy.

"Does she even know what time it is?" asked Caine, beginning to wonder whether the moon was just some illusion. There was another aspect of Red's character that Caine had very rarely come across in anyone before: she appeared to have taken an instant liking to him. His first impression normally led to people firing pointy things at him, waving pointy things at him, or cursing a lot. The rare occasions people appeared to take a liking to him were generally a pre-cursor to a more inventive attempt on his life.

Which he had to admit was part of the fun of being him.

"I think she's probably lonely, there doesn't seem to be many people around here. We can at least stay the night and have dinner with her," said Korin, a statement that inspired as much confidence as a space shuttle made of bamboo.

Drago and Caine both groaned. Images of silver platters carrying a wolf's head with an apple stuffed in its mouth flashing before their eyes. This had emerged as a distinctly worrying situation. Drago could feel lines deepening on his face.

"Just stay alert, got it?"

Korin's tone suggested he was acutely aware of the strangeness of their surroundings. He had no intention of staying the whole night, he was just hungry. His stomach was rumbling enough to excite a seismometer.

The sound of clanging pots and pans had ceased.

A moment later Red reappeared from the kitchen and headed for the door.

"Won't be too long, gotta have some vegetables with our meat o'course. Oh, and don't you rascals go peeking through my drawers," Red added while winking at Drago,

47

who blushed crimson in response. Caine looked like he'd just had a great idea.

They bid Red farewell and she set off for the other side of the square. Ringlight stretched across the sky conspicuously and the earlier cloud cover had dispersed. As the door shut, Korin turned to Caine.

"Think you can follow her without doing anything rash, stupid or dangerous?"

"Course I can," he exclaimed, offended. "They don't call me The Shadow for nothin'."

"Who calls you that?" asked Drago, giving Caine a curious look.

"People, that's who. R'spected people too." Caine trailed off, looking at the floor for a moment before rallying and standing up straight. "Righ', I'll see what the mental lass is doin', what are you goin' t'do?"

"We're going to have a look round, see whether anyone else actually lives here, and whether they own anything worth stealing. Unlikely, I know."

Having dwelt on it a little further, Korin felt he may have to ignore the pleas of his appetite and scarper. Perhaps before *they* became the meal. If there was one thing he disliked more than axe-related malfeasance, it was being eaten. At least, he assumed he disliked that more. He was now fairly confident of what was going on here. Red had mentioned she'd dated a werewolf earlier on, Korin wasn't so sure it had ever left.

Caine had already gone when Korin and Drago set out. They wandered down the road, hands quivering not far from the hilt of their swords. Rather, Korin's hand was quivering slightly. Drago's clammy hand shook violently, patently aware that the full moon was now glaring down upon them like a headmaster who'd caught a student urinating on a copy of *War and Peace*.

"I hope Red gets broccoli," said Drago shakily, past the point of making sense and too sick of the silence to prolong it, "not had broccoli for a while."

"I thought you hated broccoli?" replied Korin absently as he peered through another house window. "Same again. Right, we get Caine and we get gone. We've loitered too long already," Korin said definitively. Curiosity got the best of Drago. He moved towards the window and peered through.

"Shouldn't have looked," Drago whimpered.

The room was similar to Red's own living room except the sofa in this one had been shredded to pieces and the walls had deep scratches and red stains. Drago had a faint hope that it was fashionable foreign décor, but he decided Korin's idea was best. Scram.

The search for Caine, as it turned out, took about ten seconds.

"RUUUUNNN!"

Racing with a speed belying his age, Caine was sprinting towards Korin and Drago having appeared from beside a house just across the village.

A desperate, angry howl followed him.

Needing no second invitation Korin, who was content for being proven correct and rueful for not leaving earlier in equal measure, and Drago turned and ran in the direction of the mountain/steep hill pass.

It should be noted that if you ever find yourself being chased by werewolves the obvious direction in which to run is most definitely not uphill.

Tearing away out of the village Drago risked a look over his shoulder with another of his faint hopes, this one being that Caine was playing a practical joke. If he was, thought Drago, he'd gone to a lot of trouble. Four large hairy wolves with razor sharp fangs, salivary mouths and breath problems were bounding after them. Jaws snapped, growled, frothed. One werewolf was still wrapped partially in a red cloak. At least she left the axe behind, thought Drago. Some small comfort.

"I get why they're chasing us Caine, I honestly do," shouted Korin as he steered them in the direction of the rock lined path that led toward the river, "but why the heck are they so bloody angry?" Korin glanced accusingly at Caine who simply stared ahead, concentrating on forgetting his bunions.

The rock faces gleamed silver in the now clear ringlight but were tainted blue by the moonlight, creating a pleasant colour clash that they were unable to appreciate at this exact moment.

The path resembled a dirt track but the ground was barely visible in parts, the rocky surroundings not allowing light to breach its barricade. However, if Caine, Korin or Drago could have seen the muddier parts they may have noticed sporadic paw prints indented upon the path.

Luckily, these particular werewolves were fairly cumbersome. Too much furniture in the diet can slow you down. They weren't gaining much ground on the geriatric sprint team of Caine and Korin.

Drago was a further ten yards ahead of them. His groundwork in running had been done during a youth spent nicking gobstoppers from Broth Zolust's market stalls.

Being ahead, Drago was the first to hear the sounds of water crashing against rock up ahead but the last to recognise what this meant. He got quite a shock when he reached the summit to be confronted with a powerfully flowing river that, amidst the roar and the foam, met a vertical drop.

Drago stopped at the edge, fixated with horror at the booming waterfall in front of him.

So this is mortal peril, he thought. His fingers tingled.

Ferocious, hairy brutes right behind him (a description applicable to Caine and Korin just as accurately as the werewolves), a foaming mass of thunderous death before him.

There was little time to ponder the available options. But this didn't matter much. His mind was made up for him as he was lifted off his feet and over the edge of the waterfall by two grey-haired blurs screaming 'Geronimo'.

***

On Torvacane, the legend of Geronimo is well known.

A renowned pacifist, he negotiated peace between the tribes of the Upper Bedon Kohe, the lands much further north of Misty Mountain. Without dispute and war to placate he reinvented himself as a circus performer, specialising in being flung from a catapult towards a giant net.

He famously screamed his own name as he flew through the air.

***

The river's powerful current thrashed against its banks, teetering on the edge of overflow, the water a spectrum of shades of blue and silver. Some thirty yards or so away a small tent was glowing against the darkness of the night.

A lustrous fire burned at its opening.

This may seem like an obvious target for bandits or trolls, but thieves and thick-skinned magical creatures aren't stupid. Well, they are, but they have their own school of logic. In situations like this their thinking is that if the campers are brave enough to light themselves up like a Christmas tree then they can probably look after themselves. It's the ones trying not to be found that were worth attacking. You can't really argue with that logic. Then again, you can't really argue with trolls at all.

"The moonlight's a lot brighter here," said Amelia.

"Well the moon and the sun both orbit within the four rings. The moon isn't very far away from the planet at all right now, particularly from this area, so the strange blue light it emits shines brighter here," answered Vector.

It was true, the sun and moon orbited Torvacane. It was a peculiar arrangement, but one that Son had felt necessary. They were celestial babysitters.

And cheap ones at that.

Amelia nodded. She began to rummage through her bag, hunting for a blanket.

Vector looked crestfallen at the lack of appreciation for his knowledge. It wasn't that he needed validation. Perhaps just a pat on the back or a 'wow, you're awesome'. Not too much to ask.

But Amelia did find it interesting, she just wasn't adept at showing it. Short trips to Vertenve aside she had spent most of her childhood alone or with her father. She wanted to know more about the world and she wanted to know more about its people. Particularly wizards.

"I have a question," she said tentatively.

"Okay, fire away," encouraged Vector.

"Well, why are you and my father, and I guess most

other wizards, practically in hiding? Surely you have the power to help others?" Amelia was giving Vector that accusing look once more, as if holding him to account for running over her puppy.

"I didn't do too good a job at hiding, did I?" stated Vector, smiling politely.

"You know what I mean!"

"I do. It's a long story, I'm not sure I can do it justice."

"Injustice will do just fine."

Smart-bottom, thought Vector. He sighed and sat upright. His knees creaked like an old and battered door that had spookily eased open of its own accord.

"We did, long ago, interfere in everything," he began. The robust flow of the river nearby eased the tension in his voice. He sighed once more before continuing.

"The Wizard's Council, long ago, was a focal point of philosophical, scientific and political debate and advised many stewards and kings. But divisions developed, grew, and split the council. As the war picked up pace, we picked sides. We contributed hugely to the havoc and chaos that ensued. I'm not proud, nor is your father, but we learned long ago we cannot be trusted with power."

Amelia was sat bolt upright, leg's folded, her knees not creaking in the slightest. Jealousy flickered through Vector's mind briefly, which he found amusing.

Amelia gazed intently at Vector, taking it all in. She wore the expression of one who isn't sure they're going to like what they're about to hear. Much like a barman on karaoke night.

"It's simply in our nature, I theorize, to get carried away, for power to go to our heads. Magical power is a dangerous thing in itself and comes with responsibility.

Beyond that, we're best staying out of world affairs. You forget we wielded volatile Dragon Lords, creatures that cannot truly be controlled. Yet we were so arrogant we dismissed the occasions when they ran amok,"

Vector went on with guilt in his eyes.

"No, wizards aren't regarded too well amongst the higher echelons of Seven Cities these days, we are best not getting involved. I have one or two old friends, but little contact with them. Us wizards live alone with our books and our foibles. And our tea, of course. We deliberately live great distances from each other, to quash any temptation to band together. To be blunt, I'd say there's only a handful of us left these days."

"But surely you can help still? In small doses I'm sure you could control yourselves," Amelia said, a note of pleading in her voice.

"Yes, we probably could," said Vector, "but it isn't the only reason. Magic is unnatural, there are very few capable of utilising it safely. It cuts through the very fabric of the universe, of the world's atmosphere. And in large quantities it has the potential to rip a hole in reality."

Vector deliberately omitted that if a hole in reality were to materialise then all manner of tentacled beasts, winged demons or people who enjoy statistics could pass freely from other dimensions into this one.

Most inconvenient. Particularly if you have dinner plans.

Amelia rested her head on her knees. She hadn't noticed how cold it was until now. She pulled her blanket tightly around herself.

"Your father is a good man Amelia," said Vector, "what happened in the past, it was never our intention. We planned to do good, we thought we were the wisest amongst mortals but we were wrong. What ensued may have been partly our fault, but we weren't alone in culpability. Many men and women with darker hearts and even darker intentions pulled the strings, we were mere puppets. That is our greatest crime. Allowing ourselves to be used for evil."

Outside the tent there was a steady breeze. The only other sounds to be heard were the river and the occasional *hoot* or *chirrup*.

"No, people lost their faith in us a long time ago." Vector turned and lay back down, lost in melancholy. He hadn't relived those days for a long time and he'd never erase the guilt.

"I think faith can be refound, over time," whispered Amelia.

With this, Amelia blew out the candles and clambered into her sleeping bag.

***

Meanwhile, far away atop the citadel of Athea Hubris, King Edirp had stubbed his toe.

"AAARGH," he shouted, hopping in agony while clutching his foot. His personal door guard (yes, he has one of those) came running in at the tumult, sword raised.

He consequently lowered it at the sight of his gawky liege bouncing around the room wearing pale pink pyjamas and cursing like a sailor.

The bed chamber was the epitome of royalty. Towering four poster bed, gleaming oak furnishings, and a bulging chest full of jewellery. His shiny, fresh-looking battle armour was draped over a mannequin in the corner with his family crest emblazoned on the chest. The crest

– quarters of blue and red behind the head of a roaring lion – was actually emblazoned on everything you could possibly emblazon something on to.

"Are you okay sire?"

The door guard, whose name is unimportant for reasons that will soon become apparent, failed miserably in suppressing his amusement at such a ludicrous sight.

Edirp noticed.

"Finding this funny, are we?" As the pain subsided Edirp had turned to glower at his soon-to-be former door guard. If people could be branded with an expiration date his would simply have read, 'right about now'.

"Pass me your sword."

Panic adorned the man's face but he reluctantly handed over his sword.

"Now kiss my foot," ordered Edirp.

"Sorry sire…?"

"KISS IT BETTER YOU SIMPLETON!"

Seeing no way out of this the terrified door guard got on his knees and leant in to kiss Edirp's foot. With a light swish the sword came swooping in. The guard's last thought was how curious his body looked from five feet away.

"HERM!"

People regularly working around Edirp's quarters were accustomed to hearing his voice blaring through the walls. If the walls could talk, they'd have probably said 'shut up!'

Or words to that effect.

Herm was Edirp's unfortunate personal assistant. He was good at his job, although his efficiency was entirely motivated by fear.

As he scurried in he glanced briefly at the decapitated door guard on the ground and let out a short squeal, despite being unsurprised, then looked to his king. A skinny, watery-eyed man, Edirp reminded Herm of seafood. As well as his singular ideas about pyjamas, he inexplicably wore his crown to bed. It just can't be comfortable, thought Herm. Anyway, he returned to the task at hand.

"Another door guard, sire?"

"If you would, Herm. One of Med Tet's personal guard will do, trustworthy and reliable types I've noticed," said Edirp.

He looked down at his slippers and sighed. Yet another nice pair ruined, stained with the blood of a minion.

"And perhaps some new slippers too."

"Right away sire," replied Herm and he scurried out. His room was a short way down the hall and it was considerably smaller than Edirp's. It contained a bed, a desk and a wardrobe.

He walked towards another door behind which there was a storage space. It contained a hundred spare pairs of slippers and several extra sets of pale pink pyjamas.

Herm felt it was best not to ask why they absolutely could not be any other colour than pale pink. Those issues were seated so deep that they couldn't see the stage.

Knowing full well Edirp expected a new door guard within the half hour, Herm made his way to Med Tet's quarters carrying a spare pair of slippers and pyjamas (Edirp hadn't noticed the spatter on his legs). Herm always had the look of a man who had never fully mastered walking, too nervous to place one foot too far away from the other. So he scurried everywhere hastily like a rat whose permanent residence is the tiger enclosure of a zoo.

Hurrying down the hallways of the citadel, Herm always thought that Edirp was in the wrong line of work. As a king he was terrible. He'd been blessed with the brains and temperament of a baboon with a chronic itch. But he'd have made a superb interior designer. Red velvet rugs with gold trim, exquisite vases, classic portraits, he certainly knew how to colour co-ordinate.

Herm stopped in front of an iron door and took a deep breath. Cold stone beneath his feet, cold stone behind the door.

You can do this, he thought.

Probably.

Herm didn't like disturbing Med Tet at the best of times, let alone late at night. He expected to find him hanging upside down from his ceiling like an overgrown vampire bat.

Med Tet didn't have an aggressive posture. He was quite placid, like the ocean on calm day. You just didn't know what was stirring beneath.

Med Tet had a slow, drawling voice: it dripped malice from every syllable. A thin moustache tickled his top lip and lay there like a venomous snake ready to strike. He was forever twirling the tips.

Herm raised his hand and used it to tap tap tap on Med Tet's door, praying to Son he hadn't disturbed his sleep. Med Tet didn't dream, he just schemed subconsciously.

There was no vocal reply to Herm's knock but he caught a glimpse of an eye peering through the peephole. This was followed by a collection of noises, mostly metallic clanging and scratching. By the time the door finally opened Herm had determined that Med Tet had no less than nine locks on his door.

Standing before Herm now was a slender man with severe dark eyes and pointed features robed in black silk (robes were traditionally worn by regal council. Herm's were grey), tweaking the corner of his moustache.

"Yes, Mister Herm?"

Herm shivered, just barely suppressing a squeak.

"The king's door guard has sadly, um, passed away," said Herm, failing to prevent a nervous stuttering, "the king would like, um, one of your personal guard to take over the role."

Any other general would have sneered dismissively and angrily at Herm upon hearing this news. Herm would have welcomed that readily knowing that would be the extent of it. With Med Tet you knew that he'd get you at some point, but you wouldn't know when, where or how many fingers you'd be left with.

"Okay," said Med Tet coolly, "take Kaze, and let us hope he lasts until morning. We don't want to have to recarpet the king's chambers again, do we?"

"No, no of course not," replied Herm, shifting uncomfortably.

"Kaze is down in barrack two, I'm sure you can fetch him yourself, Herm. You do scramble down these halls much quicker than I myself can walk." And with that he turned and shut the door on Herm while he remained stood there facing the doorway. Finally regaining the power of movement, Herm set off down the stairway toward the barracks wondering why Med Tet had been so agreeable. This made him uneasy. It's a wonder a man as permanently nervous as Herm ever rose to the position of the king's personal assistant. Then again, it's probably this quality that would endear him to a king in the first place.

***

Far away at the top of Val Hilla, Son, God of Torvacane, had a headache.

Val Hilla rose unimpressively out of the Asthmatic Ocean's billowing whirlpools. They made ghastly gargling noises as if the water had drunk itself too quickly. It had been named the Asthmatic Ocean because of the peculiar wheezing noise the tide made upon the mainland shores.

Son's headache had been caused by the angry E.T Mails (extra-terrestrial mail) He'd received from other gods from different star systems. Apparently, during the night, Torvacane had made a spirited effort at crashing through interspace barriers without a passport. This displeased the other planetary gods who viewed Torvacane as a menace.

Their displeasure merely spurred Torvacane on. As with any rebel, the more you try to keep them down, the harder they rebel.

Everyone thinks it's so easy being a god but it's actually a very complex and demanding role. It requires excellent organisation, good communication skills, patience and dedication. None of this lounging around being fed grapes by beautiful men and women in a state of undress or being serenaded by heavenly choirs of angels. Not even close. Just administration, inventory, and complaints.

Son collapsed His omnipotent bottom onto His holy bean bag and sighed. Only He could have created a planet that in turn created the immense amount of paperwork He had to wade through.

At this rate, He might have to start employing demigods.

***

As morning crawled home after a long night a flock of magpies scattered. King Edirp was marching along the battlements of the citadel overlooking Athea Hubris. He stopped for a moment to gaze down at the city he had inherited. It had a rustic beauty that he felt was unmatched. Only Gredavia, with its magnificent skyitchers, could compete aesthetically, but Edirp always felt the place lacked soul. Not like Athea Hubris. Athea Hubris was brimming with soul to match its handsomeness.

Misty Mountain stretched away to the west. The city was built up and into the mountain. The citadel was an enormous stone structure, a miniature city in its own right. Flags baring the royal crest whipped in the wind, proud and tall atop the flagpoles, watching over the city. Beneath the citadel, whitewashed stone houses erupted on any remotely flat piece of land. Stables and smithies and taverns were dotted about, each in a similarly picturesque style, a result of excellent planning. And, importantly, the place was clean and well kept. The citizens had pride in the place they lived (Athea Hubris's unofficial motto being 'If you don't have your pride, you don't have your head.').

Edirp removed himself from his reverie to swipe at a low flying magpie. It was unusual for magpies to gather in flocks at all but, of late, there had been more and more of them congregating along the battlements.

The reason for this was simple.

The front line of battlement reached the side of the adjacent mountain and where the battlement met the moutain there was a hole.

It was a large and well-lit hole.

Behind this hole there was a large and well-lit tunnel.

The tunnel delved deep into Misty Mountain until it reached a glowing chasm. It had been hollowed out by the king's miners who had, quite literally, struck gold.

For a while, Edirp had been a busy man. People had queued for days at the citadel entrance to speak to his advisers. He'd become so frustrated he ordered them to approve everything. It didn't matter to him if someone wanted their wooden leg replaced with a golden one.

And that wasn't the only, ahem, appendage people wanted made of gold.

But of all the shady prospectors the king had expected to turn up in the city upon the discovery of a huge gold mine, magpies were not high on the list. And they were evolving fast. Edirp was certain he'd seen them use a pincer movement yesterday. The birds had attempted to ambush convoys of soldiers transporting gold to the newly formed mint in the citadel. While their efforts up to now had failed, they were motivated, determined and had great belief in the philosophy of 'where there's a will there's a way'. The birds were only warming up.

"Bloody magpies," muttered Edirp, indignation etched upon his face as he shook his fist toward the sky.

"Herm, why has no one dealt with this?"

Herm was once again scurrying behind Edirp, completely forgotten right up until it was time to complain about something. When that moment arrived, Herm suddenly existed again.

"Um, honestly sire, we didn't think the magpies would

be quite so persistent," replied Herm with a whimper.

"Well it seems *you* were wrong."

Herm found the king's stressing of the word 'you' worrying.

"Fetch the archers once we return," Edirp ordered as they reached the tunnel entrance before stopping as a figure appeared.

Med Tet emerged from the tunnel looking ruffled. His moustache was less curled at the tip than usual.

"Hello Med Tet," said Edirp cheerfully. Edirp's mind had a natural defence mechanism. He was incapable of entertaining the possibility that he didn't command the respect and admiration of everyone he met. The idea that someone disliked him, or, Son forbid, would plot against him, was impossible.

"Good morning my king, what brings you here so early?" Med Tet had his suspicions but he wanted them confirmed nevertheless. His behaviour had been unusual of late. Kings were supposed to sleep in late, eat unhealthy amounts of meat, hunt whatever they felt like hunting and generally be an arse. In this latter respect Edirp was a sensational king.

"I wanted to see how our new friend is doing before commencing further interrogation of our old friend in the dungeons," said Edirp, a sly grin on his face as though he were speaking in an uncrackable code. Med Tet, having somehow worked out the enigma of Edirp's speech, bowed slightly and spoke formally.

"An excellent idea, sire. I myself have been down to check everything is being attended to dutifully. I shall return to the armoury to oversee weapons' production. I have procured another significant enlistment and will be inspecting them on arrival. Fine men from what I am told, sire. I shall also have archers stationed upon the battlements, I'm sure that you do not wish for our ornithological problem to worsen."

"Fantastic, everything is in order and moving along nicely I see… Yes, fantastic," said Edirp in a semi-dreamy tone.

Med Tet took this as his signal to leave, bowed once more to the king, sneered at Herm (who had still been hoping no one had noticed him), and strode off in the direction of the citadel. He stopped to aim a kick at a particularly plump pigeon that had been using his head as target practice.

"What a good fellow, extremely useful to have around," said Edirp, eyes back in focus. Herm utilised the smile and nod technique, something he'd become all too accustomed to doing with Edirp.

A roughly hewn pathway delved deep into the mountain until it reached a spacious cavern. Wooden support beams held the tunnel firm. Herm was yet to accompany Edirp into the mountain and, as they moved along, he noticed a strange brightness that had nothing to do with the flaming torches mounted on the walls. He knew the cause of the untorvacanely light and worried his footwear wouldn't be appropriate. Was gold slippery? Herm and the king reached an opening at the end of the pathway.

"Wow," whispered Herm. His jaw hit the floor like an elephant whose parachute had failed.

A spring steamed lazily before them emitting a faint sulphurous smell. Herm couldn't see where but assumed it escaped into the mountain and out through some secret exit. It was a natural geothermal spring, warm enough to bathe in safely, with a high mineral content that might prove beneficial to Herm's nerves. The urge to take a relaxing bath nearly swallowed Herm whole. But his eyes decided to drink in the rest of his surroundings.

The walls glistened gold and the ground shone too. There were clusters of gold that had risen up as though two parts of the ground had crashed together like tectonic plates. Some had rebelled and begun to spill out. Gold appeared to have been interwoven into the rocky walls by grandmother knitters, those responsible for many a gaudy Christmas jumper.

Stretches of dust sheets lay along the floor, hammers and chisels and picks scattered across them. There were a group of dwarves arguing animatedly to their right. It suddenly seemed irresponsible to have so many sharp tools in the vicinity.

They hadn't noticed Edirp or Herm enter.

"I ain't workin' near tha' thing anymore," a heavily bearded dwarf said.

Which offered little distinction as all dwarves are heavily bearded.

"T'ain't no reward w'thout no risk," said another, the lead miner. All that distinguished him was a slightly larger helm.

"T'at's risk in finance, this is risk o' bein' eaten. T'is diff'rent."

This was followed by nods and grunts all round.

"Did someone say summat 'bout fine ants? Wha's ants got t'do with anythin'?" said the eldest and greyest of them.

"Don't worry Gumlot, s'nothin' ta do with ants."

"Good. Pesky little buggers the lot of 'em," said Gumlot. He continued complaining about ants for ten minutes.

The lead miner looked a defeated dwarf. He had one last gambit.

"Alrigh', alrigh'. 'Course, if we leave now, we forfeit ar' fee…"

There was brief silence and an exchange of glances.

"S'pose t'ain't a big dragon…"

"Sturdy lookin' curtain righ' there, prob'ly hold it off."

"Pass t'pan, le's get back t'work."

The lead miner breathed a sigh of relief. This happened at least once during every job. If it wasn't dragons to complain about, it would be a draft, or a smell, or cheap and ineffective beard trimmers.

Edirp smiled. He'd have hated to have to chop the lead miner's head off. Dwarves were so stubborn it took at least three swings.

Herm was still retrieving his jaw from the floor. It had to be around here somewhere.

Despite the gleaming gold and the mounted torches, it was apparent there was natural light sneaking in furtively from above. There must be a way out up there too, thought Herm.

Herm failed to notice that Edirp had set off walking and was stood on the far side of the spring examining a clump of gold that had taken on a phallic shape. Smiling, Edirp turned to face the wall behind him. What had escaped Herm's notice was that this wasn't a wall at all. Up close, he saw the texture was smooth.

It was a manmade partition. Crude iron hooks had been hammered into the jagged ceiling and stalactites on which to hang a thick curtain. Scorch marks littered the material.

"Come with me Herm," said Edirp with a reverence reserved for things of rare and dreadful beauty. "I want you to see something." The egglike smell of sulphur distracted Herm from the strange affection in Edirp's words.

They pushed aside the dividing curtain and slid through into a much smaller space, one where the smell was less pervasive. The cavern walls before them now were mottled limestone sporting a glistening nugget or two, but without the over-awing goldness of the previous chamber. Across from them, embedded in the uneven walls, was another curtain. This one was shivering with a gentle rhythm, just like breathing.

The space they stood in resembled an office. An office in dire need of redecorating, but an office all the same. A couple of tables and chairs and a rudimentary set of shelves that someone had hacked into the cracked limestone. On these shelves sat rows of glass vials and beakers containing liquids of assorted colours and viscosity. Herm hoped he was never thirsty enough to chance drinking any of them.

There are some who appropriate the maxim of always trying something once, which is all well and good, thought Herm. But if it's luminous green and steaming like a lava pit it's best to leave it well alone.

Occupying one of the incongruous chairs was a man nursing a nasty burn on his forearm. Bright and sharp against his dark skin, the wound oozed. Dabbing the reddish burn with a damp cloth coated in something pungent, he noticed the visitors. The man dropped what he was doing and stood to attention, causing his face to crease with pain. Edirp seemed not to notice.

"How is she this morning, soldier?" said Edirp, weighing up the man before him like a father would when his daughter brought home a new boyfriend: sceptically and suspiciously.

"Still weary sire, still weary, though she ate well during the night," came the reply. There was a note of apprehension in his voice that sailed so far over Edirp's head it scraped the ceiling.

"Excellent, excellent, and what did she eat? We must have a firm grasp of her dietary needs in order to get the best out of her," said Edirp emphatically.

"Well sire, it was Bill…"

"Ah, bill? Good, good. I'm unfamiliar with bill, some sort of herb no doubt…"

"Erm, Bill was a person… sire," said the soldier, whose name, appropriately, was Skarz.

Skarz had drawn the short straw and been promoted. Being Head Dragon Watcher (he had to be 'Head', he was the only one left with his still attached) offered plenty in the way of job enrichment but little job security. The rewards package was actually rather good but to enjoy it you had to survive your shifts first.

Poor Bill, he thought.

Skarz had figured since he was stuck down here he may as well do his best. It had begun to dawn on him he was lucky he'd been blessed with two of each limb. His burn stung terribly.

"I'm sure Dill would have been proud to have died so magnanimously, fulfilling his duty," said Edirp.

"You mean Bill, sire?"

"Enough about herbs, we have business to attend to."

Skarz and Herm exchanged a look. It was the kind of look that said: 'I know I'm here and I know you're here, but where is he?'

You can get a lot from just a look.

"I want men guarding the tunnel entrance, Herm. I

don't want just anyone wandering in here," said Edirp, gazing toward the lightly swaying curtain with an affection that bordered on affliction.

Said curtain had been replaced thirteen times already. Random bursts of flame had incinerated the current curtain's predecessors as well as one unsuspecting miner. Med Tet had seen to it that the best and most easily intimidated minds were working on fire-proofing the divider. Currently, the closest they'd come was curtain number eight. It hadn't allowed the fire to escape beyond it when the Dragon Lord sneezed. Sadly, it also exploded quite violently and nearly caused a cave-in.

"Yes sire, that will be arranged immediately," replied Herm, who was also fixated on the lightly shaking curtain, though probably for a different reason to Edirp. "Sire, I, er, it may not be my place, but, er, how exactly did we get the dragon chained up in the first place?" Herm said this very quickly. He regretted asking before he'd finished the sentence.

Edirp looked at his assistant and smiled, which was a relief to Herm. Quite suddenly, Edirp whipped around and strode back out into the larger cavern, purple robe trailing behind him.

Skarz simply stood staring after them, relieved he didn't have to deal with Edirp.

He'd take a volatile, fire-breathing dragon any day.

Edirp was positively giddy as he began strolling around the spring. He was skipping like a child in the playground. Clearly this was a tale he'd wanted to tell for some time. And so he launched into it, every detail, a great deal more than Herm's small question required or expected.

The Dragon Lord had been residing within the

mountain for decades, surviving off spring water and whatever unfortunate creatures happened upon its path. Almost fully grown, it had existed undetected all this time, unaware there was a world beyond the cave. It had likely never spread its wings properly, to Edirp's lament. When the miners had broken through and discovered the gold encrusted caves and the spring a messenger had fetched him with haste. It had been quite a shock to learn his first lead miner had been eaten, of course.

Edirp laughed to himself at that part. Herm felt a bit squeamish.

Med Tet had co-ordinated the men who endeavoured to capture the dragon and they did so by heavily tranquillizing slabs of meat placed around the cavern. The dragon had indulged, its suspicions curtailed by crippling hunger. Once knocked out, they'd chained it up and set up the first divider.

A tendency to snort in its sleep left the dwarves feeling uneasy working in close proximity. More than one beard had been set alight, leading to the addition a second partition.

Having been so heavily tranquillized the Dragon Lord was still groggy and weak and disorientated, like a groom-to-be the morning after his stag party. This made it easy to maintain its sedation from then on.

Edirp stopped walking and turned to Herm. A look of madness clouded the king's eyes.

"We all know the stories, don't we? The old wars, the wizards and the Dragon Lords. Well if they could control them, why can't I?" said Edirp, his voice curtailing to little more than a whisper. "So I read and I read, until, finally, I found what I needed. The wizards speak directly into the minds of the Dragon Lords. They soothe them until they become subordinates, mere soldiers to do their bidding. Now I am not a wizard, I do not have the power to do this. But I can gain it. Yes, and gain it I will."

Herm had been edging backwards, little by little. Suddenly, there was a splash.

"Perhaps you should be more careful, Mr Herm," shouted Edirp jovially, all signs of that burning intensity gone.

With this he spun balletically on his heels and strolled away, leaving Herm struggling to clamber out of the shimmering water. Herm dragged himself out and lay there – that hadn't been the relaxing bath he'd hoped for.

He was lucidly aware of two things. The first was that Edirp had stumbled beyond being a bit mad and into unbalanced with alarming speed. The second was that he'd need a change of clothes.

***

The River Sticks flowed quickly. Once it reached the outskirts of Vertenve it moved up a gear from 'quick' to 'rapid', probably so it could get away from Vertenve as soon as riverly possible.

The current was difficult to swim against and you'd often see assorted debris drifting along. What you don't often see is three men clinging on to a tree trunk arguing amongst themselves.

"I'm not confident about this, Caine," shouted Drago, who then swore in annoyance when yet another fish slapped him in the face.

"Fastest way round Vertenve, laddy," replied Caine before spitting water out of his mouth. "We'll be round t'foot of t'mountain in no time and there's some lovely views n'all." Caine managed his big, not particularly toothy grin. Something he regretted as more water sloshed into his mouth. Drago looked incredulous.

"You make it sound like you planned to take this route the whole time."

"Who says we dint?"

"Anyone sane!"

"An overrated quality in my eyes," added Korin, chuckling as his companions bickered like children. As the river continued to leap down their throats, the chatter subsided. All three were grasping a slender tree trunk that was acting as a taxi service. A service that was certainly not getting a tip at the end of the journey.

"I didn't know there'd be a waterfall," grumbled Drago, who hadn't recovered from having two near-death experiences in the space of half an hour.

"Well the water 'as t'get down from there some'ow, don't it?" said Caine, flashing his wide grin once more. Not having learned his lesson, Caine coughed and spluttered as Korin patted him on the back, grasping the log tightly with his other hand.

"The Sticks and Stones waterfall is a pretty well-known landmark in the Seven Cities, Drago. You really need to get out more," said Korin.

"The Sticks and Stones waterfall?"

"Yep, Sticks and Stones," answered a breathless Caine, "'cause normally when ya go over it you break ya bones."

"Last thing you're worried about after that is words," added Korin.

Drago turned pale. He frantically checked to see he hadn't broken anything. Having never broken a bone he wasn't sure how it should feel. After a short panic he concluded he was entirely intact and breathed a sigh of relief. An achievement, he concluded.

Escaping ravenous werewolves by diving over a waterfall came naturally to Caine and Korin and they were more than happy to hitch a ride on a tree trunk down the River Sticks, but it was all alien territory for Drago.

Since emerging at the foamy foot of the waterfall unharmed they'd settled in for the ride. The water wasn't too cold and there wasn't much of a breeze. This was, Korin reflected, one of their more conventional modes of travel. It wasn't the first time he'd drifted down river with Caine. It pleased him to recall there were no dangerous fish native in this stretch. The area of their bodies exposed to anything with teeth… well, it wasn't something he wished to dwell on.

Drago was bemoaning the loss of his satchel. He'd missed it somewhere in between running for his life, jumping for his life and swimming for his life. Noble plans for preparing hapless future adventurers with his detailed map were dashed. Hot meals would be harder to come by. Disaster. All Drago had left was the dagger he'd sheathed and pocketed and his sword which had somehow clung to his waist throughout the entire episode.

"What's the plan now then?" asked Drago, curious as to when their little watery adventure would end so he could be dry. He liked being dry. He couldn't remember being dry anymore. Dry was comfortable. Wet was not.

"We'll go around Vertenve," said Korin with certainty, "and get out there. We can scout the outskirts of the city for places to acquire food, drink and dry clothes."

"Then we storm Athea Hubris, takin' on every one of the bast…"

"I think it would be best to travel by the foot of the mountains. We'll be less likely to run into soldiers out that way. We'll move into the city and listen out for word of the gold mine and work out the best way in and out from there."

Korin had interrupted Caine before he'd built up a head of steam. Over the many years they'd travelled together he'd learnt a thing or two. Primarily, that if you were able to cut Caine off before he gathered momentum then the more impractical or downright potty ideas tended to slide away. He hadn't succeeded in doing this with the elephants. But that had been quite fun.

Taking on an entire army, however, seemed like something he ought to nip in the bud.

A quick change of subject was required. The water was less erratic and wild so they could speak liberally.

"Caine, back there, you didn't answer my question. Why did the werewolves seem so angry?"

Caine would have looked at his feet if he weren't floating.

"Well, I followed the lass 'til she walked into one of the buildin's," said Caine sheepishly, "and I figured it were prob'ly a shop. So I thought I'd go in and offer to help Red carry some stuff, ya know, all gentlemen-like. So I bumble in through the door…"

"Not exactly shadow-like…" said Drago.

"I was only gonna be found b'cos I wanted t'be found, ya see," Caine said, tapping the side of his nose with his index finger.

"Anyway, the werewolves?" Korin interrupted. His knowledge of werewolves was limited, but he knew enough to make an educated guess as to where this was leading.

"And," said Caine, "there were four of 'em, four girls, all real pretty and all comple'ely starkers!" Caine suddenly laughed riotously, happy that he could take the mental image with him wherever he went.

"They were naked?" Drago was unconvinced.

"Can you imagine the cost if you had to buy new clothes every month?" commented Korin sagaciously. "Stripping before the change saves a lot of money."

"Oh right. That does make sense. It hadn't occurred to me, we don't have many werewolves round my end," said Drago.

"Imagine being undressed when this grizzled old letch storms in on you," joked Korin as he splashed Caine.

"Hey," shouted Caine, "many a fine woman would love nothin' more than for me t'storm inta their boudoir in my birthday suit."

"You were chased out of Hyperia by mad priests in your birthday suit, if I recall?"

"Why are they always mad and religious?" asked Drago.

"Incense."

With no let up in the banterous oneupmanship and general musing, the three of them continued floating down river (or it could be up river, it depends which direction Torvacane is facing, something else those fine astronomers are struggling with). The shores were flanked by trees and shrubbery that rustled gently in the breeze. Beyond, pleasant green meadows basked in sunlit glory. The blueness of the water highlighted under the sunlight, it was a glorious stretch. Clean and clear. Unlike the three men currently travelling down it.

Caine had been right (a sentence that made Drago uncomfortable): there really were some lovely views.

While Drago had always felt there was a certain charm to Broth Zolust this scene was closer to what he had in mind when setting out determined to tag along with Caine and Korin. The drifting down river using a log as a float hadn't been something he'd foreseen. At least it was less embarrassing than arm bands.

The undergrowth became thicker and darker as the river slimmed as it meandered and turned. Trees lurched forward to hang out over the river, blocking the sunlight to a greater extent as they continued to drift along. Drago's feeling of hope withered with the scenery. The wind had picked up and the river was rougher. The rustling of the trees and bushes grew sinister.

And then, amongst the encroaching jungle, a clearing.

In the clearing is a peculiar house. And stood before this peculiar house is a peculiar woman. She beckons them indoors and they feel compelled to enter.

***

In the middle distance, Amelia could make out a bridge crossing the river. It was swaying. She couldn't hear at this distance, but she expected it sounded like Vector's knees.

The banks of the River Sticks had risen gradually until they were sufficiently high enough to be referred to as cliffs. They'd had no choice in that, their naming. Maybe they'd prefer to be called richards or steves? Instead they'd been pigeon-holed as cliffs irregardless of their personal opinion.

The cliffs, or richards, or steves, didn't tower above the speeding river below, but they were high enough for a person to incur that sickly feeling where your head starts to spin and your stomach drops to your knees. Amelia didn't have a fear of heights, just a fear of falling. She saw this as being perfectly rational. Reasoning that you had to be at a height to fall, logically, this led to her not being fond of heights. All of this and more was frantically skittering around her mind.

"Are there any other places to cross the river?" she enquired, examining the patterns in the sky. If she avoided looking down, she couldn't picture herself falling. But if she didn't glance to her left, she may not notice when there was an absence of cliff edge and an excess of fresh air. This would have escalated her trepidation tenfold.

"There are," replied Vector, "though none of them are twenty yards away like the bridge. Nervous?" Vector's eyes twinkled with mischievous charm. He was having fun.

"Nervous? Ha, no, of course not."

The award for least convincing line of the year had a new contender.

Vector merely smiled. He was further convinced that Amelia was a young, female version of her father. They certainly shared many traits and characteristics. An obtuse stubbornness for one, thought Vector, amusing himself. Guilty as he was at the thought, he'd begun to feel like he had his old friend back with him, or at least a shadow of him. It made him feel happy. Of late, a somewhat alien feeling. Wizards may be capable of many things ordinary men are not, but that does not mean they are indifferent to the need for companionship. They are human, they feel happiness and joy just as they feel sadness and despair. And loneliness.

Drifting amongst a cloud of reverie neither Amelia or

Vector noticed they were no longer alone on the path. A tremendous creature had appeared as if from nowhere, silent and deadly, ahead of them. Positioned directly between the bridge and where they stood. The bridge looked just as rickety and unstable upclose as it had from afar, easing to and fro like a drunk.

The creature stole Amelia's attention from the bridge. She was staring into the face of a handsome yet stern looking woman. It wasn't the face that so alarmed Amelia. It was the body of a lion the head was attached to, and the unfurled, expansive wings of an eagle that did it.

"A sphinx," whispered Vector. He'd never come across one himself. Not many people had. What worried Vector is that he suspected a large number of sphinx encounters were not recorded on account of the encounteree being mauled and eaten. Not a soothing thought. However, he had to appear calm outwardly as to not panic Amelia, assuage her as much as possible. The last thing they needed to do was spook the sphinx.

The sphinx settled itself on the path and retracted its wings, indicating it wasn't ready to maul just yet. Great, thought Vector, it likes to play with its food.

He wasn't quite sure of the appropriate etiquette in the current situation. Making up his mind hastily Vector stepped in front of Amelia, who stood frozen. The sphinx's claws glinted as if recently sharpened on a grindstone.

"Hello," said Vector. A solid start, he told himself.

"Hello," replied the sphinx. It's voice was haunting like an echo, somehow languid but effusive at the same time. A contradiction of a vocal tone if ever there was one.

"I trust you wish to cross the bridge?" said the sphinx, staring at Vector haughtily. Showing no sign of nerves, Vector held her gaze, but soon realised he had met his match. The sphinx's eyes lulled him into a light-headed daze from which he had to extricate himself. Amelia was now paying attention to the mildew that covered the grassier parts of the path, hoping she wasn't needed.

The river down below suddenly felt less like a threat and more like an option.

"That is indeed our intention," answered Vector calmly, regaining himself, "I should imagine you have a riddle for us?" Vector did his best to sound respectful. And he was respectful. He had great respect for anything that could rip him apart and eat the pieces. And if such an eventuality came to pass, he hoped he gave said creature diarrhoea.

"I have. If you answer correctly, I shall allow you to pass. If not, then your fate is sealed."

In what? he thought, lucky envelope number three? This reminded him of those horrible shows they used to put on in the old theatre in Broth Zolust. Simply the lowest form of entertainment. And it used to be such a lovely little place.

Concentrate man!

Vector nodded to himself, resolving to fix that old theatre up one day. As well as a love of the arts he also had a strong desire to remain in one piece, being ambivalent to existing as several. So he engaged his full wizardly wisdom and sharp mental acuity and concentrated all his energies.

"What is brown, but also sticky?"

This felt anti-climactic. "I'm sorry, could you repeat that?" Must have misheard, he thought.

"What is brown, but also sticky?"

Vector's erudite mind was flummoxed. This was such an asinine riddle it barely even constituted a riddle, he thought despairingly. What's brown and sticky? The obvious answer seemed outrageous, disgusting even, considering the legendary status these creatures hold. The sphinx maintained its haughty gaze, satisfied it was about to be well fed.

Perhaps it is some kind of insect, thought Vector, a moth perhaps, or a butterfly? He was no lepidopterist, to his everlasting regret. No, unlikely, they aren't the stickiest of things and they aren't entirely brown either. Something muddy maybe, like a pig. Yes, that could be it, they roll in filth all day, it could be a pig. I could really go for a bacon sandwich right about now, that would help me think. Yes, three rashers, lightly toasted bread and a cup of tea, lovely. Hang on, what was I meant to be doing?

Amelia coughed gently.

"It's a stick," she answered in the tone of one utterly confident in her indubitable correctness. A far cry from the Amelia of roughly two minutes ago that had considered leaping off a cliff, right into a literal phobia of hers. The river crashed about below, disappointed. No, Amelia had come face to face with danger and passed the test with flying colours, recovering from the early setback of being frozen with fear.

Unless she was wrong, that is.

"Bugger," said the sphinx.

Amelia took this as a positive sign.

Magnificent shoulders slumped, beautiful face demoralised, the sphinx stepped aside and retreated to the boulders it had emerged from.

"Well done Amelia, I knew you could do it, hence my

silence. Of course, I wouldn't have let it go on much longer, but congratulations all the same. You defeated the sphinx." Vector could do bravado and false confidence pretty well. In his youth, whenever he was in a sticky situation but couldn't remember how to do a certain spell, he'd just pretend he could.

This explained a few of his scars.

"Thanks," replied Amelia, giving Vector a funny look. She'd been certain she'd seen beads of sweat on his brow, and it wasn't exactly warm out…

The predicament of the sphinx was over for Vector and Amelia and this was a weight off their shoulders. The problem now, however, was the bridge. That would be the bridge that was clinging on by its fingernails, barely able to sustain its own weight, let alone the excess baggage of a wizard and a young woman.

The bridge swayed feebly in the breeze like rags on a washing line.

It was making a quiet creaking noise that prompted Amelia to say it was laughing at them. Vector himself pointed out it was an inanimate object and was unlikely to actually be laughing at them, although he didn't say this with conviction. You couldn't trust anything around these parts. Realising they were putting off the inevitable, they roused themselves and walked nervously towards the bridge. Their concentration snapped. From a few yards behind them something let out a tremendous burp.

The burp was then followed by a grubby looking glass bottle that Vector recognised. His least favourite whisky rolled noisily along the ground and over the cliff edge.

Apparently the sphinx had not reacted well to its riddle being solved. Clearly well stocked, it was now grasping between its paws another bottle of a viscous unknown liquid that looked to be bubbling aggressively. Amelia was impressed that it had managed to open the bottles without opposable thumbs.

She knew it would have been best to just go. After all, the sphinx would have eaten them had she not guessed correctly at the riddle. But she edged cautiously towards the pitiful beast and tried for a sympathetic tone.

"Erm, are you okay?"

"I am the great shhphinx, my dear, of corsh I am okay," replied the sphinx, whose elocution and lucidity of tone had curtailed exceedingly fast.

"How on Torvacane did you manage to get so drunk in the space of about five minutes?" exclaimed Vector, curiosity having overpowered his sense of self-preservation.

"Oh, I wash drunk the whole of the time, my good sir. I do shober good, don't I?"

It seemed to be appealing for approval at this moment in time so both Vector and Amelia felt obliged to nod vigorously and smile. The sphinx was swaying more than the rickety rope bridge, but with all the menace of a hairbrush. Amelia aired towards concern and asked again whether the sphinx was okay, just for reassurance.

She was not reassured.

"Well bishness hasn't been good. It's not exactly a prime, you know, prime shpot I've got here. And I can't think up no riddles no more, not good onesh," moaned the sphinx, hiccupping again. "I jusht sit here waiting, considering mort, mort, morta…"

"Mortality?" Amelia ventured an answer. She was fascinated by the part lion, part eagle and part woman amalgamation that stood (barely) before her bemoaning its lack of business in a drunken haze.

"Thash the one, mortathingy. Been considering it lots, you know, as you do. Ain't no place left in the world for us mythical creatures, not no more. Ushed to be a time when there was lots of mythical stuff around, ancient too. Not these days…"

The sphinx began to cry and sway in a pronounced fashion, totally lost in self pity. "I could have been someone, you know? Not like a proper contender, but, you know, one of those fringe contenders. Now I'm washed up, can't comes up with no riddlesh. Brown and sticky? Should have just said it was poo, shouldn't I? Leasht I'd get fed that way."

Vector warily stepped back from the sphinx and pulled at Amelia's arm, beckoning her to do the same. It had struggled to pull itself up to its full height and cast aside its bottle, which smashed into a rock. The rapid rate of erosion made Amelia wonder just what was inside the bottle.

"No mores, no mores. Time to go. Can't have little girlshes getting my riddlesh, not proper." And with this the sphinx stumbled forward, regained its composure, took a running leap over the cliff edge, and was gone.

"Do you think it will remember it has wings?" asked Amelia. It seemed unlikely. She hadn't expected it to do that, not at all. It happened far too quickly and suddenly for her to have done anything. Not that she could have stopped it. Tackling four-hundred-pound mythical beasts was not advisable.

"If it does, I doubt it shall use them," answered Vector, who was not stood at the edge. He'd answered from by the rocks that jutted out onto the path, right where the sphinx had lay in wait. Vector slipped something bottle-shaped into his cloak pocket. Amelia was staring at him and, despite his obvious guilt on this matter, he had an explanation. All good wizards have an innate ability to explain all actions until they sound like they've done the sensible thing.

"It can get very cold at night, Amelia. A few drops of this before bed could help to deal with that. You don't want to freeze do you? As far as I am concerned it would irresponsible of us to pass up the opportunity to stock up on rations such as these."

Well reasoned, thought Vector, smiling to himself.

"Drunk," muttered Amelia, although she found it quite amusing really.

"A drunk? You call me a drunk? My dear, I rarely touch the stuff. This is merely good sense."

"Sure, sure. The sense being taste."

Amelia turned to face the bridge, looked down, then turned back to face Vector. Faces can't turn green, but Amelia's did its best to try.

"You might want to pass me that bottle actually."

"Perhaps afterwards," said Vector airily, considering the task at hand, "we need to get across. I suggest you go first, you're much lighter, the bridge will certainly hold your weight."

"That's true, but then I should go second. Less likely to crash through it after you've been across." Amelia tried once more, and failed once more, to out-stare Vector. She sensed she would also lose this argument.

"My dear, it may have seemed like I was asking your opinion on the matter, but I was in fact telling you. You go first. I have many years on you and I would not be as great a loss to the world as you."

It is not just to seek out my help for this task that your father sent you to me. You will have an integral part to play in this before we are done, I am sure of it. Of course, Vector didn't say this out loud. No need to give her an inflated sense of self worth. Always a risk in the young.

And he could be wrong too. He hated being wrong.

"I knew you'd say that," moaned Amelia, looking pleadingly at Vector but knowing it would do no good.

"Do not try the puppy dog eyes Amelia, I don't like dogs. Now, the wind has died down a touch. I suggest you go now whilst it isn't shaking so much."

Amelia nodded solemnly. She shivered as she turned back to the bridge and took her first cautious step.

***

Son had finally sorted through the angry E.T Mails He'd received from across the galaxy and replied in the most humble, grovelling and apologetic way possible. He hated having to turn sycophant to defend His unruly little planet when it decided to metaphorically (and occasionally literally) do its business in the next door neighbour's garden.

But how does one house train a planet?

And does anyone make leashes large enough?

A resounding no seemed the obvious answer and Son wished He had no time to contemplate these things but, sadly, time was the very thing He had in abundance.

Strolling across His white marble floors, a must for any godly dwelling, He decided to take a further look at the three adventurers floating down the River Sticks. He had taken a liking to their outlook on life. Taking each day as it comes, living for the moment and tackling head on any problems that should arise in their lives. Mostly these were problems of their own making, but they were fun to follow regardless.

Son stood over the small circular pool of clear water that allowed Him to see everything that was happening on Torvacane. He called it His Oracle Pool. The water rippled gently as a myriad of faded colours became gradually more defined and bold and lifelike. Shapes began to form and soon these shapes took on fully realised beings.

Son was staring straight into the scene as though He was there Himself.

The trio were disembarking from a log they'd been clinging to and walking towards a house. It was a peculiar house. Son, of course, recognised it and He recognised the woman stood in its porch.

"Ooh oh," said Son.

***

Rain was falling. The kind of rain that bludgeons the ground into submission. Mean rain. What made it unusual was how this rain was falling on the entire forest surrounding them, but not this small clearing and house.

Music was playing somewhere. It sounded like a harp.

And the smell. The house smelled enticing, like a bakery in the early morning. Cookies, bread, pastries. It was a homely and comfortable smell and it fitted the cottage perfectly. Potted flowers hung from the windows, hydrangea bushes beneath them, and a neatly thatched roof sat atop the house with a little chimney puffing away. In the porch stood an old woman, short, with a slight hunch. She wore a white cardigan over a pink, floral dress. Her eyes were bright.

"Hello dears," she said in a high-pitched voice, "you all look so hungry. Do come in. We'll get you fed right up."

As she turned and entered the cottage the door remained open. Caine and Drago didn't hesitate to march right up and enter. Korin slowed enough to look at the forest surrounding the cottage. This was the Forest of Perpetual Rain, a miserable and wet area where the rain never stops. No one lived here, or so he thought. You'd need to do a lot of praying to Son to ward off these particular rains from your home. Korin doubted this was an act of god, so how did this little cottage circumvent such a powerful effect? There were no other bare patches in the expansive cover of rain. It could only be... witchcraft.

Now Korin had never had positive dealings with witches. But when Caine has made off with your flying broomstick, an attempt or two at zapping you into a frog were justified. Regardless, Korin felt he should keep a close eye on this apparently welcoming host.

But then that smell was so lovely and the music calming... He could always worry about whether this nice old lady planned to stick them in a stew once they'd been fed. After all, they'd missed the chance to eat back at Red's because, well, they didn't see eye to eye over what to have for dinner. So Korin obligingly followed his companions into the house.

"What a lovely home you have," said Drago, remembering his manners once more. On this occasion his words were true. The décor inside matched the cuteness of the exterior. Cosy armchairs and a sofa, a roaring fire, quirky trinkets, vases filled with flowers, the lounge was comforting. The kitchen had mahogany furniture to match the sideboards and, built into an alcove within the exposed brickwork, a large, black stove and oven. Pots and pans hung from the low ceiling.

The old woman appeared in the lounge where the three travellers were reclining with a tray of sweets and cakes.

"Tuck in, you youngsters. Plenty more where that came from."

Caine and Korin exchanged a glance. Neither of them had been referred to as 'youngsters' in the best part of half a century. The tray of cakes disappeared in a feeding frenzy akin to sharks. Another tray of pastries came and went in similar fashion, the laps of Caine, Korin and Drago a sea of crumbs.

"Wouldn't 'appen to 'ave a spot of apple pie, would ya?" Caine asked.

"As a matter of fact, I do, my lovely. Just a moment."

She returned with freshly baked apple pie and custard and Caine appeared to be on the verge of proposing marriage. How he intended to fit a wedding ring on a pie was another matter.

Music continued to play. It occurred to Drago that he hadn't seen a harp on the way through, something he whispered to Korin while their host dashed about serving Caine seconds and thirds.

"Something isn't right," Korin said, yawning. "The house doesn't make sense."

Drago yawned in response.

"Well if I'm boring you…" Korin said, before yawning again. Rubbing his eyes, he turned to Caine to gain his expertise only to find him lay back in his armchair and fast asleep. Moments later, he began snoring.

"Why am I so tired?" Drago asked, resting his head on

the arm of his chair. Korin looked at him through glassy eyes.

"Because, my dear, you have listened for too long to my lullaby harp spell. Three trays of desserts won't have hurt either. I am the Forest Witch and I am hungry."

Korin, clinging on to a state of wakefulness, saw a change come over the old woman. Firm and upright, her wrinkles ironed out, colour returned to her hair. "I thought two kids pushed you into an oven?" Korin muttered.

"Two children? Isn't that the one with the gingerbread house? Do you know how fragile gingerbread houses are? No, that was a different witch. And good riddance. Giving the rest of us a bad name," the witch said, a vigour returning to her words, the little old lady disguise fully faded. Stood over Korin, watching as he too succumbed to sleep, was a woman with striking sharp features, sleek black hair, wearing fine silks.

The sleep-inducing harp music subsided and the witch broke out into manic laughter. As was proper for the occasion.

***

Edirp was in a good mood. He whistled as he walked and nodded with a smile at the guards stationed upon each descending level of the dungeons. This frightened the guards. Never quite knowing what to think of the eccentricities of their king, they did their best to appear professional, subtly sliding the 'Help Wanted' section of the local newspaper out of view. Herm scurried behind the king with an apologetic look on his face. This did nothing to ease the guards' concerns.

Athea Hubris's dungeons were typical as far as dungeons go. If you've been in one, you've been in them all. Darkly stained stonework, rusty bars and very little light allowed to seep through, the kind of place people are forgotten in. On the lowest level the only light was candlelight, whenever anyone bothered to light them. The tricks the dark can play on a person's mind often saw prisoners lose their mind. Edirp didn't sleep well with all the screaming so the dungeons slipped out of usage during his reign. They had been popular with Edirp's father though. He couldn't sleep without the screaming.

"I feel like today is the day we make a breakthrough in our negotiations, Herm," said Edirp as he turned left through an arched doorway. This one led through to the cells, the cells in the deepest level. They had that macabre atmosphere and thick and musty air that all the best prisons have. You can't manufacture these qualities. It takes years of neglect.

Edirp was not possessed of patience, particularly in the area of criminal justice. He had a habit of skipping out the trial part and jumping straight to his favourite part: the execution. Which made it all the more unusual the prisoner he was visiting was still alive.

Pondering Edirp's wild misuse of the term 'negotiation' as well as his uncharacteristic persistence, Herm's gaze was drawn by the emaciated figure laid across one of the hard beds in the cell in the far right corner. They had reached the lowest level and it was every bit as creepy as Herm remembered. Spiders ruled these parts. Webs caressed large areas of the iron bars and covered them like lichen. Herm did his best not to disturb anything. The last thing he needed was to annoy the spiders, they could really hold a grudge.

The candle flames were still. Edirp casually strolled to the end cell feeling entirely comfortable with the eerie, shadowy nature of his surroundings. It must be a king thing, thought Herm.

Stopping abruptly and turning to face the lugubrious and forlorn figure of a man propped up on uncomfortable, rough-looking pillows, Edirp smiled. The candlelight illuminated the gaunt features of a frail old man dressed in dusty robes. Emilius Kaio was tired. He had intrepidly faced his tormentors without his will being broken. The same could not be said for his body.

"My good friend Emil," said Edirp amicably, "we meet again. I do hope you will be a little less rude today."

Emil raised his head, managed a sardonic smile, then spoke. "My dear Edirp, I'm afraid I plan on being twice as rude you moronic, limp excuse for a man. And don't call me friend, I am not your friend and I am quite sure that no one else would be friends with an uppity little retch like you either." Emil maintained his smile whilst staring at Edirp, who already looked like deserting the pleasantries in exchange for the thumbscrews.

"I see," replied Edirp curtly. The grinding of teeth could be heard, but he steadied himself, trying not to lose control of his emotions. "You are a stubborn one, aren't you? I was rather hoping we could sit down like mature, intelligent adults and discuss the control of my Dragon Lord. No more of the mud-slinging and torture that has become routine in our meetings."

"I find it laughable you appear to include yourself under the category of intelligent adults. You're a petulant, small-minded buffoon who holds a high position through chance and breeding, no more than that. And I will never, I repeat, never tell you a thing about Dragon Lords. I look forward to the day I am informed that its torn you to pieces, which it inevitably will." Emil broke out into an acrid laughter that echoed around the windowless dungeon.

"DO NOT LAUGH AT ME OLD MAN," screamed Edirp, whose loose control of his emotions had slipped once more, "I AM THE KING, KING OF THE CASTLE, KING OF THE KINGDOM, YOU SHOULD KISS MY FEET!"

"No thanks."

As Edirp stormed off shrieking for his torturers to report to the dungeons, toys well and truly out of the pram and out of sight, Emil lay back chuckling to himself. Knowing as he did that Edirp would call for the torturers whether Emil insulted him as creatively as possible or offered him a cup of tea, he had decided to at least have a little fun. "Too easy," he muttered, grinning.

***

Smoke puffed from the chimney above the cottage.

As Caine, Korin, and Drago each stirred from their respective slumbers they discovered their hands were bound behind the mahogany chairs they had been sat upon. They sat facing the oven and could see an orange glow mocking them through the grill.

"Wakey wakey, boys," said a voice that felt distant.

This was met with groans.

"I'd forgotten 'bout you," mumbled Caine, blinking his eyes back to life.

"Well that is rather insulting, I must say," replied the witch, licking her lips. She continued pouring spices into a cauldron full of…

"Eurgh," said Drago, "vegetables!"

The Forest Witch eyed Caine and Korin, back and forth, before setting her sights on Drago.

"First adventure, is it? How adorable. Alas, this is the bit where you perish at the hands of the wicked witch. I do hope it was worth it. What was the idea? Two old hands show you the ropes, yes? I'm afraid these two aren't quite up to scratch."

Drago glanced left and right, sandwiched as he was between the two grey old men alongside whom he was now expecting to die. He felt like a fool. What had he been thinking? Another dire situation, facing certain death, this time being cooked and eaten. It's not been my week, thought Drago.

A black cat hopped up onto the windowsill and miaowed. Yellow eyes glared at the trio and the cat let out a hiss.

"Just ignore Bubble, he's not friendly toward strangers. I don't know where Toil and Trouble have got to," said the Forest Witch, walking over to the kitchen window and looking left and right.

"Black cats, a cauldron, mysterious cottage, black dress, ya got all the witchy stuff, but ya don't look much like one. If ya pardon me sayin', miss," said Caine, shifting in his chair.

She smiled and appraised Caine. "Well I could say you don't look much like an adventuring hero, couldn't I? Not everything is as it seems. Let that be a lesson," she added, patting Caine on his mud-stained knee.

Drago couldn't comprehend the oddly jovial atmosphere. Especially as he could hear the fire in the oven stove crackling with menace. Was the Forest Witch simply playing with her food? Perhaps she's lonely, he thought. Stuck in this little hideaway with the river before it and surrounded by a nigh-on impregnable forest where it never ceases to rain, he almost felt sorry for her. Almost, but not quite.

Drago noticed Korin had been quiet for some time. He hoped this meant he was concocting an ingenious plan to spring them from their chains. Drago looked to Korin with hope in his eyes and realised he was about to speak.

"Could I have a glass of water, witch?" asked Korin.

Drago sagged. In the process of sagging, he failed to notice that Korin was paying close attention to the witch's face. Whatever it was he was looking out for, he saw it.

"I'm not your maid," she replied, a small crack in her voice. The witch recovered herself. "And it's Forest Witch, if you don't mind. I have a title and I suggest you use it."

Drago, unaware of the subtle struggle for power that had just taken place, stared at his feet glumly. The Forest Witch turned back to him. "Now how would you like to be cooked, young man? Boiled? Roasted? I could marinade you in something? I'm feeling open-minded so I'll allow you choose. Go on, choose."

Before Drago could respond, Korin jumped in.

"Oh, I bet you say this every time," said Korin, "for the love of Son, why can't we catch a break?"

Drago stared perplexed at Korin.

"Aye, we try so 'ard, ya know? Plans, good'uns too, but we never 'ave anythin' work out. All our lives, failures, that's wha' we are. We're right sorry, Drago, f'draggin' ya into our daft plans. And now we're at t'mercy of this 'ere witch," Caine added with a despondency seen only in the very worst of actors. The two old men wailed like schoolchildren, stamping their feet, on the verge of tears, in perfect unison. They were of one mind, Caine and Korin. Whether they were of sound mind was debatable, but they were certainly of one mind.

The Forest Witch edged closer, her hair falling by the sides of her face, eyeing this bizarre show with suspicion.

And Caine leapt up, barging her towards the oven. The back of her dress, covered as it was in lovely and flammable frills, caught fire.

"Run," Korin yelled.

The three men crashed through the front door with mahogany dining room chairs still strapped to their backs and trampled through the hydrangeas. Behind them they heard a wicked screech.

"Wait until she sees the flowerbed," said Korin, heading for the trees. "Into the forest, she won't follow us there."

Unsure how Korin could know that, Drago considered responding but, upon the realisation that this was not the time for a committee meeting, he followed the two crouched old men who, from a great distance, probably looked like the fastest tortoises in the world.

***

The first signs of Torvacane's rings were etched across the sky as evening drew in, casting a faint silver glow upon the land, a glow that would intensify as evening turned into night.

Amelia and Vector could see the outline of Rathendy. It appeared jagged and irate against the horizon. They would be there by morning, but as to what the plan was Amelia felt very much in the dark. She would ask Vector later though. She still felt a little shaken up. They'd both made it across the sphinx's bridge without much of a scare, prompting Vector to remark how it hadn't been so difficult after all, that they'd built it up into some kind of demon in their own minds. Then as they'd turned to set off there was a loud snapping noise and the whole thing had collapsed and crashed into the river some forty feet below.

The area that lay before them was several miles of marshland. Shallow pools of muddy water covered the ground as far as they could see, a thick mist hovering above them. You could taste the sickly smell on the air. Many battles had taken place here in the past and a large part of its make up was decomposition. Bodies to be exact. This had contributed to a stench that had left the air thick, the humidity exacerbating the smell. It was a morbid plain.

"It really puts things into perspective, doesn't it?" said Vector. The marshland was full of sorrow and memories, something that he could feel in his bones. Not a wizardly trait he was fond of.

"How so?" Amelia asked, not sure she would like the answer.

"This land, it was once fruitful and green. People lived here happily for a time, the closest thing to harmony that Torvacane has seen even. And now look at it, a wasteland. Just another example of the damage warfare causes, a symbol of death and destruction." Vector had turned away from Amelia as to hide his face for a moment. He blew his nose loudly.

"Ew," said Amelia.

"Pardon?"

"Nothing," replied Amelia hastily, "but yes, you're right. We cannot allow this to happen again. I don't feel particularly tired, bit of a second wind. If we travel by night we should be able to reach Rathendy by late morning, given a couple of hours rest later on."

"Sounds good to me," said Vector, having pulled himself together again. "And I suspect you'll be wanting to know the full extent of the plan I have concocted. I've decided to call if Operation: Save The World."

"I didn't know it had to have a name," said Amelia, suppressing a giggle, "can it not have a cooler name than that?"

Vector folded his arms in as sulky a fashion as he could muster. "I thought that was pretty cool," he muttered. "Perhaps I'm just getting old."

"No, that's a good name really. I was kidding. Operation: Save The World is cool," said Amelia, backtracking quicker than a gazelle that had stumbled into a lions only nightclub.

Ringlight now illuminated the marshland. It looked like someone had put birthday candles on a bowl of gruel. A pervasive glow shone from the pools of dirty water giving the land a haunted look, as though the very souls of the men who had died there were attempting to escape, but were being sucked back. Mildew coated the few rocks that had forced their way up and exposed themselves to light. It would be a very depressing place to travel across alone, thought Amelia. She felt lucky to have Vector by her side. Something she was certainly not prepared to admit to him.

"So," said Amelia slowly, "the plan?"

"Ah yes, the plan." Vector pulled out an old pipe from

his pocket, tapped its side with his index finger, and lit it. This was something all good wizards did before launching into a monologue. "Well…"

"What's the pipe for?"

Amelia's interruption was unwelcome. She's unaware of the rules, thought Vector, remain calm. Never stop a wizard once he's lit his pipe. These things are all about rhythm and momentum. A bit like an egg and spoon race.

"It's for the effect girl, now do you want to know the plan or not?" Vector said this a little more sharply than he'd intended, but it seemed to work.

"Sorry, carry on."

"Right." Vector cleared his throat, took a puff of his pipe and composed himself. "We need help in this and a lot of it. The steward of Rathendy, Antillia, is not like many of her peers or descendants. She is a measured and intelligent woman who will not rush into war as easily as her hot-headed ancestors. However, it is imperative that we convince her war is the only option. She has spies of her own. She will have a vague idea of what is going on in Athea Hubris. If she sends word to Vertenve then they will surely ally with Rathendy against Edirp. No other city will so our eggs are in one basket in that respect."

"Sorry to stop you but why are Vertenve the only city who would answer the call to fight Edirp?"

Vector dropped his egg and tossed his spoon away in frustration.

This was to be expected though. Vector recognised that Amelia still had much to learn about the politics of Seven Cities. Despite the disruption, he entertained her question. He'd give her a full lecture on the art of indulging a wizard and his windbagging at a later date.

"Gredavia are money hungry, they won't bother to

oppose anyone, they'll simply wait to see who comes out on top and then begin immediate trade negotiations. Slotopia are a lazy, self-satisfied bunch who won't deal with a problem unless it's on their doorstep. And Broth Zolust is a mess, their army exists merely to drink itself to death rather than die in battle," said Vector with a rueful smile. "No, Vertenve are our only likely ally."

Amelia did not reply to Vector. She clenched her fists, her knuckles turning white. The ring above was emitting its silvery glow. A beautiful sight. One of those sights that people take for granted. There were still many other beautiful sights on Torvacane, yet so many selfish people weren't willing to fight to preserve them. This, she thought, was the greatest crime of all.

Vector sensed the fury simmering under the surface, but chose to continue. "We need a diversion. Sadly, bringing war to Edirp's doorstep is the best diversion we can provide. The sooner the better, whilst we might retain some element of surprise."

This was an optimistic thought but one he held to and, hopefully, it would turn out better than the last time he'd tried to surprise someone. On that occasion, the surprisee had sprouted a second set of ears. Magic has a habit of just happening to you when you're younger, you learn to control it over time.

Vector halted and rested his hand on Amelia's shoulder.

"You need to hear this, Amelia."

For the first time, Amelia saw Vector as an old man. He seemed tired.

"Your father has been captive for some time now. You need to be prepared for the possibility that we will not find him alive. You understand this, right?" Vector was urging Amelia to not only understand but to process. He knew she would have to come to terms with this quickly if she was to continue on their quest. Without a degree of realism and balance they could very well make a wrong decision. They must think with their heads and not their hearts. Vector would never have admitted this to Amelia, but he had to consider the bigger picture: there was a very real threat to the safety of the entire populace of Seven Cities and preventing its full realisation was their priority.

Vector was stood so close Amelia could see her reflection in his eyes. And see the breadcrumbs in his beard.

"I am well aware Vector. But thank you. And, I don't know why, but for now at least, I'm sure he's still alive. I have to hope."

The silence stretched on. A bird settled on a mound nearby singing a delicate song.

It went on. Finally, Amelia spoke.

"These marshes really do stink, don't they?"

"They truly do," said Vector, "let's get a move on."

***

Antillia was in a dour mood. Each day reports reached the steward's chamber, a place she was spending more and more time in these days, of a great danger building in the north, and the pressure and onus was on her to react to it.

To her, full scale war was the last resort. It simply had to be.

Antillia knew the stories of the war well, her father had ensured that. It had been a trying time, leaving scars in many shapes and sizes, some superficial and some far deeper. And now, barely a generation on, the war machine appeared to be revving its engines again. Or at least oiling itself up.

"How has it come to this?" muttered Antillia under her breath absently, forgetting she was not alone.

"Sorry ma'm?" Heron, Antillia's assistant and confidante, long-necked and eagle-eyed, had been watching warily, milling around tidying up. At least, tidying up of a sort. The type of tidying up that teenagers across the universe are adept at, the type where you just move things back and forth.

Of late, Antillia had seemed lost in her own thoughts. This was unusual behaviour in Rathendy. Ordinarily, people shouted their thoughts very loudly in each other's faces.

"Oh, nothing Heron, nothing. I am glad you are here, I have an order to be passed onto the captain of each army barrack in RathDownTown," said Antillia, rising wearily from her throne. "I want them running drills, the armed forces have been inert for too long. And I want weapons training high on the agenda too."

"Yes ma'm, it shall be done. But they will ask why, so what should I tell them?" Heron, as adviser to the steward, was sharper than he looked. It was why Antillia had chosen him. He wasn't the usual burly berk that was promoted simply on the width of his neck.

"Tell them I want Rathendy to be proud, once more, of the men and women who would give their lives for our safety. And it doesn't hurt to keep in shape," said Antillia, glancing down at her own belly which had been developing nicely during peacetime.

"Tell them I shall be joining them too."

"As you wish, ma'm," replied Heron, already backing up and creeping toward the exit.

"As will you, Heron," said Antillia, laughing for the first time in quite a while. Heron nodded and left. Antillia could have sworn she heard something that sounded like 'bugger' from the hallway.

Antillia rose unsteadily from her seat. She really had let herself go. Or perhaps age was catching up with her? The balance of her hair had swayed from black with grey streaks to grey with black streaks. She strolled out onto the balcony and looked out across her city.

It had been a struggle, rebuilding, but things were moving along. There were a lot of upright structures at the very least, an achievement in itself considering her architects went off pure imagination and a rudimentary knowledge of physics. Building was more of a trial and error process in Rathendy.

Luckily, everything ran through her and she exercised a moderate level of restraint. Just yesterday she'd had to overrule one of the more flamboyant architects who wished to rebuild city hall as two large domes with small pink spires atop each. That had been one of the easier decisions she'd had to make.

There was still much to be done. Starting with breakfast.

"These are interesting times, that's for sure," whispered Antillia as she turned to re-enter her chamber. "I'd rather they were dull…"

***

Edirp was stood upon the battlements above his city.

"Look at them all," he said, "they have no idea…"

"Sorry sire?" Herm asked in the weary fashion of a man who'd had a long day at work and just wanted to go home.

It was only mid-morning.

"It's about time we introduced conscription, don't you think?"

This had to be a trap. It was impossible that Edirp had intentionally ended that sentence with a question mark. Herm was in a sticky situation. What to say? Veer towards the truth. Backtrack immediately if he disagrees. Good policy.

"I'm not sure that would be a popular policy, sire. Perhaps you should raise this with your advisers?'

A satisfactory answer, Herm hoped. It said a lot about the king that, as far as ideas go, this wasn't even his worst. It was still woeful, but a slight step up from keeping a Dragon Lord as a pet.

"Oh Herm, stop being such a pedant," replied Edirp, "it's difficult for them to advise me when I've identified the right course of action already."

He hadn't looked at Herm whilst saying any of this. He'd held his gaze upon the city as if waiting for it to evolve or change before his eyes. Which seemed unlikely.

The mist surrounding the mountain had settled above the city. Herm was merely grateful that his brief moment of resistance hadn't cost him any fingers.

"Yes sire, of course I see where you are coming from," answered Herm, privately thinking it was somewhere in between hopping mad and lock him up and throw away the key mental.

"Have it be known, Herm, that this afternoon I shall personally be travelling through the city accompanied by Med Tet and some of our finest soldiers and I will be hand-picking the able-bodied, adult men I feel are fit to enlist. I will allow them the evening to celebrate the honour before joining up."

They'll be banging on the citadel doors, flaming torches in hand by nightfall, thought Herm.

"Do you have all that, Herm?" Edirp had finally wrested his eyes from the city and turned to face his beleaguered and put upon assistant. Edirp had dark circles below his eyes as if he had been awake throughout the night.

"Yes sire, I have it, I shall get straight onto it," said Herm, glad that he wasn't required to deliver the so-called good news to the men of Athea Hubris. He wouldn't have made it back alive.

As Herm scurried off toward the citadel, Edirp sauntered off toward the mountain entrance, greeting the guard who had his crossbow trained on a renegade magpie that seemed hell-bent on death or glory.

***

Edirp made his way down the hollowed out tunnel into Misty Mountain. He skipped around the spring, breathing in its heady fumes.

This was, in theory, an active volcano. It was just very lazy. Magma provided the heat for the spring and the cloudy aesthetics of the mountain. There were fumaroles dotted about the outer layer of the mountain, blowing steam like unpredictable kettles, giving the appearance of mist. It coats the area and is how it came to be christened Misty Mountain (another accurate name owed to the famous yet inarticulate explorer Bumbo Clar).

Edirp cared not for the science or the gold. He was

fixated on one thing. He could hear the heavy breathing dancing through like an asthmatic sonata.

The dwarves were arguing again. This time it was about the heat. Gumlot seemed to think it was about feet.

"Chairs, that be the s'lution, if ya ask me. We need chairs."

Edirp ignored them as a scuffle broke out and shoved through the divider to the usual sight of Skarz, sitting at the table and dabbing at a fresh burn on his muscular arm with a damp cloth, cursing away. Before Edirp could say anything, he spoke.

"Sleeping currently, sire," he grunted, not looking up from his latest wound. After several late-night visits Skarz was no longer convinced he needed to show any decorum. "Should be safe to poke your head through."

He looked forward to the day the dragon was awake and feeling peckish when Edirp walked in.

"Excellent," said Edirp brightly, "I see you are taking your job as seriously as ever Skarz, you shall be honoured at some stage for your continued hard work. Have there been anymore… accidents?"

"Nothing fatal, sire, though Sid had his hair singed off along one side, got a little too close whilst she was sleeping. He's fine though, thinking of starting a band actually," answered Skarz with a grimace. He hoped Sid reneged on this plan, his idea of music was thrashing around angrily for two minutes then smashing his instrument. It'd never catch on.

Skarz elected to overlook the mention of honours, he wasn't interested in medals. He was interested in what Edirp was planning. Skarz watched with muted interest as Edirp eased the curtain aside. He looked tense, skittish even, but this was brief. Visibly relaxing, he went in.

Skarz returned to tending the scarlet burn that marked his left forearm, retrieving one of the brightly coloured liquids from his rickety shelf. There must be easier ways to get a tan, he thought.

Edirp's nervous shuffling evolved into a walk once he saw the Dragon Lord was asleep. Eyes wide in awe, he crouched down to gaze upon his greatest prize. His confidence around the beast was at an all-time high. Being in its presence felt natural.

"It won't be long. The old man weakens by the minute. His knowledge shall soon be my knowledge and I will know how to speak to you, soothe you. I'm sorry you're stuck in here, cooped up, it's simply convenient for now. You have a tendency to set people on fire which is a little disruptive in a more crowded area. Not that I care, I just don't want to be the one incinerated. So you see this isn't an act of cruelty on my part, merely a precaution. We'll need the people too, at least at first. Once we've tamed the inevitably infantile attempts at thwarting our progress from Rathendy, perhaps even Vertenve, we'll take over the world together, destroying everyone and everything in our way."

There was a clang from behind the divider. The Dragon Lord didn't stir. Edirp rose from his crouch and sighed.

"That's always the problem with people. They're always getting in the way."

Edirp steadied himself. Voicing his desires aloud had caused him to tremble slightly.

Something was amiss. Had he spoken loudly? He had slipped into a trance-like state. He pushed back through the curtain. A bowl lay on the floor, yellowy-green liquid pooling around it.

Skarz was gone.

He ran through the first divider. "Skarz!" he shouted, "it was just a joke my friend, nothing but a joke! Hahaha!"

"Musta bin a bad joke if he's run orf," whispered Greta, one of the dwarves.

Sweat began to form amongst the creases of Edirp's forehead as he desperately tried to find his man. The plan he'd meticulously calculated and implemented ever since the discovery of the Dragon Lord was in jeopardy through a lapse in concentration.

The dwarves were eyeing Edirp nervously. He was red in the face like he'd been quaffing Grog all morning.

"I'll make you rich Skarz, beyond your wildest dreams. Look around, it's all yours!" Edirp cried, exasperated and desperate.

"I'll 'ave it," said Gumlot. He was immediately shushed by the lead miner.

The gold meant nothing to Edirp. Nothing compared to wielding the ultimate power, the lone power in a crumbling world that needed putting out of its misery.

He ran off toward the tunnel.

"Must 'ave lorst a bet or summat," said Greta.

"He'll run a mighty temperature runnin' round 'ere in this 'eat."

"Aye, we ain't workin' no more in this 'eat!"

The lead miner felt like giving up. Pulling out his pipe, he lit it, puffed on it gleefully and began ignoring the entire team.

"Where's ma chair?" added Gumlot.

***

107

Edirp yelled in rage and confusion as he sprinted back up the tunnel towards the battlements. The tunnel was the only way out, wasn't it? Running wildly and paying no heed to his surroundings, Edirp tripped over a stray rock. He crashed to the ground in a series of ridiculous poses, one of which resembled Voguing. The proud king of Athea Hubris wept.

***

Skarz crawled on his hands and knees through the rocky crevice until its rough ceiling was high enough to stand up straight. A hint of light taunted him from far ahead.

It was no coincidence he'd launched himself into the spring and swam for the source. The dwarves were too busy arguing to notice him. You could always rely on dwarves to be totally unreliable witnesses. He'd figured the spring had to flow somewhere and explored a little when he'd been bored one day. That was how he'd found this little escape. It took a claustrophobic route down the mountain. If you wade through a couple of hundred yards of slender stream, down a dark and jagged tunnel, there's a gap that opens out onto the mountain path.

A path Skarz now stood upon.

"Madman," whispered Skarz to himself, "total madman."

He tried to dust himself down, dirt and muck covering his hands and knees. And his feet were wet too. This day just got worse and worse, he thought.

Skarz knew what Edirp's next move would be. He'd be public enemy number one in Athea Hubris by morning with a host of fictitious crimes to his name. He could only hope they'd try to make them interesting.

If Edirp continues unopposed the entire of Athea Hubris will burn. Its buildings and its people.

Skarz could not allow this.

He had to formulate a plan. Create subversive mutterings amongst the citizens. Once the seeds of doubt were sown he could start work on figuring out how they grow.

"Turn an entire city against its king, fair enough," he muttered with a wry smile, "life doesn't get any easier." A fleeting glance at his glistening scars and a final brief smile and he set off down the mountain.

***

The rain of the forest had soaked the three men through until they were as wet as barnacles and just as unwelcome. The forest groaned at their presence. While the Forest Witch refused to venture out into the rains, she was popular with the trees and animals. Caine was already at a disadvantage in any popularity contest by virtue of being himself, so as a group they weren't out of trouble just yet.

"Yowch," Caine yelled as he clattered the chair upon his back against a tree, breaking it up sufficiently to disentangle himself. Korin copied him and was soon free, after a short 'yelp' of his own.

"Can someone untie me?" asked Drago, his voiced raised to be heard above the torrential rain. It pittered against the muddy ground and pattered against the wide green leaves and branches of the trees.

"No can do. Ya'll 'ave to do it t'adventurer's way. Tha's a good tree, right be'ind ya. Go on lad, get it smashed," said Caine, his near-vacant grin tormenting Drago.

"He's right, Drago. We won't always be about to untie you. You need to get used to these little tricks of escapology," added Korin, a wide smile on his once-handsome features. Rain dripped from his fang earring. In fact, rain dripped from nearly everything. "And get a move on. It's raining, if you hadn't noticed."

A complaint about whether running back-first into a tree could really be called a 'trick of escapology' died in Drago's throat as he sighed, glanced over his shoulder, and ran.

"Ow!"

"Good lad," said Caine, applauding. Drago wasn't sure how sincere this was as he clambered to his feet, the material of his clothing surely more mud than linen and cotton.

Creaking echoes drifted amongst the treetops and the shadows danced. Eyes were watching them. The three men looked at each other, the persistent threats to their lives bonding them. Caine and Korin had been to the edge and back many a time but, with Drago in tow, they found themselves feeling a sense of guardianship, like they were mentoring the next generation. In a way, Drago was their legacy.

"I'm so wet, I can't tell if I'm weeing or not. Which way do we go?" Drago asked, his mood as damp as his clothing.

"Well," said Korin, crouching down and running his hand along the ground, squinting as he gazed in each direction, "it appears to run slightly downhill in this direction. I think that's our best chance of finding the river again. Everyone got everything?"

The other two grunted and the group set off walking.

Trudging through the slippery, muddy forest, tree

roots groping for them, the walk was a struggle. This forest disliked trespassers and roots grasped for the ankles of the travellers, tickling shins. By way of ensuring they weren't snatched up by malevolent trees they each took great care to watch their footing and moved swiftly. The air was thick with the smell of rain and moss. Time passed slowly. Drago realised he had a question to ask Korin.

"So why were you so certain the witch wouldn't follow us into the forest?"

"I'd heard a rumour, some time ago, that some witches don't like water. Melts them, apparently. Now I'm not sure if this is just a superstition or if there's anything in it, but the Forest Witch seemed to think so. With the consistent spell keeping the rains from her cottage, I thought I'd test the water, if you'll pardon the pun," Korin replied, grinning.

"Tree-mendous effort," added Caine, glancing at their surroundings. Drago stared blankly at his companions. Korin continued.

"I wanted to see her reaction to the mention of water, so I asked for a drink. Her face contorted just enough to convince me the very thought of it scared or disturbed her. With that, we just needed a few seconds to make a break for it."

Drago nodded and returned to his thoughts. Korin had kept his head when he'd needed it most, while he had wallowed in self-pity, waiting for death. Drago was worried. Perhaps he wasn't cut out for this life? He shook his head, mostly to himself.

"Aye lad, ya've nowt to worry about," said Caine, slapping him on the back. It was more of a squelch than a slap. "We've all bin there. No one jus' dives righ' inta this life. Takes some experience t'get ya panic head set."

Drago nodded but again didn't respond. There was, however, a small but distinguishable bounce in his step again.

Korin noticed it and smiled to himself. That old dog Caine was a softy at heart.

The undergrowth thickened as the decline steepened. They were heading downhill. Korin's confidence they would find the river soon was growing. He thought more about how they would proceed once they reached the river again. One glance at Caine and he figured they would wing it.

***

Son perused His filing cabinet. He couldn't remember how many wizards were left. He couldn't remember a lot of things. The problem is everyone expects you to know everything, but that's just unreasonable. To the casual fans, of course He was omniscient. But in reality, it was tricky to be all-knowing because all that knowledge gives you a headache, making it best to let some knowledge slide out of your head.

This was His first ever planet, after all, and everyone makes mistakes. For example, He'd given the planet itself a mind of its own. This was a mistake because it's a delinquent mind. It's a mind that wants to spray graffiti on galaxy walls, moon at Moons and refuse to pay bus fare.

He needed to focus. It was here somewhere.

Wizards can do magic and magic can be useful. In small doses. In large doses it causes no end of paperwork. You need a permit from the Court of Planetary Gods to rip holes in space and time.

Here it is. The list.

On it was the name of every living wizard still residing in Seven Cities.

Ah.

There were only two names on the list. Inconvenient. He might have to interfere if they fail and interfering meant walking amongst men, something He hadn't done in a long time. They always had such varied odours that it made Him uncomfortable. He'd just have to keep His fingers crossed. And, if required, sprout a few extra hands, and cross the fingers on those too.

***

They reached the river soon enough and began walking along the bank, confident that a plan of action would throw itself at them. Hopefully not from the trees. Drago was grateful to escape the grasping snake-like roots of the forest trees and the incessant rains, whose reach they were now stood just beyond.

Darkness had begun to creep in gradually but the ethereal light of the rings countered it quite nicely, a wispy glow emitting from the river's surface. The flow was slower here. It whistled, the water bumbling along in pleasant fashion. The incessant buzzing of all manner of creatures coloured the air, splintered by the occasional cold howl. The forest's edge was a short distance from the gritty mud path along the riverbank.

"So, what now?" Drago had grown impatient again with the languid, relaxed attitude of his companions. He'd soon calm down. The silence allowed him the opportunity to mentally run through everything that had happened to him since leaving Broth Zolust. He was just grouchy after yet another attempt on his life.

"Well I reckon walkin's a good idea. Seems we're goin' in the righ' direction, just a little slower than we'd 'oped. We can 'op back in the river and swim if ya like?" With this Caine starting jogging forward doing a poor imitation of a man swimming, arms flailing in an awkward doggypaddle-like motion. Swimming through the air, Caine disappeared around an upcoming bend and out of sight.

As he set off Drago turned to Korin and whispered: "how old is he again?" Korin looked ahead at his long-time companion with amused disdain.

"By my reckoning, he's as old as tough boots," replied Korin, now turning to Drago.

"What on Torvacane does that mean?"

"Erm, I'm not sure, I might have gotten a bit muddled there. Anyways, he's seventy-four. I think." Drago considered this as Korin attempted to work out where it was he'd gone wrong with his paraphrasing. He pinpointed the beginning, middle, and end of the sentence as the main areas of issue.

Drago was about to ask Korin how old he was, hoping to avoid sounding rude, when there was a yelp from ahead. They immediately set off at a run, swords out, only to sheathe them again once they regarded the unusual sight before them. In the Forest of Perpetual Rain lived several peaceful tribes beneath networks of simple canopies built to create small, dry villages. However, distrustful of outsiders, these villages were known to set non-lethal traps as a deterrent. Some of these traps could be forgotten about. As, it appeared, this one had been. Caine was hanging upside down with a rope wrapped around his leg and he was turning the air blue with every curse he could think of, and he knew a fair few.

"This is no time for games, Caine," shouted Korin, not trying too hard to hide his amusement, "we've got places to be and people to steal gold from you know."

Caine was trying to reach up and untie himself but was only succeeding in forcing the rope to sway, which in turn made his stomach do somersaults. The witch's array of cakes and pastries were on the verge of a reappearance but, just as his most recent meal reached the threshold, Caine crashed to ground with a thud, right into a puddle. Sitting upright and wiping mud from his face he turned to Drago who was stood by a tree, knife in hand.

"Thought I'd save you the trouble of showing me any little tricks of escapology," Drago said, grinning.

"Ya could 'ave bloody warned me!" Caine replied, his indignance unbound and his dignity (or what was left of it) gone. He rolled up a lovely mudball and hurled it at Drago, who ducked smartly and avoided it. The mudball landed with a splatter behind him.

A mightily enraged roar just beyond the trees followed this. Drago turned and stared into the abyss with trepidation. Darkness and unknown roars and howls were creeping up his top ten most hated things list. Backing up slowly, another thought occurred to him. He wasn't fond of large, yellow eyes either.

All three of these peeves together were a formula for fear, an increased likelihood of soiling oneself and sudden bursts of speed in the opposing direction.

"RUN!"

His cry bounced from tree to tree scattering the birds as Drago and his companions once again found themselves narrowly escaping a hungry enemy that bore them unwarranted enmity.

In this case, it may have been warranted. The wild animal was wearing a mud pie as a hat.

***

Antillia strolled down Warpaint Street with her head bowed and hood raised, deep in thought as she often was. She'd reached acceptance regarding what was to come.

War.

Her only source of optimism was that it could wait until after breakfast.

The sound of zealous merriment drifted from the barracks despite the lateness of the hour, yet Antillia felt no inclination to douse the fires of such riotous partying. Spirits needed to be high.

The new work out regime had been implemented over the past couple of days and the soldiers had pushed themselves hard. Some of the more perceptive men and women held suspicions, but it had been a smooth enough introduction. Her own presence will have helped as it showed the soldiers the great extent to which they were fitter than their steward. The downside of such commitment, however, was that she may be dead before she'd even gone into battle. Antillia turned back in the direction of the castle. A chill wind stopped her in her tracks and sent a shiver down her tired body. It was probably irrelevant, but the sudden notion that the situation wasn't so bad, that there was hope for this world, suddenly came to her with a jolting certainty. She couldn't identify the source of this conviction, but she continued walking on feeling fresher than her old legs could have hoped for five minutes ago.

Wind can do funny things to you.

***

Vector groaned.

"I've got boggy marsh goop all over my boots," he exclaimed, supporting himself against an old wooden post whose sign had long been stolen and used as a sled by the local youth.

They were an enthusiastic lot in Rathendy, though it was rarely channelled down useful avenues, often racing down pointless alleyways.

Vector took off his boot and proceeded to shake the filth off, but it was that stubborn sort of filth that finds all the nooks and crannies and infiltrates them expertly. It was clever filth.

"I give up," he cried, stumbling as he rammed his boot back on. "How have you crossed that horrible marsh without being soaked up to your knees?" Vector was now looking upon the surprisingly clean Amelia with curiosity born of annoyance born of filthy boots.

"I guess I'm just nimbler than you," she replied with a grin. It was true that she was very light on her feet, she could easily have been a gymnast if the sport of gymnastics existed on Torvacane. The closest thing was probably cat burglary.

The city of Rathendy was walled. Or, partially walled. About two thirds of it were circled by a twenty-foot sandstone wall. It had shallow cracks splitting the stonework, but it was sturdy and thick. Much like the people of Rathendy. Around the top, at set intervals, were beacons to be set aflame if they were under attack. At least, that's what they were built for. Now they were always aflame because the patrolling sentries disliked chilly night shifts.

Amelia and Vector wandered up to the city gate that was currently being presided over by two men in chainmail holding pikes. Or, to be precise, leaning on pikes. One of them appeared to be snoring, the other was watching the two curiously, clearly debating whether it would be worth the bother to question them at all. As they reached him he had a surge of motivation (a rare one) and clumsily stepped into their way, nearly falling over his pike in the process.

"What, um, business do you have in Rathendy?" he asked shakily. He immediately regretted this course of action.

It was Vector who answered. "We're here to begin the process that shall lead to the saving of this world and the recovery of this girl's father, a good friend of mine. So if you just stand aside and take the pointy stick with you we'll be on our way. Urgent stuff, I'm sure you understand."

The guard, who Amelia could see in the light was barely older than her and had a mop of blonde hair pulled back under his helmet, gawped at Vector for a moment before recovering himself enough to say, eyeline no higher than Vector's ankles, "oh, right, um, that seems reasonable." He promptly stepped aside, still dazed by the overly candid answer to his question.

Vector strode on with Amelia hurrying behind him feeling a little sorry for the poor young lad who was still trying to take in what had just happened, something that may take him at least the rest of his watch. She glanced back to see him scratching his head with the tip of his pike. An inadvisable act if ever she saw one.

A few seconds after she'd turned to face the city she heard a cry of 'ouch' from a short way behind her. Inevitable, she thought.

Rathendy's streets were pervaded by an unnatural gloom, an inevitability. Despite the raucous chanting from somewhere on the east side of the city Amelia could practically taste the foreboding. Perhaps it was the eeriness of the empty dark streets or just her imagination, it didn't matter. She knew the next few days could be pivotal. Looking around she wondered whether they'd begun the rebuilding process at all in Rathendy. Collapsed scaffolding seemed to be the only indication.

Some of the structures Amelia had assumed were houses were built from wood and had tin roofs. The further along she and Vector walked the sturdier the structures became, with stone and brick more frequent. Nearly all the houses connected by washing lines and rickety fences. Though the town appeared rough, it had a charm when basking under the ringlight.

She could discern a few more impressive builds dotted around, looming over the shanty houses.

Quite abruptly, Vector stopped and turned to Amelia. "You must understand, we need Rathendy. Without the diversion of immediate open warfare Edirp will have time enough to extract the secrets he needs from your father. Everyone has a breaking point. If that were to happen, we would struggle to contain Edirp and Athea Hubris."

Amelia nodded. She was taken aback by his sudden seriousness.

"You can hear the singing, yes? It will be coming from a bar by the barracks. The man who runs it is called Blaine. Tell him I sent you. He owes me one after I got him out of a sticky situation involving a rampant antelope and two hundred fire ants." Vector shivered. Those fire ants got *everywhere*.

"But anyway, he knows anyone who is anyone in Rathendy. If you hear a rumour in Rathendy, you can always trace it back to him. What we need to spread is a rumour of an impending attack from Athea Hubris. We need to get these people riled up, we need to light a fire beneath their bottoms" … Amelia choked back a chuckle… "if you'll excuse the phrase." Vector allowed himself a brief smile before giving his beard a quick twist (another wizard trait, frequent twisting of the beard infers wisdom).

"Okay, I can manage that, but where will you be?" asked Amelia.

"I'm going to pay good steward Antillia a visit. I hear she has a very rare cask of Coesustian brandy that I'm going to tempt her into opening," said Victor with a sly grin. Amelia glared at Vector for a moment before stomping off in the direction of the loud, rude songs.

With another chuckle Vector calmly proceeded toward Antillia's castle hoping to Son that she hadn't found the time to install the moat she'd always dreamed of.

***

"I'm in luck," muttered Vector as he strolled towards the open gate. At some point they'd begun creating a moat, grown bored, and discarded any plans to continue. Furthermore, they hadn't bothered refilling the dug-up area just yet. This Vector had deduced upon seeing the trench that circled roughly half the castle's walls. Much like the city wall it remained unfinished. Vector looked up at the familiar balcony that allowed Antillia to survey the entire city.

Although intrigued as to why the gate was open, Vector continued on across the sparse grounds toward the keep unchallenged. As he stepped through the threshold of the ageing keep he was met by a sleepy looking man with a slender build and pronounced bags under his eyes. "I knew you'd turn up in the middle of the night, you awkward git." Weary though he was, Heron broke into a smile. "How are you, old man?"

"I've been better my friend, and yourself?" asked Vector, returning the smile.

"Tired. And curious. But glad to see you all the same," replied Heron, extending a hand which Vector shook heartily. "Antillia is expecting you, I trust you'll be wanting a drink of something?"

To a wizard this is essentially a rhetorical question. The only real question is whether to boil the kettle or raid the cellar for something a little stronger.

"I do wonder Heron, my good man, whether you have any Coesustian brandy…" Vector rambled on absently about the merits of the lost cocktail recipes of Coesustin, infamous drink brewer and mass poisoner, and just about declared them the greatest loss Torvacane has suffered. Luckily, some of his brews remained found.

Heron, being a good listener but not particularly loquacious, nodded and approved when required to as he led Vector up the cold spiral staircase. He knew full well Antillia had anticipated Vector's parched nature.

Having reached the door to the chamber Heron bid his old friend goodnight and Vector returned the gesture and entered. Antillia sat on her uncomfortably regal chair swirling a glass of fine brandy in her hand. Another glass was laid alongside the bottle on a table that had been set in front of her with a comfy, incongruous blue armchair the other side of it.

"I thought you may be a bit more comfortable with this than a cold wooden chair," Antillia said as she rose to greet Vector.

"As always, a most hospitable host Antillia, how are you? And, come to think of it, how did you know I had arrived?" asked Vector, embracing another old friend.

"You are not the only one with spies my dear friend, although mine aren't in the form of golden eagles with names that do not suit their magnificence," Antillia answered with a laugh. "As to how I am, physically I am well. But a dark cloud hangs over us all and it most certainly affects my mood," Antillia said, this time with just a wry smile.

The two of them sat down and Antillia poured Vector a glass, examining his expression. She couldn't help but notice the twinkle in his eye. "I trust you aren't here just to relieve me of some of my favourite tipples, Vector?"

"As perceptive as ever Antillia. This is just an added bonus," said Vector, breathing in the aroma before sipping. Vector even made that approving 'aaah' noise as he drank, the noise that no one really makes when drinking something they like. It was just a reflection of how much he'd been looking forward to tasting this particular brandy. It didn't disappoint. "Spectacular," he whispered, losing his train of thought, staring glassy eyed into the swirls of the amber liquid. After a time he remembered himself.

"Ahem, yes, to business, I guess. How aware are you of what is going on in Athea Hubris Antillia?"

"Reasonably aware, although you hint at something more with your question alone. That oaf Edirp has been recruiting mercenaries, no doubt through that callous murderer Med Tet, to bolster his forces. Armaments have overtaken rebuilding as a priority as far as we can tell and there's been an unusual amount of activity around Misty Mountain. Only mining, I think…" Antillia spied Vector in expectation.

"I'm glad you've got an idea of the seriousness of the situation. However, it is far graver than you have perceived. We know of the gold, but immeasurable wealth is only scratching the surface. For a start, he has kidnapped Emil Kaio. Can you think of a reason as to why Edirp would do such a thing?" Vector's grave enquiry brought forth no initial response from the steward.

Antillia paused to contemplate for a moment, to try to understand. The silence went on and she drank deeply from her glass. Her eyes narrowed. And then a gasp of horror escaped.

"Impossible," whispered Antillia, rising skittishly and pacing up and down the room. "Do not joke about such things Vector, it's in poor taste."

Vector could see in Antillia's eyes that she knew it was true. Some innate knowledge that suddenly rushed to the surface. "I am sorry, it is the only explanation. And it could mean the end of everything. I suspect that upon discovering the gold mine they discovered the last of their kind, the last Dragon Lord, standing guard. And now Edirp seeks to tame it and use it, and you know as well as I the devastation that will ensue should he succeed. The wizarding community within Seven Cities, by my last count, is two. Hardly a force to combat a Dragon Lord. I still have some power, but inactivity… I've been dormant for so long… too long."

They sat in silence for some time, drinking steadily. If there had been a third person in the room they would actually have been able to hear their two minds ticking over such was the chaotic nature of their thoughts. This was one of those moments where you wonder whether ignorance is truly bliss. Then, of course, someone says something stupid and you feel a lot better.

"Time is of the essence then. I'll have to announce it soon. How can I put this upon their shoulders like some kind of large wooden cross to bear?" Vector wondered if this was some kind of reference. He made a mental note to look it up.

Antillia drained her glass and rose from her chair. She walked on wobbly legs towards the balcony and gazed out at her people with sorrow. At first, she thought a mist had descended, but she then concluded it was probably the drink.

Vector followed her out onto the balcony, looking beyond Rathendy at an entire world that had not yet recovered from the ravages of warfare. A broken world. But one still worth fighting for.

"These people may surprise you yet, Antillia." Stood out on the balcony under the ringlight Vector could see the fatigue etched on Antillia's face. She needed to rest. And so did Vector, now he thought about it. Or maybe a drink.

"Let us sleep," declared Vector, "decisions can wait at least until the morning. I trust Heron will have made up a guest bedroom?" Vector began making his way inside. Antillia slowly turned and followed.

"Yes, he is rather good. Care for a nightcap?" said Antillia, a hint of humour returning to her weathered face.

"You read my mind, old friend," replied Vector, clapping his hand on the weary steward's shoulder.

***

Amelia was close enough to make out what it was the men were singing now. She wasn't too impressed.

"We were born in a bin,
And cast out for our sins.
We'll drop our pants and take a lance,
Just so we can fit in!"

Pacing down the grubby streets she identified the bar in question, no doubt the bar Vector had directed her towards. She wondered if it would have a suitably crude name to match its clientele. A large sign above the door flanked by two blazing torches read: Bottoms Up. The name she could live with, it was the painting of a man mooning that she found off-putting.

"Oh well," she muttered, "time to light a fire beneath that bottom."

The interior of Bottoms Up was as she'd expected. A bar against the back wall lined with stools, most of which were chipped and cracked after being hurled at people so often, round wooden tables dotted about surrounded by grizzled looking men and women playing cards. And she also noticed the source of the rude warbling.

There were several groups of people stood up who were obviously soldiers crashing tankards together and singing merrily. The men were trying to out-man the others to impress the women and the women were keen to put the men in their place. An age-old battle.

As Amelia strode in several men's heads turned favourably and elbows nudged ribs and fingers pointed.

Amelia was ill-used to crowds and this crowd was non-too-subtle. By the time she'd reached the bar she was blushing crimson and staring at the ground.

"What you havin' miss?" said a gruff voice from behind the bar.

Amelia looked up sharply to see a tall, sturdily built man with shaggy red hair cleaning a glass with a rag that was doing more harm than good. She steadied herself and eyed up the variety of bottles set against the wall. "I'll have an ale, your choice Blaine."

The man's eyes flickered from the still dirty glass in his hands. "Comin' right up," he said, calmly placing the glass aside and selecting one he'd been more successful with. "Curious, I 'aven't seen you round before. You know my name, tis only fair I know yours." Blaine finished pulling the pint and slid it across the bar.

"My name is Amelia, I'm here to ask a favour. My friend Vector is under the impression you owe him one."

"And for what reason should I believe you even know Vector? He ain't here himself," Blaine replied.

Amelia took a large glug of her drink. "He also said I should ask you just how far the fire ants travelled up your…"

"Denny," Blaine shouted to a boy leaning against the far end of the bar speaking to a group of girls, "watch the bar." The boy called Denny waved a hand fleetingly and continued his conversation. Blaine didn't seem to care.

"Follow me."

He stepped from behind the bar and headed upstairs to much hooting and whooping from a few soldiers who became silent after a particularly malevolent stare from Blaine. Halfway up the stairs there was a very definite crashing noise from the bar.

"Shouldn't you attend to that first?" enquired Amelia curiously.

"If I attended every crash in my bar kid, I'd 'ave long since worn away the soles of my boots."

Amelia sensed Blaine was a man who didn't mince his words. She'd gathered this from his failure to mince his words. They entered a small, square room containing only a desk and two chairs, a lamp and several bookshelves jam-packed with thick and dusty volumes. Blaine collapsed into one of the chairs and gestured to the other.

"I assume this is a business trip?" asked Blaine, fiddling with a pipe and tobacco.

"Correct. Sort of. It's no sight-seeing holiday, that's for sure," Amelia said whilst crossing the room and sitting down in the second chair. "War is coming. It's practically on the doorstep and this entire place doesn't have a clue."

"You've got my attention," replied Blaine absently, still attending to his pipe. Something of a contrarian, Blaine enjoyed needling people. But while he might have appeared nonchalant, he truly was affecting his version of hanging on someone's every word.

"Vector says you're a man with connections. We need this whole place to think Edirp and his entire army are going to turn up and kick the doors down at any given moment. Can you help do that?" Amelia's gaze began to unsettle Blaine. He stood up abruptly as he lit his pipe and began circling the room like a vulture. Amelia noticed he had a slight limp.

"And how's a young girl like you mixed up in something like this?" he asked. Blaine had a knack for people, he knew where he was with people, and this girl exuded an intensity from the moment she'd sat down. Of course, that could have just been a cramp or maybe haemorrhoids, but he doubted it.

"Edirp has my father," she replied matter-of-factly, "he kidnapped him because he knows about Dragon Lords." Blaine stuttered sharply and froze upon hearing Amelia's last two words. He attempted to think up something worse but failed.

Blaine gathered himself and puffed on his pipe. He stood examining his books before turning to Amelia.

"They aren't extinct?"

Amelia shook her head.

Blaine went back to circling the room, occasionally pausing to wipe dust from a shelf with his finger. He could feel Amelia's eyes following him attentively and this brought a certain kind of pressure, unease. After a time, he spoke.

"Okay. Edirp has a Dragon Lord. He can't control it. He's a complete idiot. He's planning to attack. And he's a complete idiot. That's where we are?"

"Pretty much," replied Amelia rising to her feet, "we need to destroy the Dragon Lord, first and foremost. And what better way to distract Edirp than a full-on attack on Athea Hubris? Vertenve will join us. If we can reach the city before they realise what's happening, it could give us an advantage. Possibly, we could force a surrender without the need for bloodshed. What I do know is war will come regardless. Attacking whilst they aren't prepared gives us a shot at victory. If Edirp finds a way to control or even just unleash his Dragon Lord, we'll have a full-scale catastrophe on our hands."

"Have you got that little speech written down somewhere?"

Amelia scowled.

"Okay. Well then, I guess we should rally the troops. I should've known Vector would be the one to turn up with bad news one day. The man's a bad bleedin' omen, but a good bloke and a prompt payer of tabs. Now, you start with the boys in the bar downstairs. Keep it subtle. You've heard this 'ere, someone said this there. That lot downstairs will have told everyone within a half mile radius before the night is over. I need to head out to see a few people about t'city. By morn' there'll be a crowd outside Antillia's castle baying for blood, mark my words. Let's go." Blaine turned and stalked out. Amelia followed.

The violence in the bar had subsided for the time being. Denny was behind the bar mixing drinks for the same group of girls he'd been talking to when they'd gone upstairs. He was protecting the bar but apparently the furniture and windows were not priorities.

Blaine stopped by the bar and near enough growled, "you stay behind the bar tonight boy, and this 'ere girl drinks for free, understood?"

Denny had appeared dismissive earlier, but he looked like he knew where the line was. Eyebrows raised for just a second, keen eyes appraising Blaine's demeanour, he nodded and began pouring an ale.

"I don't really fancy drinking much…" began Amelia, but Blaine put his hand up to silence her.

"To deal with this lot, a few drinks will go down well, trust me. You take the room upstairs when it's time to retire, next door to the one we were just in, got it?"

"Yes, thank you."

Blaine nodded and strode off with as much purpose as a man with a limp could muster. Well, thought Amelia, I guess it's time to mingle.

***

Skarz had reached the end of the rocky mountain trail quickly and with just a few cuts and bruises from the occasional shortcut he took. That is to say he slipped down miniature rockslides like he'd landed on the wrong square during Snakes and Ladders.

The grim morning air bit at his face as he stared out at the forest before him. From higher up the mountain he'd been able to see beyond the forest to the coast and the Asthmatic Ocean. The sunrise and morning sky appeared like an oil painting upon the water. Sadly, he couldn't make towards that particular vista. He was to circle around the foot of the mountain and infiltrate Athea Hubris. He found it unusual to consider he had to infiltrate his home, but circumstances called for a covert approach. He would decide upon a concrete plan on the way.

Strolling to the edge of the forest he looked into the bleak mass of trees. They were unusually tall, fruit-bearing trees. In theory they had no right to be situated where they were. Then again, Torvacane rarely made sense.

Skarz could hear a high-pitched whistling noise and he couldn't quite work out where it was coming from. He peered deeper into the forest but could discern no movement.

It was getting louder.

Skarz reached for the hilt of his sword.

He realised too late the direction in which the noise was coming.

Looking up, Skarz had just enough time to establish something spherical and brown was about to hit him square on the forehead. And it did. Skarz lay prostrate on the ground as a coconut slid away, rolling away down the slope and into the forest.

***

Son didn't like interfering. He always felt it best for the people of Torvacane to solve their own problems and, in their defence, they usually did. People had plenty of practice considering they created so many. He sauntered away from the Oracle Pool, ripples fading to stillness in the now clear water. It's not your time just yet, He thought, not yet Skarz.

***

Scientists claim that there is nothing faster than the speed of light. This is wrong. The fastest thing in the universe is rumour. You'd be surprised at the overwhelming speed at which a rumour could spread, particularly through any of the Seven Cities. When you consider no one has invented television it is a little less surprising.

Gossip spread like wildfire and was only marginally less harmful to trees. Trees have feelings too, you know. By the time the ringlight dimmed and the sun had begun to rise there was a buzz amongst the folk of Rathendy. At least amongst the early risers. The only buzz the others would experience for another hour or so would be between their ears, at until their respective hangovers calmed down.

***

The birds would have sung along the battlements on a

glorious morning such as this if they hadn't learnt long ago that singing too early in the morning was a surefire way to being shot at by archers.

Sunlight crept further into the chamber. It eventually collided with the prostrate figures of a man and a woman and numerous bottles of wine and brandy. It would be several more hours before the two would stir, woken by the sussurating echo of what sounded vaguely like a crowd baying for blood.

Vector awoke with a groan, wondering why the usual ringing noise had been replaced by a low growl in between his ears. He noticed Heron had graciously left a pot of tea and two mugs out for them and fumbled for it clumsily, nearly knocking it over in the process, before pouring two cups out for Antillia and himself.

He stood up creakily and, cup of tea in hand, wandered toward the balcony for some fresh air, hoping it would ease his rapacious headache.

As his initial wake-up grogginess cleared he began to realise that the growling noise was not actually coming from his own head. Its source was altogether external to the castle.

Antillia shook herself awake, or at least not asleep, and reached for the cup of tea Vector had placed by her, taking a quick sip. Stretching whilst making an ungodly noise, her vision centred to see Vector looking back from the balcony.

"I think you ought to come and have a look at this, my friend," said Vector evenly, turning to face out across Rathendy.

Puzzled and slightly worried, Antillia rubbed her eyes, picked up her mug and ambled across the throne room to the balcony and looked down at her city.

She dropped her mug, pieces scattering as it hit the floor.

"Unbelievable," she whispered.

Half the population of Rathendy seemed to have turned up at her gate, certainly the majority of the army, all talking excitedly and anxiously amongst themselves. Some chanting war songs, some shouting battle cries, some still singing '*we were born in a bin*', all united.

"I think this is where you address your people, Antillia," Vector said with a wink.

"But I have such a headache Vector, can't it wait until, say, next week?" The answer to Antillia's question was as mean a scowl as Vector could muster. It was partially for the destruction of a perfectly good mug full of tea too.

Antillia cleared her throat and stepped forward in the most impressive way she could manage while still feeling hazy. There was now silence across the entire crowd. "My people, citizens of Rathendy."

It's funny how leaders have such sonorous voices. Probably all the practice they have shouting at people.

Antillia was quite unsure of where this speech was leading. She was winging it from here on out.

"We face a grave threat. But we have faced many before and we have always pulled through." There was a short cheer from the crowd. They're lapping this up, thought Antillia. "We have delayed for as long as we could, allowing the benefit of the doubt, but the time has come for action! Together we will tweak the nose of our enemy, poke the eye of our opponents and, erm, batter down the doors of those who stand against us. Together we shall bring peace back to Rathendy!" Antillia thrust her fist skyward and roared and the crowd responded, united by a single cause.

Behind Antillia stood Vector looking slightly bewildered. He'd have to ask just how Antillia planned to 'tweak the nose of our enemy' later on. For now, he felt a little more optimistic.

Toward the back of the crowd Blaine stood with Amelia shouting as vociferously as the rest. It had been far easier than they'd expected. Amelia had the entire bar eating out of the palm of her hand within an hour and, as they milled out, their tales went with them and mutated until not only were Athea Hubris a threat, there army of ten foot tall gargoyles were galloping toward Rathendy on unicorns that rode the clouds and spat poisonous bile from their mouths.

It was a bit like the old game, Slotopian whispers. Pass a message down a line and it would change significantly by the end.

Combine it with alcohol and the message evolves into something hitherto unknown to the universe.

***

As the crowd dispersed in a less than orderly fashion Amelia and Blaine marched toward the castle. They took advantage of the lax security to walk straight into the heart of the courtyard and right through the front door.

"Hardly seems like a city at war," remarked Blaine, sneering at the lack of urgency around him.

"To be fair we've only been at war about fifteen minutes," replied Amelia. She had to admit that it was quite startling at how placid people seemed in and around the castle. Everyone else in Rathendy was irate with life itself. Antillia's influence, perhaps?

They finally bumped into someone having entered the

castle hall. A tired looking man addressed them as if he'd been expecting them. Apparently, Vector hadn't just been drinking all night, thought Amelia, which she found fairly shocking.

"Hello, my name is Heron, I trust you are Amelia and Blaine?"

"Yes," answered Blaine, "how did you know?" he said in a distrustful manner. After a lifetime of cynicism, he wasn't about to alter his habits.

"Vector guessed you'd be quite forthright in your attempt to enter the castle, and here you are walking through the front door," said Heron chuckling, unruffled by Blaine's directness.

"We could have been anyone though, how were you sure?" Blaine continued in his line of questioning rigidly, disappointment at the appalling standard of protection for the steward evident.

"Vector said that one of you would be quiet and blonde and the other would be inquisitive and fiery," Heron replied, "now if you'd like to follow me." Heron led the way up the staircase with Amelia following and curiously eyeing up her surroundings. Blaine grumbled to himself as he limped after them.

The padding of footsteps announced their arrival to Antillia and Vector long before Heron barged through the door without knocking. Something else Blaine incorporated into his grumbles.

Amelia had never set foot in a castle before, let alone a steward's chamber. She imagined that most weren't decaying as much as this one. The walls were stained in the corners where rainwater had leaked in and the corners of the carpeting were frayed, although it did retain some resonance of nobility. It was a bit like a retired racehorse.

They sat down around a long table that could have done with a polish.

"So," Antillia began, gazing at the faces surrounding her, "now we're all here, how exactly do you think we should proceed? I assume that there is a master plan afoot," she said looking hopefully at Vector and then to Amelia.

"Well, no, not exactly," came Vector's rather limp response.

"Is that not what the two of you were supposed to be concocting last night instead of dangerous drinks?" asked Amelia indignantly, glaring at the sheepish looking pair whilst pointing at the empty bottles poking out from behind the curtains. A feeble attempt to conceal them.

"You wouldn't be so angry if you'd ever tried a Super Mocha Lava-Tinted Rose Blossom Firecrackle Spritzer…"

The following five minutes were probably the most uncomfortable five minutes of Vector's and Antillia's lives. For a steward and a wizard to cower before the wrath of a petite young woman who had accumulated momentum equivalent to that of a hurricane was quite something to behold. Blaine could barely disguise his glee at witnessing such a rare event.

Once Amelia's irate lecture was complete, they finally set about discussing tactics, battle plans and so forth. This, naturally, took a long time and included several takeaway meals and a few games of trying to throw the scrunched-up paper into the bin from as far away as possible. Eventually the floor was full of paper and the bin contained nothing but the pungent remains of an Insert Fairytale Character's Name (The Most Magical Take-Out Food Across The Land!) anchovy pizza.

The morning passed to afternoon before sinking into evening and, for the most part, the day had been productive. Vector and Amelia were to take two horses and ride to Vertenve and convince Ivan, steward of Vertenve, to support the fight against Edirp and Athea Hubris by any means possible. Blaine was to continue his subversive propaganda campaign within Rathendy to ensure any doubters were converted. And Antillia was to oversee the gradual mobilization of the armed forces, a tedious task in itself considering the general disorganization of Rathendy's citizens. The most important thing was they had a plan. Quite how it had taken a full day to formulate was a matter that they didn't feel the need to dwell on.

Torvacane's rings were startling against the night sky by the time the horses were ready and their packs stuffed with provisions. Amelia and Vector had already bid farewell to Blaine earlier. Antillia and Heron lingered to say a final goodbye.

As Heron helped Amelia finish packing Vector and Antillia took the opportunity to shuffle aside a moment. Although they had partaken a large amount of alcohol the previous evening, they'd also discussed in depth several aspects of coming events that they decided to keep between themselves.

"Are you certain Ivan will send troops?" she asked in an anxious whisper, her eyes drifting toward Amelia and Heron to see they didn't overhear.

"I assure you old friend, I will meet you ten days from now at Hogback ridge. Ivan is so easy to manipulate he may as well have strings protruding from his back," Vector replied.

A gust of wind blew through the castle gate as

Amelia's horse whinnied loudly and reared, causing a succession of items to fall out of one of the saddle packs. Another gust of wind carried Amelia's resulting swears toward the stables. This minor uproar had settled Antillia, now content that they would not overhear any of their conversation.

She nodded slowly in reply to Vector before her face turned grave once more. "Do you think she can save her father?"

"Yes, I believe so. He was always a resilient old fart so I don't think they could break him mentally. It's more a question of whether his old bones can handle it. As I mentioned last night, with the aid of those two daft marauders and their, for want of a better word, protégé, I fully expect them to retrieve him. Then it's simply a matter of facing down the Dragon Lord and destroying it…" The two stared at each other for a moment before breaking out into laughter – gallows humour – at the ridiculous nature of the challenge ahead.

Amelia had mounted her horse and was staring incredulously at the giggling old-timers before her. She wondered whether they ever took anything completely seriously. She'd assumed magic abuse had sent Vector a little bit funny in the brain, but she had no explanation for Antillia. "Come on," she yelled, "time to go!"

"See you in Athea Hubris' throne room for tea and biscuits," said Antillia as she shook Vector by the hand.

"Aye, I'll see you then," responded Vector, taking her hand heartily. With that he mounted his horse and he and Amelia set off through the city and onwards to Vertenve. As they left the city Amelia noticed the guard who'd attempted to stop them upon their arrival was wearing an eye patch and she afforded herself a little smile.

Before she knew it, they'd passed by the edge of the boggy morass around Rathendy and were crossing open land once more, the rings dominating the sky and betraying the space before them.

***

Emil had grown used to the sound of water dripping onto stone. So much so, he'd begun making a game of how many drops there were in a day and then tried to see whether the next day could beat the previous day. The current record holder was last Thursday. He felt Sunday had been a little unfortunate though because he'd lost count. Being tortured can have that effect on you.

He felt weak, but he dragged himself upright so he could face the man who'd just arrived outside his cell holding a lantern.

"Hello Med Tet," said Emil in a shaky voice, "fancy seeing you here."

"Emil, I'm afraid I haven't come here to exchange pleasantries. I'm after information, information I believe you can provide. However, the interesting thing about the information I require is that you will be willing to give it to me." Med Tet opened the cell and placed the lantern on the end of the bed.

Even the light appeared to cower from Med Tet. He might have found this upsetting because he was actually trying exceedingly hard to be friendly. His sneer was less sneery than usual.

"Oh really. Well I'm more than happy to hear you out Med Tet but, though I'm no clairvoyant, I foresee disappointment in your immediate future," said Emil, grinning broadly, a small flow of energy returning to his muscles. All he had at the moment were these few brief conversations to amuse himself with.

"I wish to know how to slay a Dragon Lord. What is its weakness?"

Emil's grin shrank. He went back to counting the water droplets for a time.

"I did say I was no clairvoyant. Before I answer, I wish to know why?"

Med Tet's sneer returned, natural instinct being a hard thing to suppress. Emil may as well have waved a slab of meat in front of a tiger and expected it to sit there calmly minding its own business.

Med Tet took a step closer, his arrogant face inches from Emil's. "Because, you fool, if Edirp sets that beast loose there will be nothing left. You know that, I know that, it's obvious. What's the use in owning a world of ash? I have my own ambitions," stated Med Tet in hushed tones, though his confidence allowed him to speak of such ambition without hesitation and little concern for who might overhear, "and they most certainly do not involve setting everything on fire." Med Tet's voice carried down the dark corridor, spitting venom at the shadows.

Emil appraised the man stood before him.

He was definitely still evil, no doubt about that. Just look at that moustache, thought Emil. But under the circumstances he was the lesser evil. Something that would probably have disappointed Med Tet. Emil disliked the idea of destroying what was, up until now, an innocent creature, but he knew it could not be allowed freedom, the risk to the populace being too great.

"They always used to say the soft underbelly was their weakness," he whispered, "and this is true, partially, but it takes a hell of a lot to expose such a minor weakness. No, the best bet was always the eyes. You take away the eyes and it descends into an incredible panic. It'll thrash around initially but the creature can't handle such an acceleration in its heartbeat. Shortly after it suffers a massive heart attack and dies. That is the most effective way to vanquish a Dragon Lord. It takes an incredible or lucky shot to expose it."

Med Tet stared at Emil for some time, mulling over what he'd just heard. It seemed so simple now he knew. Once the Dragon Lord is out of the way it will be Edirp next. Or perhaps the other way around, he was in rather a playful mood today.

Public opinion is already on the cusp of turning. Edirp's preposterous idea of conscription was met with predictable abhorrence. The armed forces had been fleshed out sufficiently with men whose loyalty Med Tet had purchased. What use was adding a collection of farmers who didn't want to be there? Either way, Edirp had played into Med Tet's hands nicely by turning an already tenuous public opinion against himself.

Everything was ready.

"I shouldn't get too far ahead of yourself though," added Emil, "this Dragon Lord of yours has been cooped up for so long it may have developed different instincts entirely from the Dragon Lords we once knew."

And it may prove to be the death of you, he added privately.

It seemed to Emil that there was to be a shift in power shortly in Athea Hubris. Med Tet was preparing to make his move.

Edirp and the dragon were in his way.

Sadly for Med Tet, when a Dragon Lord is in the way

of where you're trying to get to you rarely reach said destination. Unless you've developed a kind of fire-proof, indestructible battle suit, that is. But Emil imagined he'd have heard of such a suit by now, so the very thought of it seemed a tad implausible.

"I shouldn't be too confident in your dreams of my demise, you're failing to see that I simply have to outwit Edirp," said Med Tet.

He'll be in charge by morning, thought Emil.

Med Tet grabbed the lantern and stalked out, leaving the cell open, and headed for the stairs. Abruptly he stopped and, without turning around, called out, "I suggest you attempt to remove yourself from our evil clutches, Emil. That is, of course, if your legs can carry you!" Med Tet continued on up the stairs, laughter trailing faintly behind him.

Emil lay in the dark again contemplating his options. He could attempt to escape, but how far could he really get before he was spotted and locked up again?

And why exactly would Med Tet allow him the opportunity?

Edirp would certainly be perturbed by what he deems as his only chance of controlling the Dragon Lord vanishing. It could easily tip him over the edge. The alternative would be remaining locked up and suffering through further torture. When Emil considered this, it made the decision a tad easier. With considerable effort he pulled himself up and swung his legs off of the bed and grabbed his cloak and walking stick.

***

The noticeable thing about the good guys in a lot of

stories is that, when someone or something is needed, at the most opportune moment, it presents itself. At this moment in time what Emil needed was an unexpectedly deserted route out of the dungeons, a route that would remain deserted for as long as it took his battered body to heave itself out of there.

He also needed sustenance. With energy levels desperately low, bread and water would suffice. Emil's luck was in and the corridors were empty, the soldiers out running drills and manoeuvres. Only a couple of levels up, right by the mess hall, there was a small room that appeared to be a storage space for the army kitchens. The luxury of convenience should not be underestimated.

***

Edirp was sat alone in his chamber deep in thought.

He had a problem.

Not one of those usual and predictable ruling problems like who to make his new queen or whether to execute his current queen. This was a highly unusual problem.

His dragon babysitter was on the run.

Skarz was the only man who knew the full extent of Edirp's glorious plan of travelling the world with his dragon, erasing it piece by burning piece. Life could be so unfair, thought Edirp.

As he cursed his ill fortune there was a tap on the door to disturb his reverie. Herm scurried in and bowed as low as he could manage without toppling over. He was anxious because he had some bad news and he truly hated delivering bad news. He'd always found that the old phrase 'don't beat the messenger over the head with a candlestick' was a shamefully ignored one.

"Sire, we've a minor problem in the mine," said Herm quietly, ready to throw his hands up to protect his head as best they could. To his surprise, Edirp burst out into a fit of laughter which Herm found to be far more unsettling.

Gathering himself, Edirp spoke breathlessly: "you're saying we have a minor problem with the miners in the mines. Is that what you're saying, Herm?"

"Yes sire," replied Herm. He couldn't help but feel Edirp had exacerbated the hilarity of his sentence somewhat. He supposed kings weren't renowned for their sense of humour. After all, they often found those hopeless jesters amusing.

"The miners are annoyed that nothing has been done about the magpie problem. They're tired of receiving a severe pecking while transferring the gold back to the citadel mint."

Edirp was still wheezing but Herm continued stubbornly.

"They're just leaving bags of gold lying around the mine until the problem is dealt with."

Herm had expected his laying out of the issue to change Edirp's surprisingly chipper mood, but he continued to giggle to himself. Herm even saw him wipe away a tear before finally rising from his chair.

"Tell them to take a break, Herm. I'm sure we can delay the process while the magpies are dealt with. I hear they're flying in convoy systems now. Quite remarkable really. Perhaps we should study their rapid evolution more closely," said Edirp airily.

He wasn't concerned. He wouldn't need gold when the time was right. It would probably be a heavy inconvenience trying to haul all that gold around on just the one dragon. "I'll have it sorted out soon enough. The magpies might even lose interest if there are no transfers for a few days."

"As you wish, sire," said Herm, bowing so low that this time he stumbled forward and landed in a heap. Edirp laughed raucously as Herm got up and left, his cheeks flushing a deep crimson with embarrassment.

The door swung shut behind him and Edirp was once again alone in his chamber. This was, of course, when Edirp was at his most dangerous because there was no one around to interrupt his mind from gaining that inexorable momentum which would often lead to his more outlandish ideas. In this way he was quite similar to Caine. When left alone he was a danger to both himself and anyone within a fifty-yard radius.

It was during this particular bout of lone thought that produced Edirp's worst idea yet.

"No more delays," he whispered to himself, a manic quality to his tone. "Time to set her free."

He had no idea the gender of the dragon. It's just a masculine thing to refer to something you own as female. It's a form of deep-seated sexism that no amount of flaming underwear can overcome.

Rising from his chair he made for the door but, upon opening it, he found the way to be blocked.

"Med Tet, what are you doing here?" said Edirp. He failed to contain his irritation at the timing of this visit. Did they not realise he was about to embark on his destiny?

It was a few seconds before Edirp realised that Med Tet was not alone and there were several hard-faced soldiers stood behind him.

"May we enter, sire?" asked Med Tet coolly, eyes

flickering around the room to ensure they were alone. Not that it mattered. It was just less messy without collateral damage.

"Now is not really an appropriate time as it happens…" began Edirp.

"I'm afraid it is urgent sire, we must insist," interjected Med Tet, swiftly entering the chamber followed by his intimidating squad of guards. From down the corridor Herm was watching on, nervous at where exactly this action was leading. He had a feeling it may be time to pack his bags and scarper whilst the going was still, well, not good, but he was alive.

A rather taken aback Edirp pulled himself up to his full mediocre height and retorted angrily: "now see here Med Tet, this is entirely out of order. I have half a mind to have you arrested on the spot and thrown into the dungeons!"

"That sounds like a relatively close assessment of what's going on here sire, I congratulate you. However, it is the other way around. We are here to arrest you for the crime of murder. The murder we are referring to is that of your late door guard whose name still remains unimportant. Even a king cannot break the law and for that you are to be arrested immediately and locked up in the dungeons until further notice regarding your sentence. As it happens, we have a fresh, recently vacated cell ready and waiting for you."

The calm expression on Med Tet's face did not falter. Unblinking, he remained there twisting his moustache with that malevolent charm he'd mastered.

In contrast the unmitigated fury and utter incredulousness on Edirp's face gave him the appearance of a tomato that had just been told its only purpose in life was to be thrown at a man in the stocks. Edirp was hauled down the corridor screaming 'I am the king of the castle' at the top of his lungs. He wasn't one to go quietly. Herm stood gawking gormlessly as his former employer was dragged away.

As far as boding goes, this was not boding well.

Med Tet noticed Herm squirming at the end of the corridor as he watched on with satisfaction. Herm realised too late that he'd been spotted and could do nothing but remain frozen to the spot, trembling like a child on his first day of school. Before he knew it, Med Tet was stood in front of him and it suddenly occurred to Herm the extent to which Med Tet could tower over a person effortlessly. At least it felt that way to Herm. This was it, thought Herm, what a wasted life.

"I am not an intolerant man, Herm, despite what you may think of me. You are relinquished of your position and have precisely one hour to be on your way, else I may lose my temper. Are we clear?" he stated. He was really enjoying himself now.

"Yes sir, thank you sir," replied Herm gratefully. He sprinted, or more accurately moved as fast as his little legs would carry him, in the direction of his quarters to hurriedly pack and then get as far away from this place as he possibly could.

Working for Edirp had been a difficult experience, but Herm felt a little sad at how it had worked out. He could at least count it as an achievement that he had survived with his health intact, although he couldn't say the same for his nerves. He near enough crashed through the door to his chamber, began throwing his few belongings into a bag, and collected all the money he had saved in a neatly carved wooden box underneath his bed. It wasn't much but it was enough to get him far away from Athea Hubris.

Perhaps he'd head for Gredavia, find himself a job in one of their famous Skyitchers. He then dismissed this as he had a fear of heights. The citadel was bad enough.

Well, never mind, that wasn't what he had to worry about currently. He slammed the door behind him as he scurried frenetically down the stairs, out of the citadel and out into the vastness of the world that had so frightened him previously, but now seemed far less terrifying than the small fragment of it he'd spent his life in so far.

After Herm had run off Med Tet had strolled casually into the deposed king's chamber and had a quick look around. "Hmm, time for a change in décor I think."

***

Despite an apparent changing of the guard there wasn't exactly a change of motives. That Athea Hubris was now essentially under the control of a far more calculating and intelligent and motivated man was hardly cause for celebration. News would spread over the course of the following day that Edirp had been involved in an unfortunate accident. Whilst on his way to the mines he'd been set upon by magpies and toppled over the edge of the citadel's high walls and plummeted to his death. In essence, this is what actually happened.

If you replace the word 'magpies' with 'men'.

And the word 'toppled' with 'thrown'.

It's true what they say about it being tough at the top: it's a long way down and the ground has a habit of happening to you when you fall.

Thus ended the reign of King Edirp of Athea Hubris. It hadn't been a long one, nor a particularly successful one, but he'd set in motion a series of events, events that were now inevitable. It was easy for Med Tet to assert his position at the top of the tree. He revoked the policy of conscription before mentioning briefly that until further notice he would be in control. And when he said further notice he meant when he felt like notifying people he was no longer in charge. Which might be a while.

He didn't like the term 'king' because he disliked the idea of being associated with Edirp and his ilk. The enmity and disdain he felt for Edirp had led to a change in plan. Leaving him in the cells to rot meant that, as ridiculous a man as he was, he would remain a future threat to Med Tet's authority. At least, he would for as long as he lived. Therefore a more permanent solution was required. No more king, no more lineage. Only Med Tet and the role he would carve out for himself. He'd clarify his title once he settled in.

Over the next few days rumours detailing a threat to the city began circulating, gradually veering further and further from the truth until some people were anticipating a horde of mountain trolls breaking down the city gates at any moment. Of course, in such dire circumstances, the people of Athea Hubris would wish to protect themselves and their families. The armed forces announced that in light of recent news (they weren't specific: 'never give a face to the enemy', according to Med Tet) they were accepting volunteers. This played into the proud citizens' mind-sets and they volunteered in great numbers. Determined volunteers made better soldiers than reluctant conscripts. Med Tet stood atop the citadel wall gazing down at line after line of Hubrisians signing up. People are too easy, he thought, if you press the right buttons.

***

Son didn't like it. He'd never imagined someone evil but also clever would actually have complete control over an entire city. The problem with these intelligent types is that they think things through. This means their evil plans may actually come to fruition, which is just not on. The God of Torvacane was having a bad enough day as it was, He'd lost at chess to Himself eighteen times and couldn't work out how. He was loathe to reconsider His Latvian Gambit opening but His opponent, Himself, seemed to be adept at countering it.

As well as His chess grievances He'd also seen, whilst looking into the Oracle Pool, an entire flock of sheep disappear into thin air. He wasn't certain yet, but He thought the Big Bad Wolf may be dabbling in the black arts, which is never a good thing because everyone knows that to use magic safely you need opposable thumbs.

These were trivial issues in comparison to Med Tet assuming power in Athea Hubris. If He had a lump of gold for every time He regretted giving people free will He could have filled a thousand temples to Himself.

I may have to interfere further here, He thought.

But how?

There was always the option of just smiting him, flick him off the battlements with a divine gust of wind. But that sets a precedent that god(s) will always interject when things go wrong, and Son had always declared that He would not be that kind of god. And He thought about poor Skarz, who was going to have one heck of a headache when he woke up, a headache for nothing now Edirp was deposed. What to do with him?

Ah, He thought, that's it.

***

Skarz stirred. He couldn't be sure, but he was fairly confident someone had cleaved his head in two and he was now in hell. Hell sure looks familiar, he thought.

"Did anyone get the registration of that horse drawn cart?" he muttered, dragging himself to his feet. Twenty feet or so away he clasped eyes on his attacker.

"I never did like coconuts, but I guess it can be of some use." Skarz walked over and cracked it open with the butt of his sword. He was hungry and thirsty so this would have to do.

He stood upright and surveyed the area. At least I'm still where I fell, he thought, things could be worse. Looking to the sky he could see it was clouding over and the clouds looked displeased. It would be easier to walk through the city with dulled light and rain. He pulled his hood over his head and sheathed his sword.

Having established his whereabouts he set off on the path around the foot of the mountain that led straight back into Athea Hubris. He had no idea how long he'd been out for or whether Edirp had unleashed the Dragon Lord already, which would be an utter disaster. He needed to know.

***

Caine, Korin and Drago had finally reached Vertenve. While it wasn't part of the original plan to stop and visit, bypassing the opportunity for a stiff drink now seemed an entirely absurd thought. And they needed something to wash the tiger down with anyway as it had proven a tad salty.

"So this is Vertenve," said Drago, gazing around slack jawed as they strolled down the street, "it all looks so, erm, modern." Each building appeared to exist merely to outdo the previous one with ever more flamboyant architecture and lurid colours. One shop looked like the offspring of a flamingo and a giraffe.

"A crypt is modern compared with Broth Zolust lad, but aye, you've got a point. It's all scaffolding over yonder though so don't be fooled, they've got a long way to go just like everyone else," replied Korin.

He turned into a classy looking bar called The Itchy Nose. The large carved letters were painted a vivid purple and were illuminated by miniature candles. This must be what was classed as 'trendy' around here, thought Drago. He also registered that the three-foot-tall letters were carved out of wood, a health and safety hazard louder than the décor. The three rugged, dishevelled men strolled through the arched doorway and made their way toward the counter.

"Three pints of Grog, pal," said Caine to the barman.

The slightly bewildered looking man glanced at each of the three travellers momentarily before answering in an unusual accent Drago hadn't heard before. "Are you sure you wouldn't prefer one of our many wines? Or we have a new type of beer that people are loving at the moment called Large Ear."

Caine leaned further over the bar and beckoned the man closer. The man leaned in nervously. Grinning his semi-toothy grin, Caine said: "we'll 'ave three pints of Grog mate, in dirty glasses, warm, and ya'll bring 'em over to that table in the corner. Okay?"

The barman wasn't a dim man. He detected the threatening undertone of Caine's overly friendly request and almost fell over his own feet dashing into the back in the vain hope of finding three dirty glasses, a quite alien concept to him.

The three of them collapsed into incredibly comfy chairs with strange, zigzagging patterns on. "You didn't have to scare him quite so much, Caine. You know how people get when you do the whole leaning over the bar thing, it gives them the creeps," scolded Korin.

"It were pretty funny though, I thought 'e might wet 'imself," Caine said with undisguised pride.

"Alright, alright, but we're trying not to attract attention to ourselves, okay? Incognito, yes? Some people might have long memories around here."

Drago's ears pricked up as his stomach fell. He could sense a bout of worry coming on. "Long memories? Why should it matter that people may have long memories around here?"

"Well there's a chance, by which I mean we certainly did, raid the old treasury. It was a few years ago, of course. I bet they forgot all about it pretty quickly really," answered Korin.

"How much did you take?" asked Drago, praying to Son it was a bit of loose change.

"Everything!" roared Caine, jovially slapping a laughing Korin on the back. A few heads turned at the sound of raised voices. Disapproving whispers followed. The petrified barman came over and put the drinks on the table, snatching the bronze knoblets Drago had laid out as payment, before scuttling away without even looking at Caine. It wasn't that Caine was intimidating as such, he just had an aura of volatility that was almost tangible.

After swigging from his glass, Korin wiped his chin

and then cleared his throat. "I say we stay here for the night and stock up a little. It's not like the gold is going anywhere. We aren't on a time limit. We could even do a little sight-seeing." He hadn't travelled in some years now. There was a chance that Vertenve could hold some mild interest these days. It had forever been in the shadow of the great imperious cities of Gredavia and Athea Hubris, but perhaps the tide was changing. They certainly possessed a wider variety of paint than the other cities.

"I'm easy either way. Seem like a buncha wet blankets this lot, I don't reckon there's much fun to be 'ad 'ere," replied Caine, looking around and staring at the barman. A high-pitched squeak and the sound of swift-moving feet and the barman disappeared into the back area.

"You never know, they might just surprise you…" said a distracted Korin. "I think we'd best be going. Out the back exit."

Outside the front window was a group of official looking men surrounded by soldiers with big swords. Someone who had previously been sat near the entrance, one of the disapproving whisperers no less, was speaking to the officials and pointing in the direction of Caine, Korin and Drago.

Apparently, they did have long memories. "Bottoms up, boys," said Korin and sank the rest of his Grog. The others followed suit (Drago did it in two tries, which wasn't bad for him) and they rushed toward the bar, hopped over it, and ran into the back.

"You can't be in here!" squealed the barman.

"Outta the way ya weasel," Caine growled, prompting a further squeal. There was no time for pleasantries. They could hear raised voices from the bar area and a few cries of 'they went that way'.

"Snitches," Caine grumbled.

Crashing through the next door, they found themselves in a modern looking kitchen where some of the surfaces were made of metal, a rare and incredible sight for natives of Broth Zolust. An angry looking man in a white hat ran at them yelling and holding a large saucepan and ladle aggressively. As he lunged, Korin adjusted and used the man's momentum to lift him off his feet and straight through the window, which shattered loudly as he smashed through it.

Drago looked accusingly at Korin. "He had a stupid moustache." Drago nodded in acceptance of this fact.

The first soldier appeared in the doorway behind them running far too fast. He'd barely regained his balance when he was knocked unconscious by a flying steel pan. The anguished cries coming from beyond the doorway seemed to indicate that too many men had attempted to rush through at once and knocked several wine casks over. It was a cacophony of shattering glass.

Korin pointed to the door at the far end of the kitchen and the three of them sprinted for it, Caine knocking everything he could lay his hands on to the ground behind them to create a culinary obstacle course of diabolical proportions.

The door opened out into an alley that ran behind the stretch of shops and bars along the street. The colour co-ordinating was less ostentatious behind the façade. This was a regulation alleyway complete with bin bags and general waste. It felt like home.

They raced down the alleyway, Caine occasionally sending an overly full bin sprawling, not to hinder their pursuers but more for fun. The commotion coming from the kitchen behind the closed door was enough to indicate they had time. The wall to their left was small, maybe six feet or so. Rowan trees with delicate, feathery leaves and red berries hung over the top. Rowan trees were said to symbolise courage, wisdom, and protection, according to Vertenve's archivists. As Caine, Korin, and Drago pulled themselves over the wall, they trampled upon these values. Caine actually fell on them.

Beyond the wall was a residential area which Korin figured would be easier to lose the chasing soldiers in. Assuming they ever navigated the kitchen of doom. Now stood among a clutch of trees at the back end of a small, well-kept garden adorned with bright flowers, they surveyed their surroundings. Colour was clearly the big thing in Vertenve. Caine, naturally, landed on a small bush with unusual orange flowers, trampling it into the soil.

"We need somewhere to lie low," whispered Drago as they made their way across the garden. Korin nodded in reply but Caine didn't seem to be paying attention. He was waving. Drago's first thought was that he'd finally lost the plot, or whatever thin grasp of reality he still had, but then he noticed a young girl, aged maybe seven or eight, stood at the window. She waved back and smiled.

"This is no time to go soft on us Caine," said Korin, pulling Caine toward the side of the house where there was a gate and way out onto the street.

"As if I'd ever go soft. Just didn't want 'er runnin' off and tellin' mummy straight away. Just cleverness," grunted Caine in reply, taking mock offence at the suggestion he'd gone soft.

They were in an affluent neighbourhood. The houses had front gardens as well as back gardens, so they had to be well-off. They relaxed a little. No longer hearing the sound of clumsiness behind them, it seemed they had lost the soldiers. They continued walking down the street taking in the pleasant scenery.

"So much for travelling incognito then." Drago was peeved they couldn't go one day without being chased by someone, but he couldn't help but see the funny side too. He began to wonder at just how extensive Caine and Korin's history of mischief was. It had taken approximately fifteen minutes for trouble to find them upon entering the city, which had to be some kind of record. And if it wasn't, Caine and Korin probably held it from a previous trip.

It was now clear to Drago that attempting to keep their journey as simple and uneventful as possible was futile. If he didn't embrace the random, haphazard approach to life that they championed then he may as well turn around and go home. Drago felt this moment, right now, was one he'd remember, one that changed his outlook on life.

"Pipe down numbnuts," said Caine, "we tried real 'ard to not attract attention. These things just 'ave an 'abit of 'appening around us. A lot."

"To be fair, you did threaten the barman a little. That was unnecessary," added Korin, chuckling with that little twinkle in his eye that he had when he wasn't being serious. His eyes were almost always twinkling.

"Well if 'e'd just given us some Grog right away I wouldn't 'ave 'ad to," replied Caine.

"Yeah, yeah, alright. Anyway, we need to find a place to spend the night soon, and a nice, warm meal wouldn't go amiss. Drago, what's your opinion on breaking and entering?" asked Korin.

"I suspect my opinion on the matter isn't going to

affect what we do anyway, so I guess I'm all for it," came the beleaguered reply.

***

The afternoon passed relatively peacefully for a change. The residential road they found themselves on circled back around toward the street they'd been chased out of. The street was now heavily patrolled. This didn't worry Korin or Caine. Increased patrol presence was something they considered a compliment.

They picked a nice house built from red brick with a quaint square garden in front surrounded by rose bushes. The cute effect the entire street seemed to be trying to convey made Caine feel slightly nauseous, so he was grateful to discover a drinks cabinet in the living room that was well stocked.

The house was currently empty, the owners most likely working. This suited the trio as they could scarper when the owners returned in the evening. A fat ginger cat perched on the dining table was engaging Drago in a series of staring contests and winning comfortably.

Opening a bottle of brandy and pouring three glasses, Caine collapsed into an armchair. "Is it a standard 'cover of darkness' escape, aye? Them soldiers were incontinent," Caine grunted whilst itching his elbow.

"Incompetent," Drago said.

"Aye, that too," replied Caine, oblivious to his error.

"I think that's the best plan of action," Korin interjected. It was far too late to correct any glitches in Caine's vocabulary. "We'll raid the kitchen and get some rest, try to commandeer three horses and hightail it out of the city. Wake me up in an hour or so, alright?" Korin kicked off his boots and lay down on the sofa.

Caine had also nodded off, although that could be because he'd picked out the strongest alcohol in the cabinet and necked several shots in quick succession.

Drago decided to take a nap too. He didn't want to be slowing them down later on, especially if they were travelling into the night. He slumped into the remaining armchair and relaxed, suddenly realising he was very tired indeed.

***

Drago awoke to find himself in his own bed in his dreary little house in Broth Zolust, a plain home that offered him nothing. He could hear his mother shouting for Graeme. It took him a moment to remember that he was Graeme. He really wished she would call him Drago.

He climbed out of bed and threw on his red dressing gown and stumbled down the stairs. He'd had such a peculiar dream where he'd gone on a big adventure and spent the entire time being chased. It had been distressing but oddly thrilling.

As he reached the foot of the stairs his mother greeted him. "There's someone at the door for you dear, says he's a friend of yours." His mother left the front door ajar and strolled back into the front room calmly. Drago walked out and opened the door properly to find himself staring into the brutish, steaming face of a large dragon.

"I don't believe we've met before," he exclaimed as a billowing wave of fire raced from the dragon's mouth and slammed against his house and Drago himself with a loud *whoosh*.

***

Drago woke up. "Just a dream," he muttered, "just a dream." He looked up to find the living room of a quaint little house in Vertenve to be packed full of soldiers in grey jerkins with green undershirts holding crossbows and swords and pointing most of them at Caine, Korin and himself.

"Another dream, eh? This is getting a bit silly, how many times can I be dreaming that I'm dreaming? I guess this is the part where we heroically vanquish all our foes in the face of impossible odds?" he said, looking at the other two expectantly. Korin was shaking his head, lips pursed. The nearest uniformed man slapped Drago in the face.

"Ouch," he grumbled.

"On your feet," shouted one of the soldiers aggressively. The three of them slowly ambled to their feet and were promptly frogmarched out of the house and up the road. As they rounded the corner Korin noticed a sign attached to a signpost.

'Nayborhood Watch In Operation, Criminales Beeware!'

"Bugger."

***

Even the most experienced men in any field have to guard against complacency. Not having a lookout when you have half the city guard searching for you? A tad naïve to say the least and it had Korin kicking himself all the way to the steward's palace (a grand but garish structure he'd obviously designed himself).

As they were escorted through the streets Drago grew increasingly worried at how many faces, both young and old, were poking out of doors or looking through windows. Street acts, buskers, dancers, acrobats, third-rate magicians, they'd all stopped what they were doing to gawp.

Just how long were the memories of the people of Vertenve?

And had Caine and Korin emitted any crucial details in their tale of looting the treasury? Because the faces Drago saw lining the streets were expressing a fervent desire to see their small party punished. And he hadn't even done anything wrong!

"What on Torvacane did you do?" whispered Drago sharply to Caine. Before Caine could answer Drago received a swift sword butt to the stomach. Caine glared at the soldier responsible but even his pugnacious attitude remained under wraps for now and he kept quiet. However subdued Caine appeared now, Drago suspected a fuse had been lit. There would be fireworks soon enough.

The colours of the buildings became less garish and grotesque the closer to the palace they were until they were mostly surrounded by scaffolding and building work.

Even the palace was not completely finished. Drago could easily place it in his top three most unpleasant sights of all time. Picture a large hand holding a bowling pin around the bottom, then imagine a baby has eaten an entire set of crayons and sicked them up all over it.

As they reached the end of the rows of peculiar buildings the way opened up onto an expansive garden before the palace. There were curious statues dotted around that Drago assumed were what passed for tasteful art and a tall fountain in the centre. As they were marched past it, they saw there were hundreds of bronze knoblets littering the bottom of the pool. It would be a modest haul but Caine and Korin made a mental note just in case they found themselves coming back this way unattended. This was why a good adventurer always carried a spare looting bag.

Marched through the gaudy door they were hit with the thick stench of paint. The entrance hall was covered with paint-splashed white drip sheets. Tins of paint lay everywhere and a few workmen on ladders were going about their jobs quietly.

The next room was much further along the redecoration process. Designed as a great banquet hall, long stretched wooden tables made to seat a hundred people were spaced equidistantly from one end of the hall to the other, and regal portraits hung from the walls. There was still some painting being done and a few men in overalls were sanding down the tables. At the head of the hall was a raised platform with a table facing the rest of the room. Several impressive wooden chairs were draped in red and green velvet. Sat in the middle chair, the highest up, was a short man with beady eyes and the kind of patchwork beard you'd expect to see on a teenager. He stood up and addressed the approaching party.

"Do you like what I've done with the place? It will be the envy of all the cities once everything is complete. Yes, the envy of them all!"

Drago, Caine and Korin were ushered forwards to face the diminutive steward.

"I think, perhaps, you won't know me. It's been a

while since you were here in Vertenve from what my advisers have told me. My name is Ivan, steward of Vertenve Ivan actually, and I am most pleased to make your acquaintance."

"The pleasure is all ours, I'm sure," replied Korin politely. He felt slightly uneasy under the watchful gaze of Ivan's dark beady eyes. They were like two marbles glistening malevolently and he was the jack they were targeting. Quirky metaphors aside, he suspected this was not the time for his or Caine's penchant for mocking authority figures. Tempting though it might be.

"Yes, yes, I suppose it is," replied Ivan. "Now I believe you owe us quite a large amount of gold, quite a large amount indeed…" – Ivan was one of those people who had a tendency to repeat themselves, as if to reinforce the message. It was an annoying trait and one that Korin loathed – "…so we'll be wanting that back. Yes, we'll be wanting it all back."

"Well it just so 'appens that, what with all t'commotion, I dropped me change purse some way back there. All three of us will jus' nip back and look for it. Then we'll be 'appy to sort out t'minor details." Caine flashed his semi-toothy grin to Korin, who shook his head and grimaced.

"MOCK ME, WILL YOU!?" Ivan shouted, standing on his chair. He was barely over five feet tall. He pulled back slightly and glowered at his three prisoners. He continued in a more restrained fashion.

"I will not invite men into my own court, my own court, and have them mock me in front of my subjects. My own subjects! This is not on, not on at all! Take them away and lock them up until they see sense," said Ivan, lowering himself back into his chair.

163

Caine and Korin had been friends and companions for many years. Too many, Caine would often joke. Over these many years they'd developed signals for all manner of situations. A birdcall for the approach of sentries, a whistle for when to take cover, a cough for when to surprise attack their captors.

Korin coughed.

Caine roared and charged at the nearest soldier, elbowing him in the gut and wrestling his sword from its sheath. Despite his hands being bound he could still handle a sword, a by-product of the frequency with which courts had tied Caine up. He sliced through Korin's binds and threw the sword to him and he repaid the favour. This happened so quickly no one else had reacted.

"GET THEM, GET THEM!" screamed Ivan, jumping up and down on his chair. A chair that creaked beneath him despite his small stature.

The group of guards bore down on them and Korin engaged three of them in a sword fight at once. Caine ducked and weaved before tackling two and bashing their heads together. Drago, whose hands were still bound, decided if you can't beat the crazy old codgers you may as well join them. He narrowly avoided the sword that came flashing down at him. It crashed into the dining table with a thud and knocked several silver goblets flying.

As the man attempted to heave the sword from its current location embedded deeply in the table, Drago took the chance to slice through his binds. Then he promptly punched the sword's owner in the face.

The vociferous tumult began to attract a crowd. Decorators mainly. Caine sent a man crashing through the nearest table and received polite applause from the audience. Another man lay unconscious surrounded by overturned tins of red paint. It would have appeared as a gruesome crime scene to someone just entering the hall.

Korin now stood on one of the banquet tables swiping at anyone unfortunate enough to be within range and Drago was throwing tin after tin of paint at oncoming guards. A lovely moving rainbow surrounded him.

Above the hubbub they could hear Ivan, marching up and down his table like a rabid football fan, screaming: "GET INTO THEM YOU COWARDS, COME ON, 'AVE IT, 'AVE IT!"

It had taken the steward of Vertenve less than two minutes to degenerate into a common yob. He was now pumping his fists in an awkward, uncoordinated fashion like a children's toy whose batteries were slowly dying.

More guards had run through at the sounds of Ivan's cries and had joined the fray. The freshly sanded and polished tables were now a combination of orange, yellow, maroon, purple, green and blue. Some of the painters felt the fight had improved the room.

Caine, Korin and Drago were all engaged in swordfights and had taken to the long, grand, and colourful banquet tables. As well as using the swords they were able to kick cutlery and plates off the table as faux projectiles (reminding Caine of the time he and Korin had looted a temple with just a fork and a spoon between them). Clanging and clashing – sword on sword, knife and fork on chain mail – reverberated around the hall. Boots bounded across wooden tabletops and an increasingly hoarse Ivan continued his vehement cheerleading. It was like an orchestra, whose instruments had been sent to the wrong venue, had been forced to play whatever they could lay their hands on.

Surveying the madness from the doorway was a tall,

slender man in light blue robes and a young blonde girl with a look of dismay on her face. "This is who you're relying on to help us?" she asked incredulously.

The old man sighed and looked at her. "Yes dear, I'm afraid you'll just have to trust me on this one."

The three men on the tables had slowly worked their way nearer to the door and were ready to make a break for it. It was at this point, on the cusp of escape, that they noticed the two newcomers stood in the doorway. Vector felt it was time to announce himself.

In a surprisingly sonorous voice, he exclaimed: "PUT A STOP TO THIS NONSENSE AT ONCE!"

And it worked, everyone's attention was now on him. Although he did notice one of the old men aim a last kick at a guard.

"Ivan," he said in a measured tone as he and his female companion strode across the hall, "I should think you'd have had a better idea of who it is you were attempting to lock up here and been a bit more careful. These men are quite notorious you see. I wouldn't have even bothered trying in the first place personally." The pair had strolled through the entire debacle and come to a stop before the steward, who was still stood on the table with his fists clenched.

Initially speechless, he came to his senses to mutter, in a slightly strained voice: "I recognise you, but from long ago." The steward was only thirty and had not been around during the war, but Vector had passed through Vertenve a few times in his youth. He was known to Ivan's father, Creed.

"Yes, I recognise you. But what are you doing here? And I should think twice before advising me how to run my own court," he said, his vocal chords easing now he'd taken a rest from his role as cheerleader.

"I am here because your city is in great peril, as are they all," replied Vector. "I think it wise if we retire to somewhere more private to discuss the situation."

While not being the sharpest tool in the box, a little voice somewhere in Ivan's mind was telling him to respect the presence of this lanky old man. It contravened his urge to let the bizarre show continue, but after a deep breath he began to nod to himself. "Yes, yes of course, I see you are serious. I have a private study through here, we can use that." Ivan gestured toward a door to his left. He began to march in that direction before doing a comically exaggerated double-take and spinning back round. "What do I do with the three troublemakers? They are wanted fugitives in Vertenve," he declared.

"Well, you can try arresting them again if you like? Or perhaps it would be better if they came with us. As it happens, I'd like to speak to them myself." Vector turned to look upon the three adventurers, pleased he'd finally caught up with them.

They were gone.

"Oh, bugger."

***

Amelia looked on in disbelief at the trail of multi-coloured footprints leading toward the doorway she and Vector had entered through just minutes before. The three men, fugitives as Ivan had said, had been stood on the tables.

She couldn't grasp how such old men had moved so swiftly. Worst of all they'd be difficult to relocate, but Vector believed they were necessary to the success of their plan. Despite her reluctance she had to have faith in Vector, and this extended to having faith in the three strangers who, apparently, were wanted criminals in Vertenve.

Excellent, she thought, just brilliant.

"Well, what are we going to do now, eh?"

"Relax dear, this won't take a moment. I haven't done this for some time, don't be alarmed, should be back in a jiffy," replied Vector in a less than convincing manner. Nerves crept into his voice, giving it the jangly tone of one stood at a great height and looking down. Arms folded, Amelia tutted and shook her head.

Vector knelt down and clapped his hands together in front of him. There was a brief flash, where Vector's outline seemed to blur, and then he was still, frozen to the spot and as a rigid as a day-old corpse. Amelia stared at him, dumbstruck, until several minutes had passed. Ivan slowly sidled over to where the now stiff Vector knelt and poked him a couple of times.

"Erm, is he alright?"

***

Vector had forgotten how good this felt! His essence soaring through the air unnoticed by all the people he passed, on the lookout for a trace of the three men he sought. He did a few somersaults and shouted 'whoop' a few times before getting down to the serious business of finding the three adventurers. With his senses heightened in this form he could practically smell Caine. Admittedly, a heightened sense of smell wasn't often required to detect Caine's odour, but he was a considerable distance away. Not for long though.

Vector navigated the side streets, nothing but a speeding ball of light, impossible to see with the naked eye, lunging around corners without worrying about bumping into anyone.

This was utter freedom.

He could feel them now. They'd made it surprisingly far, so they must have sprinted at a fair pace. Such a shame their energy had been wasted. Vector could see them now, leaning against a wall trying to catch their breath. He shot past them and the ball of light burst with a crack to reveal a towering, ethereal shade bearing Vector's features, glaring at the three panting men. The younger man had a look of pure astonishment on his face tinged with fear. The other two appeared irritated, as if they had forgotten to buy milk and really fancied a cup of tea. The man with the ponytail and fanged earring kicked a can on the floor.

"I forgot he could do that."

***

Athea Hubris was a hub of activity. Long lines of men were being assigned weapons in the city centre and then appointed commanding officers to report to.

Miners were rushing back and forth between the treasury and the mine heavily laden with bulky sacks. The dwarf contractors had a full armed guard to scare off any potential thieves, but mainly to deter the ever-growing number of magpies who were now affecting kamikaze tactics to get their wings on some gold. It didn't seem to occur to the birds that if they actually procured some gold, they weren't anatomically designed to transport it.

Med Tet was residing in his office, which he had

turned into a kind of war room complete with maps and diagrams on the walls. Sat amongst the paraphernalia of a devious and imperialistic mind, he was surrounded by his most trusted and most sycophantic generals. They were big dumb men who enjoyed beating things (people to be precise). Med Tet encouraged this which is why they stayed loyal. His biggest, dumbest general had just informed him that Rathendy had mobilised its armed forces and had begun the march to Athea Hubris. This news delighted him.

"Gentleman, let them come. Once within sight of the city we shall ride out to meet them. They cannot hope to overpower us, they won't even reach the city gates," he announced triumphantly to a general murmur of approval. This is why they were his most trusted generals, they generally agreed with everything he said.

"I suggest you all go and mingle with the new recruits. Be friendly, we need to keep them on our side, they won't be as willing to die for the cause if the cause is being championed by mean-spirited gargoyles," said Med Tet.

He dismissed them and they filed out of the room looking confused, having never been ordered to be friendly before. It was a notion as alien to them as dental hygiene and regular bathing.

Med Tet raised himself from his seat and began pacing the room.

What do you do with an irate dragon? It was a question that had been plaguing him for some time now. The Hubrisian public were blissfully unaware of the monster that also called the city home. The miners knew, and so did a select group of soldiers, all sworn to secrecy by Edirp. Although Med Tet didn't rank many of this select circle as being particularly bright, he believed they might notice if the dragon suddenly wasn't there. It had to be dealt with swiftly and quietly. Perhaps, if the dragon was attempting to escape, it would of course be for the good of Athea Hubris to prevent it reaching the city. Yes, that was it!

Med Tet stopped pacing and curled his moustache. It seemed like the sort of thing people should do when they came up with a plan. He would recall his generals later on after they'd made a feeble effort at a meet and greet with the new recruits and relay to them his intentions regarding the dragon. Given the delicacy of the situation he had envisaged, the possibility of a quick fix and the disposal of the creature was the ideal for Med Tet. And then he could get onto the serious matter of world domination.

Med Tet smiled.

***

Grasping a walking stick with one hand and leaning against a wall with the other, a tired and panting old man rested.

It was a long walk from the dungeons, up the stairs then back down again to the city. Emil had been a relatively secret prisoner, therefore soldiers on patrol didn't recognise him.

Once clear of the dungeons several people had been gracious enough to help such a weak, lost, confused and frail old man make his way back to the city. Emil thought he'd laid it on a bit thick with the last guard because he'd reeled off back stories of at least seventeen fictional grandchildren. The poor lad was probably pleased to see the back of him.

Taking a quick breather, he had a look round. He didn't have any money, which was likely to prove a stumbling block if he wanted a roof over his head tonight that wasn't supported by a row of metal bars. He may have to resort to a few wizardly mind tricks. He wasn't as accomplished as his old friend Vector was, but he could probably convince someone he'd already paid for a room, a large glass of brandy and a hot water bottle.

The street contained an array of picturesque, cottage-like buildings, whitewashed stone, and thatched roofs aplenty. Several had signs hanging above the doors denoting their trade or products; a grocer, a healer, a blacksmith's forge, and so forth.

That explained the consistent, clashing metallic sound piercing the usual city rumblings.

A short way ahead on his left was what Emil wanted: an inn. He pushed off from the wall and steadied himself on his stick.

The street was not busy. A woman finished sweeping up outside her home and bustled back in complaining about fighting a losing battle, which felt like an omen. And Emil knew from experience omens were never good.

The evening had drawn in and a ring snaked across the skyline, a few stars dotted around it. Emil noticed a young black man had emerged from beside the omen-spouting woman's house, and he was staring at him quite intently. As soon as Emil made eye contact, the young man looked away, but remained where he stood. He had the look of a man trying to blend in, head bowed slightly, a cautious rigidity to his stance. But Emil thought it would prove difficult to blend in anywhere with such glistening scars on his well-muscled arms. Emil wondered why he didn't just wear longer sleeves. As the man approached Emil his eyeline shifted nervously from left to right. He was trying so hard to be inconspicuous he appeared tremendously conspicuous.

He stopped and stood in front of Emil.

"I know you."

"No you don't."

"Yes I do."

"I'm afraid you don't."

"I most certainly do."

"Well that settles it then, if you're certain, how do you know me?"

"I saw them bringing you in, or rather dragging you in. Heading straight down to the dungeons." The man inclined his head up toward the citadel.

"Oh," muttered Emil. Typical, he'd made it all the way down here and now he was going to be sent right back up there. "I don't know what you're talking about," he said, reverting back to playing ignorant.

"You don't have to worry because I don't work for Edirp anymore. We had a, er, disagreement. He seemed to believe himself entirely sane and I believed otherwise. It put a strain on our working relationship." The man chuckled and held out a hand, "my name's Skarz."

"I'll bet it is. My name is Emil, my dear boy, and I would readily shake your hand, but I fear I would overbalance and collapse if I tried. How about we make our way up to that inn over there and sit down. I think we may have rather a lot to discuss."

With Skarz for additional support Emil made it safely into the inn. There were several beaten rosewood tables to the right and the room had a strange, inescapable fragrance. Flowers and ale. The room was empty aside from a portly man sat behind the counter.

Now the portly man was called Ted. He hadn't always been portly, but weight has a tendency to drift south over the years until it settles around the middle and, given Ted's age, it was entirely understandable. Especially as he spent a lot of those years sat down. He stirred from attending his bookkeeping to address the rough looking pair ambling into his inn. One of them looked like a strong wind would finish him off if he didn't get a strong drink down him quickly.

Emil was loathe to abuse his power, but needs must.

Emil waved his hand in front of Ted's eyes before clicking his fingers twice. It was like turning the lights off in Ted's head.

They walked to a table and Emil lowered himself into a corner-seat as the lumbering innkeeper poured him a drink with a vacant, blank expression on his face.

"I think I might have overdone it slightly," murmured Emil as he studied the innkeeper's face. He was now drooling. Having filled Emil's glass to the point of overflow, Ted slowly ambled back to his counter.

"Never mind eh, it'll wear off by morning," Emil said, turning his attention to Skarz, who was sat across from him. "So, you mentioned Edirp?"

"Yes, he's completely lost his mind, wants to destroy the entire world. But it's so much worse than you could ever imagine…" Skarz drew a deep breath, his face muscles working hard to convey a severity beyond anything his face muscles had ever had cause to convey. "You see, he has a Dragon Lord, it's cooped up in the mountain…"

Emil held up a withered hand.

"I must stop you there. You're labouring under the impression I know nothing of the situation. I was kidnapped so that they may learn how to control the Dragon Lord, though I did not reveal anything to them. I must also assure you that Edirp is no longer a threat," said Emil. The look of shock upon the roughly hewn face staring back at him suggested Skarz was a little behind the times. He motioned to speak but Emil beat him to it. "Where have you been laddy?"

Skarz hesitated. He would never admit to being knocked out cold by a renegade coconut.

"I had an accident escaping the mountain... I've been out of it for a couple of days maybe, what's happened?"

Emil regaled Skarz with the details of what had been going on during his brief spell away from the city. How Edirp had been the victim of a mutiny, how Med Tet now controlled the city and wished to do away with the inconvenience of an uncontrollable Dragon Lord and seize control of the world for himself. Piece by piece.

"Med Tet, I am afraid to say, is rather more organised than Edirp. I'm hoping that the Dragon Lord does away with him before he builds up a head of steam on the imperialistic front," said Emil.

"I thought you said you told Med Tet how to kill the dragon?" replied Skarz.

"Well, I told him how to right royally pee it off, but," Emil paused to take a swig of his drink, "not how to kill it. Dragon Lords are deeply magical creatures, if he really thinks a poke in the eye will finish it off then he's a lot dumber than he appears. Another dragon could do it. Or otherwise strong magic and lot of firepower... Anyway, so long as it stays in that mountain there won't be any problems." As soon as Emil finished his sentence, he realised something was wrong. Skarz suddenly looked nervous and, maybe, a little guilty.

"Then we may have a slight problem."

"Yes?"

"Well, we've been keeping it well sedated. But, er, the tunnel down is pretty large and there's a gap up top, it could probably force its way out if it felt like it…"

"Go on…"

"And, erm, I thought that, if it was going to rip Edirp limb from limb, it best not be sedated, so I, er…"

"Oh no."

"Stopped sedating it. None of the meat stored for the coming week or so contains any sedatives at all." Skarz's face flushed red to match his bright scars. He'd spoken almost entirely to the floor because he daren't look up at Emil, who sounded like he was choking on his brandy.

***

Deep within the Misty Mountain, the Dragon Lord stirred.

Slowly opening its eyes, it surveyed its surroundings. Its head clearer than it had felt in weeks, it stretched its limbs.

This light is bright, overwhelming.

The brightness was strange to it now. For so long, it was accustomed to the shine that seeped through from above. That was before these little creatures turned up and, somehow, the mountain chasm it called home had become a prison. But that didn't matter now. It felt groggy. It craved an open space, somewhere to truly stretch its wings, to hurl the metaphorical and literal shackles into the ether. For so long an alien numbness had controlled its urges.

Thick folds before the eyes of the beast stirred and

opened and a little creature on two legs edged inside, into its territory, and placed something on the floor.

I cannot trust what it brings.

The Dragon Lord had not roared properly in some time. Its throat felt dry, but it had never heard of lozenges. After too long under painful, unnatural restrictions, the creature rose.

But I can trust it.

The cry was deafening, the flames all consuming. The Dragon Lord felt alive once more.

***

Drago, Caine and Korin reluctantly slouched back into the grand, paint-spattered hall of Ivan's palace. A couple of the decorators applauded and cheered as a result of the earlier entertainment. They were quickly silenced by Ivan himself.

"GUARDS! Seize them, seize them!"

A few guards edged forward nervously, still nursing bumps and bruises from their previous encounter.

"Oh pipe down Ivan, you're embarrassing yourself," said Vector. He wobbled slightly and Amelia grabbed his arm to steady him. Not having left his body behind for many years, Vector's limbs were suffering from his high-speed jaunt around Vertenve in spirit form. Patience for Ivan's foibles was in short supply.

Ivan was stunned and a little hurt. Few subjects have the gall to speak to a steward in such a way, leaving said steward with little practice in dealing with such an approach. "Well, they should at least pay back what they stole," he declared, legs apart, chest puffed out in an odd stance. He thought it was impressive. The effect was closer to that of a pigeon with a toothbrush up its bottom.

"How about we promise not to steal anything this time round?" said Caine, grinning his semi-toothy grin.

"Can't say fairer than that," added Korin.

Ivan looked about ready to explode.

***

They passed through a maze of hallways draped in paintings of past stewards. Drago couldn't help but notice that Vertenve's upper echelons came in all shapes and sizes. A handsome and rotund woman in a colourful and elaborate dress, complete with a wide ruff, caught Drago's eye. The inscription beneath her painting read: *'The revered Michelina Starr, known for her court's spectacular banquets'*.

"I wish I could have been there," Drago said, smiling.

Vector led the way with Amelia as the others followed, Ivan looking rather dejected. He was muttering to himself and appeared volatile, on the verge of meltdown even. Drago could just about catch him saying, 'my castle, my own castle,' under his breath. Perhaps wrestling with the reality of a continental war and the irritation at being told what to do in his own court, yes, his own court, was causing Ivan issues, thought Drago.

Ahead of them, Amelia cast a brief glance back and turned to Vector, speaking quietly. "I thought we wanted Ivan on our side?" she asked, furtively confirming Ivan was still in his own irate little world and wouldn't overhear.

"My dear," replied Vector, making no effort to conceal his words, "Ivan and Vertenve are incapable of helping, I assure you. I am here only to humour the good steward Antillia of Rathendy." Amelia stared at Vector, baffled by this open declaration. She was just about to halt proceedings and cause a ruckus about them wasting their time, and her father's time, by being here if that was the case, when Vector winked.

She had a bad feeling about this.

Not a minor feeling, a bad inkling, for example, but a negative tsunami of feeling.

They entered a large square room filled with bean bags and unusual objects, some of which appeared broken beyond repair. Amongst other peculiar creations there were shards of glass hanging from a large frame in one corner, a wardrobe made of clay, several ornate tea pots seemingly glued together and one ghastly painting of a giraffe.

The room was cold. An open fireplace sat empty and unlit.

They had all filed in and were taking in the bizarre implements around the room when Caine spoke.

"What on Torvacane is tha'?" he asked, pointing at the painting of the giraffe.

Momentarily distracted from his grumbling, Ivan perked up a little and answered: "I'm sure you noticed that lining our halls are paintings of my illustrious ancestors, and this is to be mine," he said proudly.

Caine squinted, turned his head to the left, and then angled it to the right, before facing Ivan. "Nah, looks more like a giraffe, tha' does."

"Got kind of a bird-like quality to it if you ask me," Drago piped up.

"It's a landscape of the moon."

"T'moon? I've never seen t'moon look like a giraffe!"

"You haven't been looking closely enough then."

Ivan was on the verge of boiling over again. "I'll have you know that this painting was painted by the finest squarist painter in Vertenve, Poblob Saxo. He's very well respected amongst contemporary artists."

"Aren't artists supposed to be good at painting?"

"Not these modern types, no idea what they're doin' if ya ask me."

"I think," said Vector, in one of those authoritative voices designed to break up minor disagreements, "we should set aside discussion of the contemporary art scene for the time being, each pull up a bean bag and get to the matter at hand. We all have a role to play going forward. And you, perhaps a round of tea?"

Vector was addressing the steward of Vertenve, Ivan, whose face resembled a tomato that had grown a goatee. Biting his lip, Ivan nodded at a servant to indicate he follow up on Vector's request. It would prove a challenge finding a teapot Poblob Saxo hadn't included in his installation art project (tentatively titled: *Potty for Tea*).

While awaiting their drinks, and while Ivan seethed, the group collapsed into a bean bag apiece. Amelia chose a purple one and eyed the ragtag bunch that were about to discuss how to save the world and help her save her father. Two old letches past their sell-by-date, one young pretender who couldn't keep them under control, an angry little man muttering to himself under his breath and an old wizard who seemed determined to infuriate the steward to the point where he might just try to suffocate him with an orange bean bag.

It seemed a little bit hopeless.

"So," said Caine, "somethin' 'bout the world bein' in peril wasn't it? Sounds like fun, what's the plan?"

"Fun?" asked Amelia, "how can you possibly associate the word peril with fun? That's like associating the word delicious with manure!"

"Or beautiful with Caine," Drago added.

"Oi! I've 'ad women fightin' over my 'andsome mug in the past."

The mention of mugs was prescient as the tea arrived and was distributed to welcoming, cold hands. Amelia in particular grasped hers with ten digits, hoping the warmth would spread to her unhappy toes.

"I think we may be getting a little off track again," Vector began. "I have grave news for you all, news which should help our little group concentrate on the task at hand. I am appalled to have to inform you all that Athea Hubris intends to wage war on the entire continent. Med Tet has already recruited many mercenaries using his underground contacts and, even now, more flock towards the city."

"Hang on, hang on," said Ivan, "what about Edirp, what about Edirp I say? What's he doing letting Med Tet run the show?"

"It was Edirp who started off the proceedings, and he who perpetrated the greatest crime. However, he has fallen from power. Quite literally, in fact," replied Vector, not so much as glancing at Ivan.

"And the, er, greatest crime?" asked Korin.

"Yes, yes, that brings us onto the most horrific and serious part of this sordid episode. Upon mining the Misty Mountain, they made a discovery. And not just the discovery which, I imagine, brings you three gentlemen to this part of the world," Vector nodded to Caine, Korin and Drago, a brief smile gracing his face. "Alive, hidden deep within the mountain, was a Dragon Lord."

It should be next to impossible to fall off a bean bag. A chair yes, you could fall off a chair if you tried hard enough, but to fall off a bean bag you would have to hurl yourself with great effort, comically flailing your entire body as you go.

Upon hearing this news, Ivan fell off his bean bag.

The room was silent, apart from the coughing and spluttering coming from Ivan who had also spilled tea down his robes. And choked on the mouthful of tea he had drunk a moment previously. It was a bad thirty seconds for Ivan.

No one was paying him any attention. A servant took pity and helped turn him upright.

After a short snippet of time in which everyone shifted uncomfortably, Korin spoke.

"How can they possibly control it, there are few wizards left, and certainly none young enough or evil enough to help." He looked earnestly at Vector. They weren't strangers to each other's reputations.

"That is where my young friend Amelia here comes in. My dear." Vector gestured to Amelia, who had remained quiet so far. She had not anticipated having to address the group.

"Er, yes. My father is Emil Kaio, a wizard who controlled Dragon Lords. But he is very old. He was kidnapped by Edirp and is still being held there. I, I must rescue him, he's all I have." She took a long sip of her tea. Five pairs of eyes were fixed upon her and she avoided every one of them.

"Well then I guess we should get to Athea Hubris and save him," said Korin, addressing Amelia directly. He smiled at her. Fortunately, it was Korin and not Caine who spoke, because Caine's less than full smile could appear sinister even when he meant well.

"Which means we'll need a plan," said Drago. He'd become quite tired of rushing into things and letting everything clumsily fall into place.

"Why don't we jus' rush inta the place and let everythin' fall inta place as we go?" asked Caine. Drago groaned.

"That does usually work for us," said Korin in support.

"VERTENVE WILL HELP!" shouted Ivan, exploding as much as is possible from a bean bag. Having pulled himself upright, he was just about taller than Vector sat down. "You come in here, ruin my banquet hall, yes ruin my banquet hall and insult me, make your little plans to save the world, save the world eh?! And don't expect me to do anything about it? No, not me. Vertenve will not merely stand by and let some tyrant with an overgrown lizard take over the world." The sheer effort of this rousing, manic speech led Ivan to collapse back into his bean bag.

"That is most noble Ivan, we thank you for your help," said Vector, nodding at Ivan and holding his gaze. "Now, the question is how we go about it. I don't think there's any question that we must strike soon. If we allow Athea Hubris to continue adding to its armed forces, we will have allowed them to become too strong. Antillia and her army ride for Hogback Ridge. Ivan, you must meet her there. Together you should be able to withstand the might of Med Tet's forces and push them back."

"Then that leaves us," said Korin, looking knowingly at Vector.

"Yes, I believe you fellows are up to the job."

"And the job is…?" asked Drago.

"Findin' our way into Athea Hubris, rescuing the girl's father, killin' or otherwise subduin' the Dragon Lord, and makin' away with as much gold as we can lay our 'ands on," said Caine. "Did I miss anythin' out?"

"No, I think that just about covers it. Maybe punch Med Tet right on the nose if we get chance, that might be fun."

"Well that settles it. Ivan, I believe you have an army to rouse," said Vector authoritatively. Ivan looked as though, for one moment, he thought of arguing. Most likely words along the lines of 'my own palace' being repeated over and over again. Sense finally got the better of him and he left with nothing but a grunted goodbye.

Amelia felt buoyed. They were finally, certainly, going to do something. But where did she fit in? It occurred to her that Vector hadn't specified where she would be during the entire thing. Why? She suspected she knew, and she wasn't about to allow him to keep her on the sidelines.

"I want to go with them," she declared, pointing at Drago, whose line of vision immediately encompassed his boots and not much else.

Vector looked Amelia up and down, noting her resemblance to a crouched tiger. Tigers like to maul. Vector had the wherewithal to recognise when he himself was about to be subject to a mauling.

"Okay."

"I will not take no for an answer, I refuse to be left… Hang on, what?" said a baffled Amelia.

"Okay, I have no grounds to prevent you. So far you have shown yourself to be a capable and strong-willed young woman, who I daresay has a few more tricks up her blouse sleeve. I'll supervise Ivan. Son only knows what trouble he'll get into attempting to do things on his own."

"Right," she said, "okay then… Well then, I guess this is goodbye."

"Only for now, my dear. We'll be sipping tea and eating biscuits in the citadel of Athea Hubris before you know it." Vector smiled warmly at Amelia and turned to exit. A moment later he had the stuffing knocked out of him.

"My dear," he gasped, "if you wanted a hug you should have just asked. I'm really quite frail, you know." He turned around and embraced Amelia properly, his beard tickling her face. In the background Caine suppressed a sniffle.

Amelia let go and stumbled backwards, sobbing lightly. Vector turned to Korin and nodded. "She's all yours." He afforded one last smile and departed.

Korin stepped forward and patted her on the shoulder, looking pleadingly to Caine and Drago for help. They both also tried to put their hands on her shoulder and found there was very little shoulder left, so Caine patted her on the back instead.

"I think we ought to leave. The sooner we get going the sooner we work out what to do," said Korin.

"We'll need horses," Drago chipped in, "I'm sure Ivan will allow us a couple."

"Ya don't ask for 'orses boy, ya just take 'em," said Caine, slapping him heartily on the back and striding out of the room. Drago looked to Korin for help, but he laughed and followed Caine.

"Erm, I, er, suppose we should get going then?" he said timidly to Amelia.

***

All parties were prepared and had begun to converge on Athea Hubris. Like the crescendo of an orchestral piece, things were building. The armoury in Athea Hubris bustled with the clanging and screeching of metal being fashioned and perfected, men and women vacated Vertenve and Rathendy in their droves, marching on their destination with haste and fervour.

Son didn't like their enthusiasm.

He retreated from His Oracle Pool and stared out across the Asthmatic Ocean. The rings shone vividly, enhancing each singular ripple of water, each wave glittering as if diamond encrusted.

He'd created all of this. Yet He couldn't fix it.

He knew He should have just stuck to sea monkeys. But no, He had to create real organic life. And give it free will too! Who, in this vast universe, gives life free will? He'd heard of one god who'd done the same, once upon a time. It did not end well.

He needed someone to help Him organise this madness. Luckily, a personal assistant had just become available. Provided the newly free PA wasn't eaten by a rogue Dragon Lord, Son would have to look him up.

***

The streets of Vertenve bustled noisily as cohort after cohort of soldiers advanced toward the western gate. The western gate wasn't, in the classical sense, a gate. It was more of a concept. Ivan felt cities should have towering gates because they're majestic and imposing. However, they hadn't got around to building a gate yet, so it was effectively a place where the city stopped and somewhere else began.

At the tail end of the departing fighters was Vector, ambling along with a section of infantrymen. He looked upon the faces of the citizens waving goodbye, their sadness almost tangible. This weighed heavily on his conscience, but he was used to carrying such burdens.

The day was already fading, a thin ring growing brighter before his very eyes. They planned to march through the night and much of tomorrow to make up time. The road was not a treacherous one and there was nothing but open plains between Vertenve and Hogback Ridge. The ridge was a different story altogether. Uneven and rocky like Caine's home cooking, it is a difficult path to take. Fortunately, they would be able to pass by it rather than crossing it before meeting Antillia to the north and making for Athea Hubris.

Vector was looking forward to seeing the infamous flying pigs, a phenomenon of this peculiar world he hadn't yet seen. And he wasn't the only one. He'd overheard several soldiers discussing it merrily as they went. You could almost forget why you were going there in the first place, but only for a moment…

They were heading into battle.

They were going to war.

And possibly to do a spot of sight-seeing along the way.

**

Four days had passed. During this period, Rathendy had set up camp near Hogback Ridge and were waiting patiently for Vector and Vertenve's army, fending off the occasional flying pig attack.

A small guerrilla force consisting of three men and a woman had reached the Wearisome Woodland of Mist. Passing through it would take them to the foot of the Misty Mountain.

"What on Torvacane is that?" declared Drago, pointing at a thick, green vine dangling from a tree barely ten yards away. It was hissing. And oozing. All manner of disgusting and threatening phenomena.

"That's a boomslag. Evolved from snakes, I believe. The pesky so-and-sos fuse into the trees and linger there, waiting for anyone to pass below, then they drop and hook you round the throat. That hissing is tiny pores that ooze acid. Probably should have mentioned them actually," said Korin.

"How do you know all that?" asked Amelia.

"I have a strong sense of self-preservation," replied Korin. "Swords at the ready, just in case," he added, drawing his own.

Amelia, caught up in the spirit of things back in Vertenve, had raided the palace for supplies before their departure. She was jangling like a bag of marbles by the time she left the armoury. Reluctantly, she'd lightened her load when Drago asked if she were capable of safely navigating a flight of stairs. But she was packing a bow and a quiver full of arrows, and a serviceable if worn sword. The group had also taken two horses and numerous food supplies. Caine had insisted they 'charge it to their bill', which the head chef didn't take too kindly to, resulting in him chasing them out of the kitchens with a meat cleaver. This was the second time a chef had attacked them in Vertenve, leading Drago to conclude Vertenvian chefs were passionate people. They seemed to care more for their kitchen than their lives.

The trees were spread thinly, as if the forest were balding. The breeze was chilly, but they'd also *borrowed* extra cloaks. Amelia had to admit these guys knew how to utilise their surroundings. Resourceful though they were, she still felt they were taking a haphazard approach to the whole mission. The plan was to sneak in via Misty Mountain and, in Caine's words, 'have some fun'. The actual method of entering the city or finding her father or the dragon or anything useful at all had not been discussed, which she found quite frustrating. But Vector had trusted them, planning their involvement from the beginning. She had to have faith.

"Have you let one rip?" shouted Caine whilst glaring at Drago, "that stinks!"

Drago blushed and swivelled to face Caine and return fire but stopped abruptly. The colour that had rushed to his cheeks had drained away so completely that he looked like he'd seen his own ghost. "We, er, have a problem," he whispered, pointing over Caine's shoulder.

The others turned around grasping their swords tightly to be confronted by the cause of the overwhelming stench.

A pile of brownish sludge was edging towards them. It had a vaguely human shape but with no visible features, just a sloping mass of viscous goo.

"A fireaker," muttered Korin, not taking his eyes off the creature.

"What's that, exactly?" asked Amelia nervously.

"Well, it's that thing right there."

"Thanks."

"You're welcome."

The creature roared straight from its gut. The smell

grew more grotesque to the point where Drago felt faint. Sparks flew from rolls of gooey flab as it edged forward. Suddenly, a savage flame burst from a gaping mouth in its gut, barely missing them as they dove aside.

"How do we kill it," said Amelia, hauling herself up from the ground. She winced as she brushed mud from a graze on her arm.

Occasionally, you're able to dredge up a memory that has been repressed for many years, right at the exact moment you need it. Caine had one of those moments.

"You two, try and annoy it inta firin' again," he yelled as he lunged for the nearest puddle and began rolling the mud into a ball, "Korin, get over 'ere and 'elp."

"Are you kidding!?" Drago replied. He and Amelia were currently hidden behind the width of a pine trunk. Higher up, its leaves had caught fire. "You want us to play with the fire-breathing pile of dung while you make mud castles?" There was a time and a place for everything, thought Drago, and Caine always chose wrong.

There was a crack from above and a branch came falling down right where they were standing. Or it would have been right where they were standing if Amelia hadn't dragged them both away at the last moment.

"Um, thanks."

"Don't mention it. Now grab some of these stones. As much as I hate to admit it, they do seem to know what they're talking about... some of the time."

No, they pretend to know what they're talking about before stumbling from one situation to the next, thought Drago. He didn't feel like arguing with Amelia and it didn't seem an appropriate time. And anyway, his mum had brought him up not to argue with a lady. It was part of being a gentleman. Or perhaps it was to stop him questioning his mother's decisions? A startling realisation he would have to process another time.

"Oh alright," he conceded, grabbing a handful of stones.

The fireaker continued to edge forward, belching sparks from its midriff like Caine after a Totulgnian curry. Crackling noises waltzed alongside the fireaker's languid squelching. The creature appeared to be as stable and capable of calm as a rhinoceros with several large haemorrhoids. Most of the nearby trees were aflame, the leaves burning up quickly, bright orange ashes flickering to the ground. It might have been pretty, poetic even, if it didn't smell as badly as a chiropodist's hands after a long day at work.

Korin and Caine had rolled up two balls of mud about the size of basketballs and were waiting to the side, motioning the others forward.

"Here goes nothing," muttered Drago as he and Amelia braced themselves for their assault armed with a handful of jagged stones. This was not the sort of weaponry Amelia had in mind when rummaging through the Vertenve armoury. It had crossed her mind to test out her aim with the bow and arrows, but this wasn't the moment for a practice run.

A particularly loud wheeze was followed by a voice shouting 'now'.

They leapt.

Moments later a bouquet of pheasants took flight, disturbed by a rasping explosion.

***

Med Tet had changed his mind. He now had a significant army that was littered with mercenaries loyal to him. It seemed a crying shame to keep them locked up, like clipping a falcon's wings. They would meet the armies of Rathendy and Vertenve head on and the battle would rage by Hogback Ridge. It seemed foolish to allow it to take place close enough to the city for it to be infiltrated.

Like any tyrant he had no intention of doing any fighting himself, it was the duty of others to die for him. That was rule number one in the 'Mercyless Tyyrrant Handbuk' written by Blad the Inhaler (he had terrible asthma) centuries ago.

There was a knock at the door.

"Enter."

Mootley, his newly appointed right hand man, sloped in. He was the largest and stupidest of his generals and therefore the most qualified man for the job of field marshal.

"Field Marshal Mootley, just the man. I have instructions for you. You are to take our entire forces and march to Hogback Ridge, whereby you shall engage the enemy and emerge victorious. Is that clear?" said Med Tet.

"Yes sir," said Field Marshal Mootley. He saluted sharply. A little too sharply. Rubbing his right eye, he did an about turn and exited.

Med Tet leant back in his chair and relaxed. The wheels were greased and would soon be in motion. By his estimation he should be able to declare himself the first emperor of Seven Cities within six months. He'd need to change his name, something with a bit more prestige and sophistication, but also something that represented the briskness of his rise to power.

Perhaps something with gust in it?
Or maybe breeze.
No, he'd got it.
Emperor Auwindus.

***

Traditionally, trees are brown. It's a fact. The trees surrounding Drago and his companions were also brown. But they were a browner shade of brown than tree trunk brown. Murkier.

As the fireaker started convulsing violently the four of them were forced to dive for cover, and not a moment too soon. It had exploded with enough force to cover the immediate area with thick brown sludge. It dripped from branches, it stained the ground, and it entirely changed a nearby bear's species.

There were no words required for the next step of their journey. Their desire to put as much forest between them and the stench violating their current location was stronger than Samson during his Bon Jovi phase. They briskly gathered whatever belongings hadn't been sullied by sludge and set off in the direction of Misty Mountain.

Visible above the trees, ringlight illuminated its snowy peak like ice cream atop a particularly unappetising jelly. The peak was doing what peaks do, peaking.

They trudged on through the Wearisome Woodland of Mist in silence. The mist descended, sneaking up on them like a non-corporeal mugger. With this there was a distinct drop in temperature causing Amelia to shiver, even in her thick cloak. The adrenaline had subsided from the earlier attack too, which didn't help.

"Ii thhhink it's timmee to makeee camp and builldd a

fireee," she said, "we cannnn't seeeee our hannndddss inn ffffront of ourrr facceeess." Amelia didn't wait for a reaction from the others, she slung her bag to the ground and stood there hugging herself so tightly it was as though she might fall apart if she let go.

"Did she say somethin' about faeces?" asked Caine, whose teeth would have been chattering had they all still been in his mouth.

"Let's hope not," replied Korin. He recognised there was no point going any further now, there was too great a risk of getting lost in conditions such as these.

They hastily set up their tents in the shadow of a thick-trunked tree that sheltered them from the wind and lit a fire. They were familiar with the field of thought popular amongst the creatures of Torvacane. If someone is bold enough to light a fire when far away from civilisation it is probably because they can handle anything drawn towards it. In this case it was safe to light a fire because, no matter how bright, it was unlikely to be seen by anyone beyond ten yards away.

Drago had settled down on a log by the fire. Amelia had quietly joined him. They sat there for some time staring into the fire, just trying to stay warm. After a while longer Amelia rested her head on Drago's shoulder.

Amelia wanted to forget everything, everything that was going on, and just rest. But she knew she couldn't and that made her angry. Angry at feeling so powerless and then angry for despairing. Right now, she just wanted to rest her head on Drago's dumb shoulder. Drago simply sat still, continuing to stare into the fire.

It wasn't that he hadn't noticed Amelia leaning on him. But a state of paralysis had come over him. An internal debate sparked in his brain as to whether he'd rather go another round with the fireaker than acknowledge Amelia's presence.

Or move at all for that matter.

Caine and Korin returned from a brief walk around the camp collecting wood for the fire and also to ensure there was nothing too dangerous lingering nearby. They'd seen an unusual looking bear with a powerful odour, but it was moving in a daze in the opposite direction. Aside from that there were no boomslags or anything else of note.

Caine noticed the pair, nudged Korin, and pointed at them whilst flashing his semi-toothy grin.

"I'll take first watch," whispered Korin, lowering himself onto his bag and fishing a pipe out from his pocket. Caine nodded and entered his tent and pulled the zipper down.

Korin looked across at the two youngsters wistfully. He produced a blanket from his bag and threw it across to Drago who caught it clumsily, nearly knocking Amelia off the log.

"Get some sleep you two, I have a feeling tomorrow could be a very long day," he said, striking a match and lighting his pipe. The smoke was immediately lost to the mist.

"Yeah, uh, yeah you're probably right," replied Drago, glancing nervously at Amelia. She wearily stood up, nodded at Korin, and slipped into the tent. Drago remained sat on the log. He looked up to see Korin chuckling and shaking his head.

"Go on, I'm sure you can both squeeze in there. It's getting cold."

Drago stood up and gazed up at the night sky, then out towards Misty Mountain, or where he was confident it lay through the fog. Everything went beyond Misty Mountain now, beyond the gold, beyond a childish yearning for adventure. This was something epic and he was right in the middle of it. The ringlight filtering through the trees illuminated his anxious face. He hadn't expected this. To find he was caught up in events much too big for him and the damsel in distress was actually in distress. Everything felt too real.

He took one last glance at the sky, ducked into the tent, and pulled down the zipper.

The night passed uneventfully.

***

There were threatening clouds in the sky, the kind of clouds that have several gold teeth and a heart tattoo saying 'Mom'. It had been a tough few days marching a thousand or so reluctant men and women across a dreary landscape. Vector shared their discontent. He himself was in the midst of an unprecedented situation; he hadn't had a cup of tea for almost a week.

Hogback Ridge rose ruggedly in the distance like a drunk from the gutter. There were hordes of tents set up a short way before the ridge. Antillia had made good time.

An eagle approached from the north flying low. A few soldiers gasped as it whistled over their heads before gracefully pulling up and landing on Vector's shoulder. It looked agitated. Terry wasn't one for crowds.

"News?" muttered Vector, ignoring the excited murmurs from the men. The crowds weren't sure whether Vector had noticed the large bird of prey sitting on his shoulder.

Private Bryan and Private Bluster were walking nearby

and looked on in fascination.

"'ere, is 'e talkin' to a bird?" asked Private Bryan, who only believed in eighteen letters of the alphabet.

"I think so, certainly looks that way, don't it," replied Private Bluster, rubbing her eyes out of concern for their reliability.

"Bu' ya can't talk t'birds, fac' o' life."

"I don't think anyone's told 'im that," said Private Bluster, wide brown eyes fixed on Vector, her face wearing the kind of expression reserved for only the very top bracket of bizarre behaviour.

After a few hushed words from Vector and much wing gesticulating from Terry, the bald eagle hopped from its perch and flapped in a flustered manner for a moment before gaining some momentum and flying away, disappearing, very slowly, from sight.

Having watched the eagle soaring off until their eyes watered, Privates Bryan and Bluster turned to look at Vector again with the sort of nervous eagerness of a child asking their teacher a question.

But Vector wasn't there.

He had already broken free from the ambling army and was pushing his horse as hard as was reasonable. There would be no point speaking to Ivan, he was as much use as air holes in a coffin. No, he had to reach Antillia with haste. This news was extremely worrying. By his estimations, the opposing army would appear on the horizon by morning with the express purpose of annoying him a great deal.

After all, no one wants a surprise battle before breakfast. If Vector had wanted that he'd have settled down and got married.

Antillia was waiting by the edge of the camp, wearing

fitted battle garments such as her leather jerkin, padded trousers and swordbelt. No doubt she had spotted the mass of people moving inexorably towards her and wanted to appear up for the fight.

Vector eased up into a trot, giving his horse a pat for its hard work once he'd dug his heels in. Vector dismounted and Antillia approached to embrace her friend but hesitated, sensing a subtle perturbment in Vector's aura. It also helped that Vector declared clearly in words that he had worrying news.

"Am I to understand your racing here wasn't just to see my pretty face all the sooner?" said Antillia in the darkly jovial tone of one whose last request before being beheaded was a haircut.

"Alas, no, I don't believe anyone has ever been in such a hurry," replied Vector, affording a laugh before the serious business began. "We have a problem."

"You've forgotten to pack spare socks?" suggested Antillia.

"Oh dear, you know, I *have* forgotten to pack spare socks. This just keeps getting worse. Alas, I rushed here for another reason. Med Tet's army will be here by dawn tomorrow."

"Ah."

***

Emil and Skarz had watched patiently as Athea Hubris emptied. There were so many people passing through it had looked like the road itself had come alive. They saw this as an opportunity. Med Tet clearly felt there was no threat from within the city, else he wouldn't have left himself so exposed. They hoped to disprove his theory.

The plan relied a little too heavily on their acting ability, thought Emil, but it was either talk their way into the citadel or bludgeon their way in. Emil, feeling he was a few years past his bludgeoning best, had opted for the former. He was confident that the time between Skarz escaping Edirp and the usurper Med Tet snatching power was sufficiently short that no bounty had been placed on Skarz's head. Most likely they could simply walk right in under the guise of soldier escorting escaped prisoner back to the dungeons.

Of course, something being likely isn't the same as something being certain.

***

The morning arrived, as it has a habit of doing.

They'd reached the foot of Misty Mountain during the course of the morning and followed it around before happening upon the source of a rough but distinct path that led them up the mountain.

At least, it led far enough.

Far enough that the climb could only be described as 'marginally perilous' and the drop onto the citadel battlements as 'insignificant'. Caine and Korin had described the mountainside scramble in typically insouciant terms. Amelia eyed Drago with a newfound respect, even wonderment, because he'd survived so far with these two barmy old men.

It was still cold, but the morning fog had subsided. The last thing they needed was to be climbing a mountain whilst half-blind. Inconveniences were hardly in short supply.

After a short breakfast they were ready to begin their assault on the mountain. You can't climb a mountain if you haven't eaten breakfast; it is, after all, the most important meal of the day.

The ascent, for a change, was an uneventful procession for the most part. Amelia had a short spate of nerves when she looked down after being told not to look down. That aside, they were able to reach the end of the mountain path by late morning. From the threshold they could look down at the entire of Athea Hubris. It was eerily quiet. Apart from a flock of magpies swooping down across the parapet at set intervals.

Before them was a section of mountainside, rocky, jagged, with a short and flat ledge that could be traversed. Another twenty feet and this ledge came to an end above the citadel battlements. Silently, Korin led the way and the others followed.

Inching out onto the ever-shortening ledge, the four of them held their breath, kept their backs tight against the mountainside, and shimmied with as much care as a gassy groom stood at the altar. Sidling along the remainder of the cliff edge, eyes avoiding the emptiness below, several tense minutes passed until the guerrilla force were directly above the mine entrance. It remained a steep drop, though not the certain death of mere moments prior. They would be able to skirt down the jagged rockface until the drop was what one might call manageable. There was no patrol, which struck them as odd, but you can't complain about a slice of luck.

They were due an entire cake of luck by this point, thought Drago. Alas, their slice of luck, or cake of luck, was undercooked. Or under-baked. Under... done.

A tinkling sound from above caused them to look up,

at which point they saw stones and small rocks crumbling down.

"OW! I hope they don't get any bigger," said Drago, rubbing the top of his head. Another stone threatened to clip him as it tumbled past. There was some disturbance further up the mountain.

"Nothin' t'worry 'bout," said Caine, "ya get the odd tremor round mountains, dislodges a few rocks."

Caine could not have been more wrong.

The stones running down the trembling rock face lessened in number until they were no more, and everything was silent.

"Right, I think we'd better get a move on…" Korin began, but he was interrupted by the increasing volume of what sounded like screaming. Louder and louder it grew until a man appeared from the entrance into the mountain below them. The interesting thing about the man emerging from the mountain was that he was on fire.

"Oh no," gasped Amelia, "shouldn't we help him?" she said, and made to scramble down the cliff. Korin grabbed her by the arm and held firmly as she protested.

"It's too late for him," he said solemnly. And he was right. The man toppled straight over the edge of the battlements. His screams not dying out until he hit the ground.

"That was horrible," whispered Amelia, leaning back against the rock face.

"I think we should be more worried about what set him on fire," said Korin, exchanging a knowing glance with Caine that Drago didn't miss. "We need to move fast, come on." Korin sat down and began to creep down the mountainside, dragging his bottom south. The others made to follow suit but froze.

It wasn't a scream that perforated the quiet. It was a great ferocious roar.

***

The remaining people in Athea Hubris were gazing up toward the mountain nervously. Most had heard the roar and stepped outside to see what was happening. It's funny how people hear something that sounds dangerous and immediately step out into the open to have a closer look. Some sort of in-built anti-survival instinct.

Mumbled sounds of distress and fear could be heard throughout the city as the rumbling continued. This disrupted Emil and Skarz's plan somewhat, but there was an upside. The guards had seen the flaming man crash to the ground, leaving the entrance clear. This they could take advantage of.

They climbed the steps onto the first level. The citadel was layered. There were three levels that included barracks, mess hall, training room and washrooms before they reached the stone spiral staircase that led up to the battlements. The battlements, of course, stretched across towards the mountain and the mine entrance. A walkway, flanked by statues of past monarchs and a deep and deadly abyss, connected the battlements to the main castle in which Med Tet resided. Beneath the castle were the dungeons that Emil knew so well.

They climbed up yet more stairs but froze upon hearing a thunderous roar. Dulled by its passage through the thick stone walls it was thunderous nevertheless. Emil and Skarz stared wide-eyed for several seconds. An extremely angry and large inconvenience sounded like it was waiting for them just a couple more flights of stairs up. It wasn't until they reached the third floor that they met anyone. A guard came running down the staircase from the battlements, evidently not the bravest guard in the guard, and skidded to a halt upon seeing Emil and Skarz. The man's momentum and bulk almost toppled him over.

"Hey, what are you doing here?" he shouted, slightly wheezily but in a braver tone than was a true reflection of how he felt. He attempted to puff his chest out, but it failed to protrude as far as his belly.

The first true test of their plan had arisen. Could they convince the guard of their story? They realised that they didn't exactly look like prisoner and escort, Emil's hands weren't even bound.

Skarz, who hadn't been particularly comfortable with the original plan anyway, marched in a determined fashion straight up to the guard, who looked a little taken aback, and flattened him with a right hook that knocked him out cold.

"I never liked that guy," he muttered, shaking the soreness from his hand.

"Fair enough," replied Emil lightly, "I shall have to remember to never annoy you in any way, shape or form."

They ascended the final staircase, Emil propelling himself with the aid of his stick, to be greeted by glaring sunshine from which they had to shield their eyes. After acclimatising to the brightness, they could see an unusual collection of people in front of the mine entrance untangling limbs, picking each other up and dusting off dirt from their clothing.

There was a thinning brown cloud settling along the mountainside above them.

***

"Well that hurt quite a lot," declared Drago, rubbing his backside. They'd skidded down the slope with urgency in response to the roar, which seemed a rash decision right now but entirely sensible a minute ago. His bottom certainly regretted it.

They picked themselves up and began to brush off the debris and dirt. Looking around, Drago saw an unusually large group of magpies circling above. He found this vaguely unsettling, but he couldn't put his finger on why. So engrossed was he with the ornithological mystery flying above, Drago failed to notice two men were staring at them all from across the crenelated parapet.

"I reckon someone mighta noticed us," said Caine, poking Drago on the forehead before reaching for his sword.

"Wait," said Amelia. Her tone of voice immediately caught their attention; it was as though she were attempting to speak whilst being unable to breathe.

"What's wrong lass?" asked Caine.

"That's my father."

"Oh. Well that's convenient."

"I don't recognise the other man."

"Could be inconvenient."

"This whole trip is just a series of inconvenient events."

"Aye."

They heard a cry and saw the smaller of the two men, and evidently the elder, begin running towards them. It wasn't much of a run as there was little speed involved, a closer description being a reckless meander.

It was the thought that counts.

Sensing little danger, Amelia set off at a sprint.

"Aw, ain't that nice?"

"Should we run after her, just in case?" posed Drago.

"Nah," replied Korin, "the other fellow would hardly have let him run off if he was trouble."

"Yeah, I get that, but she'll finish her dad off running into him at that speed."

***

Amelia maintained some presence of mind and slowed down before wrapping her arms around her father. It felt like an eternity since she'd seen him, and he looked at least an eternity older.

"What have they done to you?" she cried, although it was muffled as she had her face pressed firmly into her father's frail person.

"Nothing a good meal and stiff drink can't fix Amelia, my wonderful, wonderful daughter! I take it you found Vector? But where is he?" Emil said whilst looking over her shoulder at the rough looking trio accompanying her.

The others had sidled up to the reunion party anxiously. None were particularly comfortable with this sort of powerfully emotional scene. Skarz stood looking surly behind Emil; Drago stared at his feet behind Amelia whilst Caine and Korin glanced around and mentally mapped the area, escape routes, likely locations of gold reserves, and so forth. You can't turn off a lifetime of natural thieving instinct.

The place seemed quite deserted, which suited them fine. It's easier to search without having to fight people, which was another inconvenience.

What passed was a brief and awkward introduction

followed by the swapping of information until each was caught up on the general gist of the situation. There wasn't time for a proper re-acquaintance as ill deeds were afoot. The conversation didn't take long but was frequently punctured by Torvacane-shaking rumbles from the mountain. Rubble and rocky debris continued to scatter down the mountainside.

"So we have a choice, Med Tet or the Dragon Lord?" stated Korin.

"Not sure I fancy the dragon, if I'm being perfectly honest," said Drago. This one seemed like a no-brainer and it worried him that the others didn't seem to share his inclination towards not attempting to tackle a scaly, fire-breathing monster. It was the kind of disagreement he felt like he'd been having for a long, long time now.

"It could be fun though lad," said Caine encouragingly, slapping Drago on the back. He flinched.

"I need to actually teach you the real meaning of the word fun one of these days, you seem to have it confused with something else," mumbled Drago.

"The dragon can wait," interrupted Skarz, who had been almost entirely silent throughout, "it should take it a long time to smash its way up through the mountain." Amelia was surprised at the softness of his voice, he looked so battle-hardened and gruff. She was about to speak up in agreement when Korin interjected.

"I think our decision is about to be made for us." He nodded in the direction of the citadel. Its door was opening slowly. Stepping out was Med Tet, flanked by six large men who probably had names like Ripper and Gouger and Frank.

The continued tremors caused by what was an assumedly irate Dragon Lord bashing and flaming its way through thick mountain rock had finally caused Med Tet to leave the sanctuary of the citadel, reluctant though he was to do so.

He noticed the gathering ahead of him, just across the wide stone walkway. Med Tet made a mental note to destroy the statues of past monarchs and erase any history he wasn't a part of. He also noted the drop either side of the walkway. The drop was significant enough that if you knocked a rock over the side it would make that eerie prolonged whistling noise that's so very off-putting before finally finding something solid to land on.

"Well, well," muttered Med Tet, curling the end of his moustache menacingly.

It was less menacing when he was curling it at people thirty feet away.

He quickly dropped his hand. He surveyed the small group and could identify no real threat, just a couple of old men, a whelp, a girl, and an extremely feeble old man. The last one looked a tad more formidable, but he was only one man.

And Med Tet wouldn't be doing any of the fighting anyway.

"Men, I don't like troublemakers, dispose of them. Apart from the small old man with the stick, I want him brought to me. Go."

The soldiers drew their swords and began to advance down the walkway looking very much like proof of the missing link in the evolutionary line (a theory put forward by the naturalist Bulldog Goshdarnit, who insisted humans had to have evolved from apes after he had smelled his teenage son's bedroom).

***

"What do we do now?" asked Drago, looking to Korin. He hoped he might appeal to his marginally more sensible nature. Caine already had his sword in his hand and was licking his lips in delight.

This is often a misused phrase. But on this occasion, Caine was literally licking his lips.

"Don't worry, we can take these guys no problem, don't worry about their size. Amelia, I think perhaps you should get your father out of here. No offence old man but I don't think you look up for a fight right now," said Korin with authority. This was a moment for fast and sharp decisions.

Then again, their foes were making extremely slow progress across the walkway. Korin probably had time to light his pipe and have a smoke.

"Did you just call me 'old man'?" replied Emil, chuckling. "You're one to talk! Alas, you are right, there's no place for me here. We can hide out downstairs, come find us when you're done."

Amelia looked about ready to complain. She wanted to fight, but her father was frail, she had to look after him now.

Korin nodded and he turned along with Caine, Skarz and a reluctant Drago to walk out and meet the gorilla men bumbling towards them. Guerillas vs gorillas, as a boxing promoter might put it. Emil and Amelia started to retreat, but something caught their eye. A black and white blur fizzed towards the soldiers and moments later was followed by a cry of agony. Suddenly, there was a state of disarray halfway along the walkway.

The magpies were soaring down and attacking the

soldiers. These were the men Med Tet had employed to use crossbows to deter the magpies' frequent raids on the gold miners. The vengeful magpies were now flying kamikaze-style at the unprepared soldiers, who proceeded to flap and flounder, apparently forgetting they were holding swords.

One of the men cried out and ran in the direction he was facing.

Unfortunately, in his disorientation, he'd failed to notice he was running right at the low wall framing the walkway. He did not make the eerie whistling noise that a stone would have.

The magpies abandoned their organised air raids for all-out attack, a mass of pecking and scratching raining down upon men who were swinging wildly in all directions. It was a minor miracle they didn't strike each other.

There are three rankings of miracle. A major miracle is the real deal, walking on water type happening that is God of Torvacane Son's favourite party trick. A medium miracle is around the level of convincing your other half you've been in work until the early hours and not the pub. A minor miracle is simply luck.

Korin and the others continued to stare on in perplexed astonishment, unsure of what to do. The soldiers were gradually cutting the magpie numbers down, black and white feathers scattered across the grey stone floor. The birds were finally beginning to pull back having caused maximum damage and confusion.

"I think perhaps now is the opportune moment to attack," said Korin, stepping forward purposefully.

"Are you sure?" asked Drago.

There was no time for anyone to answer the question.

A Caine shaped blur rushed past Drago shouting loudly. Not shouting words but a dull and aggressive wail that could be confused for an orca mating cry.

Korin shrugged his shoulders and dashed after him.

The magpies were in full retreat. The remaining beleaguered soldiers wanted to shower in an ideal world, covered in feathers, blood and droppings as they were. But they had no time as two old men pounced on them followed by two younger men.

The short, economical jabs and slashes of Caine and Korin were proving impossible to break through. They were remarkably strong considering they looked like they needed dusting down and popping on a shelf.

Skarz actually was as strong as he looked, hammering his broadsword against the increasingly weaker attempts to block it.

And Drago, well, Drago was spirited.

One by one, Med Tet's guard fell.

Drago was starkly aware he had his back to the low wall and the steep drop while an angry looking Ripper bore down upon him. Their swords clashed. Drago's heel touched the wall. He continued deflecting blows, but Ripper was very big.

They say the bigger they are, the harder they fall. Simple physics, it makes sense. Which is why, when big things fall, you should make certain you aren't beneath them.

Skarz swung round and cracked Ripper on the back of the head with the butt of his sword. Drago saw the sudden blanking of Ripper's features. He saw them getting very close to his face.

Ripper stumbled and toppled right onto Drago, taking him over the edge.

"Drago!"

***

Med Tet was slowly backing away toward the citadel, aware that this was suddenly a treacherous situation. Gouger, Frank and the others all lay prostrate upon the walkway, while Ripper had fallen over the edge. For a moment, he thought he saw small yellow birds revolving round Gouger's head.

He blinked and rubbed his eyes. The birds were gone. At least, the little yellow ones were.

The black and white birds, on the other hand, the angry, motivated and regrouped black and white birds, were very much still there. And they were swooping round, blocking his route into the safety of the citadel.

Their beaks glinted maliciously in the sunlight as if made of sharpened steel.

Med Tet ran.

***

Drago could see Ripper disappearing from sight but was curious as to why he wasn't following him.

"One, two, three, pull!" said a voice from above. He wondered whether it was Son, but that seemed unlikely. The sun glared down, he couldn't make out the face properly, but he imagined the face of Son was a little less, er, weathered.

Someone had hold of his ankles. He felt a sharp tug.

"Ow, that hurt!" Drago yelled.

"You're welcome," came a strained grunt.

They heaved. It took a few goes, but they pulled their

young friend back over the side, and all four of them collapsed in a heap. Usually, Drago's heart would be doing its best to pound through his ribcage, but, in this instance, he was fairly sure it had ceased to do anything.

A slap on the back from Caine reminded it to beat again.

"That were close," said Caine, familiar semi-toothy grin in place.

"Aye, you should be more careful lad," said Skarz.

"You knocked him onto me!"

"I meant for you to dodge."

"Well I'm sorry but I didn't get that message."

They could all hear something, a kind of humming in the distance, edging closer. They couldn't quite put a name to it.

"I feel like we're forgetting something," said Korin, looking to the sky. "Ah, yes," he added, sweeping his hair back into its ponytail, "that's it."

The humming grew louder, graduating into a fully-fledged noise. It was a familiar fully-fledged noise. Not as familiar as, say, your mother's voice. But perhaps a distant relative who you don't see that often but have always quite liked, a second cousin perhaps?

"I'm sure there's something else we're missing here," said Skarz, getting to his feet. At that moment, a figure rushed past him, screaming. Then, a black and white cloud flew past too.

"Oh yeah."

Med Tet flailed his hands above his head, protecting himself as best he could. The incessant pecking had him flustered. And he was never flustered. He kept running, he just wanted to get away.

How could things have gone so sour? he thought.

Emperor Auwindus, first emperor of Seven Cities. Continents living in fear, Son himself would have bowed down. And it's come to this, being chased by these winged fiends.

"Should we shout to him or what?" said Drago.

"Nah," replied Skarz, "he's got it coming. I think this is what's called irony."

Med Tet kept running, straight over the edge of the battlements.

***

The universe might have started with a bang. General consensus is it started with a bang. Even Son wasn't sure, he'd heard it started over a game of cards, but that's another story altogether. Another common theory, or perhaps just turn of phrase, is that it ends with a whimper.

This seems unlikely.

Things rarely end with a whimper. At least not physical things. Med Tet's reign, for lack of an appropriate word, ended with a whimper. Med Tet the man ended with more of a *splat*.

The orchestra had no conductor. And now it had no first chair violinist. But despite this, it continued to play. Not as fluently, and without any measure of control.

***

The rumbling from Misty Mountain began again, but louder, like a stomach that's had a disagreement with a ghost pepper. Rocks slid down the side crashing down onto the citadel. In the shadow of the mountain, the city streets bustled with activity as people investigated the source of the hubbub.

"'ere, t'aint 'ruptin' is it?"

"Pardon?"

"Ya know, 'ruptin'?"

"Erm, I don't know. I think there is a chance it is erupting though."

"Lak a said."

"Erm, yes."

This conversation was perforated by another rippling roar, a roar that differed from the previous efforts. This was *clear*. Either the wild creature and source of the guttural cry had learned to enunciate better, or it was out in the open.

Curious inhabitants, scared, wary, angry, bemused, and one man claiming the end was nigh (although it was a Tuesday, so this wasn't unusual). All eyes were fixed on Misty Mountain's peak. Flames burst from it violently.

"O' 'eck."

"My sentiments exactly."

***

This feels good. I can breathe.

The Dragon Lord emerged through crumbling sediment, its hot breath melting the snow which sloshed about the mountain peak.

It's very bright. I smell… meat. I hear noises, unfamiliar noises.

The Dragon Lord stretched its legs and wings, light bouncing off its turquoise scales, and voiced its approval at freedom once more. The mountain shook. Its senses were adjusting, enjoying the opportunity to exercise their full potential, to give in to natural instinct. There was live food down in the city and, much like a great white shark, the dragon could hear their hearts beating, feel the vibrations of their voices. But in the distance, there were many more, so many more, out in open space. A dragon buffet. This was too inviting.

And now to escape.

The Dragon Lord leapt, its wings undulating and pushing against the air. It soared high, its shadow caressing the houses below, and it dived down toward the city.

***

Screams rang out. The dragon was gliding low over Athea Hubris, the whitewashed city built upon the rolling hills next to Misty Mountain. As the shadow fell, people scattered, diving into houses, into alleys, others just diving under carts. One man upturned a wheelbarrow and quivered away in darkness.

A burst of flames set alight a handful of thatched roofs. But this was simply a practice run. As soon as the Dragon Lord was above them, he was past them, gliding away from the scared citizenry and away from the city.

Someone tapped on an upturned wheelbarrow. A hairy head poked out.

"Cor, d'yu see tha'? Look lak a dragon, din't it?" said the hairy head.

"Yes, yes it did. Erm, you are aware that this wheelbarrow contained manure, yes?"

"Aye, migh' b'time for me an'al barth."

"Yes, quite."

The hairy-headed man clambered out of the wheelbarrow and trundled off down the street, watching the people running round collecting buckets of water from the well to douse the burning roofs.

***

Emil and Amelia had returned to the battlements, curiosity gaining the upper hand. Even men as wise as Emil adhere to the human rule: if one hears something that sounds dangerous you automatically investigate further and out in the open.

It should be noted this is a general rule and is not always followed. Some people, upon hearing something that sounds dangerous, curl up into a ball and cover their ears. Like hedgehogs. This makes hedgehogs the wisest creatures in the universe.

The Dragon Lord was a mere speck on the horizon, the size of an ant, which was how everyone in Athea Hubris liked it. An aerial view of the city allowed for a full view of the damage the dragon had caused with nought but a single breath. A dozen houses were still aflame and scorch marks trailed down the hillside.

"Where do you think it's going?" said Drago, shielding his eyes from the sun, still trying to track the dragon. The group had assembled along the battlement and the magpies still circled above. Skarz eyed them nervously, unsure whether the greater threat remained with them.

"Worryingly, I suspect for the most open and obvious food source. Can you think where that is?" said Emil. He sat down and crossed his legs.

"The battle," answered Korin. "We'll never get there in time, Vector's on his own."

The group collectively bowed their heads like mourners, assuming the odds were against Vector. Which they were. But if there's one thing that Emil had learnt over the years it was to never bet against a crafty old sod. And never had a phrase more directly applied to a man than 'crafty old sod' applied to Vector.

"I think perhaps I can warn him in time," said Emil, closing his eyes. "It's been a while since I've done this, one of Vector's tricks. He was always a bit sore that I was faster than him," he added, chuckling.

"Father!"

"It's alright, he knows what he's doing," said Korin, his hand on Amelia's shoulder before she could react.

She would have been too late.

He was already gone, soaring out over the city, chasing the dragon (something he absolutely had not done since his youth).

***

The sun beat down upon the open, sparse land beside the mottled ridge. It seemed they'd have a nice day for it, thought Vector, which wasn't much comfort.

The armies of Rathendy and Vertenve were lined up in compact blocks, side by side. Vector stood at the head with Antillia and Ivan. They could see the opposing force lined up ahead of them, the grass a fresh green between them with a few dandelions blowing in the breeze. Large wooden contraptions like over-sized crossbows were set up in front of the line beside Vector and the two stewards. He noted Athea Hubris had none. At least they won points for intimidation.

Flying pigs could be heard squealing as they flew about the ridge; even they sensed impending danger. Squealing aside, the field maintained a nervous silence. This silence, and a few men's resolve, was promptly broken by a ghostly apparition.

Or, to be exact, an old man shouting 'booga booga boo' at a handful of men with newly green complexions.

"Now Emil, is this really the time?" asked Vector, who couldn't help but feel he'd have done the same thing.

"Hello there chaps. Oh, and chappess," said the translucent essence of an old man, nodding politely to Antillia. There were gasps from those near enough to see who hadn't been subjected to cheap scares. Some men assumed they were hallucinating and thought hard about what they'd eaten in the past twenty-four hours. Some thought that god had aged poorly. Private Bryan and Private Bluster were talking animatedly to anyone who would listen.

"More o' them wizard tricks, seen 'em before, ain't we," said Bluster, nodding her head and winking at Bryan.

"Ay, we's expe'ts o' t'trade," added Bryan, tapping his nose, "bin der 'n' bought t'tunic."

Their voices stood out amongst the excited bustling of the men and women in the vicinity. Fingers pointed, heads nodded, jaws hung low and eyes widened until people were unrecognisable for all of these overblown traits.

"Well, this is a surprise," said Vector, mildly taken aback that Emil was still borrowing his tricks, "I assume you've been reacquainted with your daughter?"

"I have indeed old friend, thank you for looking after her."

"I'm quite sure it was the other way round," Vector replied with a grin. "I am happy to see you've recovered your strength enough to project yourself here, and I must also assume there's a purpose to this fleeting visit?"

Antillia looked on with interest, hoping some new development meant they could all go home and have a drink instead of battle. Ivan was bouncing on tiptoe, irate that no one was addressing him directly. He settled for fiddling with his wispy goatee.

"Yes, I'm afraid things have become slightly more complicated. The good news is this: Med Tet is dead. The bad news is the Dragon Lord isn't. And, erm, it's taken off in your direction, it'll be with you in a few minutes. Sorry about that old chap."

"That is inconvenient…" muttered Vector, his face scrunched in concentration. It was the face of one trying to dredge an idea or memory from the deepest recesses of his mind. Incidentally, it was the same face one pulls when receiving a football to the groin.

"Yes, I think we'll be okay. Thanks for the head's up Emil, we might have struggled without prior warning."

"Least I could do Vector, good luck! And hello Antillia, you're looking well, despite the circumstances," Emil added.

"Good to see you're free and healthy," Antillia replied.

Ivan had ceased hopping and was trying his hand at squinting, his eyes fixed on the horizon. The situation had grasped him by the throat and had him hovering inches from the ground. Metaphorically.

"I best be going. Amelia will be worrying. I shall see you soon, hopefully." With this, there was a flash of light and Emil's essence evaporated.

"I guess from your calmness you have a plan?" said Antillia, turning to Vector.

"I do. I suggest you point those siege weapons a little higher, and line the archers beside them. Drop the infantry back, they'll be in the way. We'll need to throw everything at it. With a bit of luck, I should be able to incapacitate the beast long enough to prevent it unleashing any counter-attack."

"Vector, are you sure you're up to it?"

"Nope, not at all," he replied, smiling wryly, "but it seems to be our only option. Unless you class dying painfully as an option. If you do, then I believe we have a choice."

"You always had a way with words, Vector," said Antillia, returning the smile, her white hair crossing her face in the breeze. "Ivan, let's get our archers gathered."

Ivan nodded solemnly. The impending arrival of the Dragon Lord had curtailed his argumentative nature. Vector stepped forward and gazed into the distance. He liked to gaze into the distance, he felt like people always took you seriously after a good gaze into the distance. The sky was beginning to cloud over. A storm was coming.

"Better put away the picnic basket," said Vector.

***

Son could see there was no way to prevent this final confrontation. He was a well-read god, He knew how these things were supposed to go, and they never happened on a pleasant summer's day. No. The clouds should be dark and brooding, the rain should lash down and thunder should roll. This felt like all He could contribute at this stage.

So He provided it. An appropriate setting for the final battle.

He grabbed his popcorn, poured himself a sweet ambeer nectar (alcoholic drink of the gods) and settled by the Oracle Pool.

***

The weather had deteriorated. Rain had begun to tumble lightly, and the sky had darkened. There was a flash of lightning. Vector could see it approaching. There was another flash, but this time it was of flame.

He wasn't the only one who'd noticed. There were cries coming from the men and women behind him. A couple of thousand people collectively shrinking, in a figurative sense, to the size of small children. And it wasn't just amongst those from Rathendy and Vertenve. Heads were turning on the other side too.

The thing about hiring mercenaries is that they are just that: mercenaries. Loyalty isn't in their nature and you're fooling yourself if you think otherwise. Already, men were breaking off from the cohorts and running in any direction in which they couldn't see a dragon. As it happened, this was most directions. From above, the army of Athea Hubris looked like a bleeding wound, spreading as a pool of blood might.

The dragon was close now. It manoeuvred into a dive above the main body of Hubrisian soldiers, who were situated to the north. Flames licked the grass, charring the ground and erasing the pleasant aroma, replacing it with the smell of smoke and fire. Soldiers leapt out of the way, scattering as best they could.

People ran. Some rolled. A desperate attempt to put themselves out.

The Dragon Lord roared above the nearby grumble of thunder. Rain persisted down. Troops shifted uneasily behind Vector and he could hear their fear. No doubt the

Dragon Lord could smell it.

It was upon them.

I can smell them, taste them. Is this fear? What noises are these they make?

I care not, it is time to feast.

"HOLD YOUR GROUND," yelled Antillia, her sword raised. "ARCHERS, READY, ENGINEERS, READY!"

Vector could hear the spring-loaded siege weapons screeching and clanging as cogs did what cogs do.

He could feel the Dragon Lord now. He could feel its mind and it was a comparatively simple one for a dragon of its estimated age. Years of living a sheltered life doesn't aid intellectual development. Vector, assuming the dragon hatched from an egg around the end of the war, calculated its age as around half a century. Young for a dragon, young enough to consider this one juvenile, unpredictable. But this was an angry and wild mind, a mind experiencing freedom for the first time and realising what it's been missing.

"We are one, beast," he muttered, raising his arms. Blue light shot from the palms of Vector's hands and danced in circles like a twister, flickering wildly, before rushing skyward toward the dragon.

Antillia stood behind Vector, watching on in awe and horror at the beast above them, feeling helpless. She could hear Vector and he was muttering in an arcane language.

What is this intrusion?

No, who are you?

I AM YOUR MASTER, BEAST! You will succumb. You will SUCCUMB!

The dragon juddered in mid-air between the two

opposing armies. Arrows rained down from the other side. The remaining Hubrisian soldiers had regrouped and were doing all they could to bring it down.

"ARCHERS, FIRE!" shouted Antillia, looking to Vector. He'd dropped to his knees. "Vector," she cried, "hang in there."

Blue light engulfed Vector and he shook within this blazing sphere, his limbs rigid. Hold still you bugger, he thought. The dragon writhed in mid-air, blasts of virulent flame shooting left and right with little control. And there it remained, hovering, struggling to throw Vector out of its head. The infantrymen had retreated behind their shields, some helping cover the archers, protecting themselves as best they could from the sporadic bursts of fire.

Arrows were penetrating its thick hide, gradually weakening it through the sheer volume of the attack. Vector could feel it. Its resolve was fading.

No, no, not after all this time.

Get out… get out… get out…

GET OUT!

Vector cried tamely, and fell forward, throwing his hands out to catch himself. Antillia hauled him back to his feet.

"It's free," he whispered, "hit it with everything."

Antillia turned frantically. "ENGINEERS, FIRE!"

The Dragon Lord swooped with its mouth opened wide and, forming deep within its gut, a rush of flame burst forth. Vector moved quicker than his old bones were accustomed to moving.

An enormous shield of blue light raced upward to meet the flames head on, negating them with a deafening crash. Lightning flashed again and colours flared across the sky, Vector's magic holding firm.

Siege weapons unleashed thick iron arrows which thudded into the Dragon Lord. Its wailing shook the planet to its core, the tremors knocking some soldiers off their feet. Another volley collided with the dragon and, finally, its will broke.

It fell from the sky. Soldiers scattered, pulling comrades with them as the beast crashed to the ground with a deafening *thud*. It twitched, the men surrounding it looking on nervously.

"Just check its pulse, mate, you're t'most qualified."

"How am I qualified?!"

"Din't you own a goldfish once? They got scales like."

The beast ceased to move, its last breath escaped, and its heart stopped beating.

The rain slowed and the thunder and lightning eased. Silence had returned to the field of battle. Men and women gathered their senses and tended to injured friends. Antillia supported Vector, who looked pale.

"One last effort, then we can rest," said Vector.

"You don't think we'll have to fight, not after all that?" Ivan piped up.

"No, no I don't think so. Their numbers look fairly depleted, most seem to have run off at the sight of the dragon. We should be able to sort this. Allow me." He stepped forward shakily, ran his open-palmed hand across his mouth, and spoke. His voice commanded the entire field. It could probably be heard for miles around.

"MEN OF ATHEA HUBRIS, WE DO NOT WISH TO CONTINUE WITH SUCH A SENSELESS BATTLE. WE HAVE CONFIRMATION MED TET IS DEAD, YOU ARE UNDER NO ORDERS TO FIGHT. WE WISH TO RETURN TO YOUR GREAT

CITY AND SORT OUT OUR DIFFERENCES IN A CIVIL MANNER. SEND AN APPOINTED ENVOY TO THE MIDDLE OF THIS FIELD TO MEET WITH STEWARDS ANTILLIA AND IVAN OF RATHENDY AND VERTENVE. THERE IS NO NEED FOR FURTHER LOSS OF LIFE."

Vector stepped back and leant on Antillia again. "That's me just about done, I demand you take me to a pub," he said, laughing weakly.

"I think I'll join you on that one," replied Antillia, "come on, we'll have to sort this out first."

They set off for the centre of the field, Ivan snapping at their heels like an obedient but annoying puppy.

***

High above the field floated a translucent old man. He breathed a sigh of relief. Well, not necessarily breathed, because he was nought but an essence, but it looked like he breathed, and it looked like it was in relief.

"Well that was close."

The essence dispersed once more.

***

The distant storm seemed to have calmed down. Amelia sat staring at the gaunt, apparently lifeless form of her father. She received quite a shock when he suddenly shouted 'booga booga boo'.

"Don't do that!"

"Sorry my dear, couldn't resist. Now help me up."

Between Amelia and Skarz they pulled Emil to his feet. He was a little disorientated, re-entering your own body has a habit of throwing you off. It's not like riding a bicycle, for example. Emil tried to move his left leg forward but instead kicked Skarz in the shin with his right.

"Ow."

"Sorry, this is harder than it looks you know."

"Clearly."

Drago cleared his throat. It wasn't something he was prone to doing, but he felt they needed a little focus in this moment. They'd all been waiting anxiously for news. Well, most of them.

Caine and Korin were nowhere to be seen.

Before Drago could follow up his throat clearing, Emil spoke, having regained some semblance of balance.

"Where are the other two?" asked Emil, chortling to himself. When it concerned those two, thought Emil, he felt he could make an accurate guess.

"Said they were looking for something to eat," answered Drago innocently.

"In the treasury?" replied Emil. It was Drago's turn to lose focus.

"Erm… no, why would they be… oh no, those crafty buggers, they better not have left without me!" Drago turned and ran toward the main building and treasury, stopped abruptly, and ran back. "Did we win?"

"Yes, we won," said Emil.

"Good." He span around once more to run off again, then pulled up sharply again, his hamstrings ready to make a formal complaint. Two grinning old men, one grin slightly more spacious than the other, were trundling up the walkway pushing wheelbarrows containing suspiciously lumpy sacks.

"I don't know if I'm supposed to allow this," said

Skarz, his arms folded. After some consideration, he decided they could get away with it. Upon further consideration, he decided they'd have found a method of getting away with it whether he tried to stop them or not. They just had a knack for deception.

"Alrigh' chaps... and chap-esses, good news I 'ope?" shouted Caine merrily.

"The battle never happened, the Dragon Lord is dead, and the world is, seemingly, safe," said Emil, who was feeling rather tired after such an eventful day.

"Great," said Caine, slapping Drago on the back, "best be off then laddy."

"What, right now?"

"Yep, dunno 'ow long it'll take, but someone'll notice they're a bit short in t'gold department eventually. Someone more inclined t'disagree with our point of view than good ol' Skarz 'ere."

"Unusually, Caine's right. It's time for us to scoot whilst we can. We can, er, find a horse and cart perhaps on our way out," added Korin.

"All that gold," said Amelia indignantly, "and you're still going to steal horses?"

"Force of 'abit," replied Caine.

"Well then I guess this is goodbye," she said, holding out her hand, "it's been a, erm, I don't know if pleasure is the appropriate word."

"I think that word you're searching for is 'experience'," added Drago, who knew exactly where she was coming from. His 'experience' of Caine and Korin had affected his nerves permanently.

Drago moved to shake Amelia's hand as she began to adjust to hug him. He hesitated, and so did she. The others were looking on, Drago was painfully aware of this, but somewhere in the deepest recesses of his mind there was a spark. There's no telling what caused it, or whether the spark meant anything, but it was most definitely a spark. He wrapped his arms around Amelia and hugged her. Even she was surprised.

"See you around," he said.

"Yeah, see you," she answered.

The trio embraced the others and said their goodbyes, and set off toward the barracks, then made their way down the stone spiral staircase. Leaving the wheelbarrows at the top and lugging the sacks down, they reached the bottom and looked around. Gold, unsurprisingly, is very heavy. They wouldn't get far at this pace. The rule of convenient happenings for heroes shouldn't really kick in when the heroes are stealing. But, well, they *were* heroes.

"Would ya look at that," said Caine, pointing to something by a house with a scorched roof. "An 'orse and cart, ain't that lucky?" he added, grinning his semi-toothy grin.

"This is turning into a very good day," said Korin.

Drago just sighed, disappointed that he could no longer be bothered disapproving of petty theft.

***

Son burped and decided He'd had quite enough beer for one day. He shook the alcohol from His holy system.

Things had worked out fine. He'd been worried back there, but the wizards and their friends had come through. The prospect of all the paperwork He'd soon receive over the escape and eventual destruction of the last Dragon Lord was daunting. He remembered His earlier thought.

Always act in the moment lest you forget. Wise words, He thought, despite this being something He'd already put off. He disappeared with a *pop*, only a small wisp of smoke remaining.

***

Herm was huddled into the back of a carriage on his way to Gredavia. He'd been lucky and caught the last one for the day. Nervous as ever, he glanced surreptitiously at the other faces in there with him. They seemed friendly enough.

Suddenly, there was a *pop*, and there was someone sat next to him. He could have sworn the seat had been unoccupied. But then, he couldn't quite recall it not being occupied either.

It had been a trying few weeks. Closing his eyes, he sat back.

Hello, Herm. I am Son, God of Torvacane.

Herm didn't reply. This was most certainly in his mind. Hopefully, if he stayed quiet, the voice would go away.

Don't be like that, Herm, I know you've had a tough time. But so have I. Do you have any idea how much effort goes into the day to day running of a planet? I have a proposition.

Herm could still hear the voice, but he wasn't certain he was hearing it with his ears, instead it seemed to be *everywhere*. He decided to play along. If the stress of working under Edirp, the dragon, Med Tet, and so on had caused him to go insane he figured it was best to just embrace it. It was to be expected, really.

I need a personal assistant, said the voice, I hear

you're a good one, and, currently, are looking for employment. **Come with me to Val Hilla. The salary is generous, you can have Sundays off and three weeks holiday a year**.

"Four weeks," said Herm. A few people looked around uneasily. The man seemed to be talking to himself.

Sorry?

"Four weeks holiday," replied Herm, "and it's a deal." He held out his hand.

Deal, said the voice, and something cold surrounded Herm's hand. There was another *pop*, and Herm disappeared along with the figure that may or may not have been sat next to him. A wisp of smoke remained.

One man seated in the carriage that day dedicated the remainder of his years to researching the theory of spontaneous combustion. His results proved inconclusive but, for a short window, his work was a hot topic in the world of science.

***

Two days later, the armies of Rathendy and Vertenve prepared to depart Athea Hubris. It had been a non-stop two days in which the bars and inns enjoyed roaring trade. A portly bar and inn owner named Ted did spectacularly well out of it, Emil had seen to that. He retired two weeks later and married a woman half his age and a third of his waist size and lived out the rest of his days in perpetual bliss.

It would be a long journey home for the soldiers, but just another part of the journey Seven Cities was still undertaking. Rebuilding could continue without the threat of war. This was a good thing. Probably. Antillia was unsure whether returning to the tribulations of supervising her flamboyant architects was actually a case of drawing the short straw. Another round with the Dragon Lord suddenly sounded inviting.

Instead of joining in the partying, Antillia, Vector and Ivan had taken part in an assembly held in the citadel. Along with Skarz, Emil and Amelia and a small host of the more enlightened (translation: rich) peoples of Athea Hubris, they had agreed a new direction for the city.

It was to become a democracy.

An idea previously unheard of and utterly unheralded within Seven Cities, but the steady decline of the monarchy's grasp of reality and of living left them with little option.

Skarz had declined the chance to take part in the first governing, citing his dislike for having to talk to people as his sole reason.

The trace of a ring remained in the sky as the sun rose on the third morning. Vector and Antillia stood atop the citadel battlement watching the sunrise.

"This is a bit too romantic," said Antillia.

"True, very true, I feel as uncomfortable as you. To the mess hall?" added Vector.

There were a few early risers milling around on autopilot. One man was pouring milk over his hand. Vector assumed this was due to being tired, but he was about ready to believe anything at this stage of life. Ivan was sat at a table alone, muttering away to himself. He hadn't taken so easily to eating with the masses.

"Morning Ivan," said Vector cheerily, "feeling less murderous today?"

"Oh, hello Vector, yes, hello there. And Antillia too,

how cosy. Not quite, they don't even have pheasant, no, not even pheasant. How can one eat breakfast when they don't have pheasant?" Ivan asked in earnest.

"Appalling isn't it?" agreed Antillia, "you'll be back in Vertenve and your palace before you know it. Then you can eat all the pheasant you want and forget about cereal altogether."

"That day cannot come quick enough," he replied fervently. With this last comment, Ivan rose and stalked out. He began muttering under his breath again by the door. It was going to be a long journey back to Vertenve for anyone within earshot of Ivan. Or, possibly, a very entertaining one.

They grabbed bowls and poured cereal and milk into them, skilfully avoiding their hands with the milk. They were clearly morning people.

A few more people filed groggily into the mess hall, fumbling with various articles of clothing. The wizard in his freshly laundered blue robes and the steward in a simple deep purple dress robe sat down and ate in silence. It's always tricky to eat and talk, especially when you're sat opposite the other person. Vector fetched them each a cup of tea once they'd finished eating, then Antillia spoke.

"I've been thinking Vector, I'm curious as to what your plans are after we leave here?"

"I have none of note. Return to my cottage, try to deter the pigeons from flying into my windows, upkeep the garden storm, that sort of thing. What have you been thinking?"

"Well, you know, I've got quite a lot of Coesustian brandy to get through, and you know Heron doesn't drink. And it's such a large castle too, so, well… I was wondering whether you'd consider staying around

Rathendy for a while…?"

"I think that sunrise has gotten to you Antillia, are you asking me to move in with you?" said Vector, bursting into raucous laughter. A few tired eyes widened from nearby tables. Vector had maintained an air of dignified wisdom since arriving back in Athea Hubris for image purposes. Most had seen his exploits with the dragon. People seemed to think he was cool, to Amelia's everlasting surprise.

"Oh do shut up, Vector," said Antillia, laughing along too.

"Go on then, I'll stay until the wine cellar is empty."

"We maintain a constant level of stock down there."

"Looks like I'll be around for a while then."

They shook on it and made their way down to the city. Everything was packed already, and the next few hours saw the departure of everyone. The people of Athea Hubris littered the streets, waving to the friends they'd made in just two short days, days that had been a remarkable step forward for inter-city relations. It was a lovely day and the buzz of conversation and general excitement coloured the scene.

Spirits were high once more with people looking forward to getting out of bed in the morning. Vector could have sworn he saw a grown man skipping earlier.

The men and women of Vertenve left first, and a surprisingly pleasant goodbye was said to Ivan. He was in a better mood than earlier, possibly because he'd woken up fully, or possibly the happy faces crowding the streets had cheered him. The likely reason was the prospect of pheasant in the not too distant future.

Finally, the soldiers from Rathendy streamed steadily out of the city to begin their long trek home.

"You'll have to visit us in Rathendy, Emil, and you too Amelia," said Vector, turning and smiling. His face had aged, battling with a Dragon Lord can have that effect on you. But the twinkle in his eye remained.

"Yes, perhaps once I've fully recovered my strength we can travel down, it's been a while since I've been out that way. And I'm sure Amelia has caught the travelling bug now!" added Emil.

"I wouldn't be so sure…" she said.

"Anyway, we must take our leave else the army will get lost. I think perhaps we could have a better look at these flying pigs on our way back Antillia? They're fascinating, I'd never have believed they exist had I not seen them with my own eyes," said Vector. The lines his face had developed suddenly smoothed, boyish excitement shedding years off him.

"I think we can afford to take the scenic route," said Antillia, smiling. Truly smiling. She could scarcely remember the last time she'd had cause to smile.

They each embraced and said a final goodbye. Skarz, stood beyond the group, nodded and raised his arm. That must be what he calls a wave, thought Vector. Skarz had agreed to house Amelia and Emil for a few days whilst Emil regained enough strength to travel home.

Antillia and Vector mounted their horses and waved one last time and left. Kicking the horses into life, they shifted into a canter. They couldn't afford to let anyone else lead the way for too long else they'd soon be lost. Antillia knew her people weren't renowned for their sense of direction.

In fact, her people weren't renowned at all.

Amelia watched them go and saw an eagle swoop down and land on Vector's shoulder. She also noticed two soldiers jumping up and down excitedly and pointing at Terry. Odd people, she thought.

They made their way back through the city, the crowds slowly thinning, the excitement over, the exotic (for Athea Hubris at least) strangers gone.

It was back to ordinary life for everyone now.

Amelia wasn't sure what to do. What do you do after you've been through something like this? She'd travelled hundreds of miles, seen unimaginable things, and met some, ahem, interesting characters. And now it was back to life.

It was a dull prospect.

At least, it would have been. But Drago had promised. As they said goodbye, he'd whispered into her ear. She could look forward to his return. She'd never really had a friend her age before.

"Are you coming, Amelia?" shouted her father. Both he and Skarz were stood a short way ahead. Amelia smiled. She could decide what to do, and where to go, another time. When Drago came back for her. For now, she was going to spend some time with her father.

She ran on and caught them up. They strolled back merrily through Athea Hubris, the first democratic state of Seven Cities. They had brought peace in their time, she thought.

It was noon.

Peace should last until at least supper.

The End

Author's Note

When I first wrote *Beyond Misty Mountain* it took me around three years. I struggled with motivation to plough on writing, went through long droughts, then had to remember my own story before picking up the threads again. It was a difficult process.

But this is precisely why it's so important to me.

By proving to myself I could not only complete a novel but also self-publish it (originally, I formatted the entire thing myself and published via Smashwords – this time I've used the wonderful WriteIntoPrint.com), I believe I set myself on a writer's path for life. I was just twenty-three when I self-published in October 2013.

I had always loved fantastical novels (from *Harry Potter* to *Lord of the Rings* to *Discworld*) and so I set out to write my own fantasy novel, something to exist in the shadow of these behemoths of the genre (or maybe 'bask in the light of' is more accurate?). Being young and silly I wanted to write something that was silly and fun and didn't take itself too seriously. While I have refined the text a little and improved upon a few elements, this version is still largely the novel I wrote and published as a young and naïve man of twenty-three. As a naïve and slightly less young man, I see it as a novel that embraces nonsense and irreverence and the general silliness that is part of being human. In essence, pure escapism.

I hope you as a reader enjoy its charms and recognise it for the light-hearted bit of fun it was intended to be. And for this edition, please also enjoy two further Tales from Torvacane: *The High Roller*, and *The Running of the Elephants*.

The High Roller

A Tale from Torvacane

Down the Boulevard they say money never sleeps. This is because if it did its pockets would be empty by morning. The Boulevard is Broth Zolust's famed central strip, adorned with establishments to satisfy humanity's every dark whim and discreet enough not to tell your spouse. Down the Boulevard, Alcap Noe makes the rules, break the rules, then puts them back together again.

Once a month a high stakes card game known as the Big Roller takes place in Alcap Noe's personal residence, which is situated just a blind alley or two from the Boulevard itself. The buy-in varies depending on how cheerful Alcap Noe is feeling. Today, it was set at a hundred bronze knoblets apiece (although you could place something up as collateral. Say, for example, your house). By all accounts, this was a reasonable price and it was attracting a great deal of interest from all of the city's well-known gamblers. Some of the more impetuous, carefree, and downright reckless Zolustians were also drawn to the idea of participating. Within the Parallelogram pub, right at the far end of the Boulevard, one such man was arguing his case.

"I'ma tellin' ya Korin, I can win the thing," said a man whose best years looked far behind him, along with plenty of his teeth. Firm of jaw and light of hair, the man had a scar down his left cheek.

"You don't even know how to play the game," sighed Korin, exasperated, absently retying his long grey hair into a ponytail. This was the thirteenth time today Caine had insisted he was going to take part in the Big Roller, a fact that represented quite aptly the luck his old friend often had in just about anything he chose to do.

"I've bin learnin' though, ain't I? Old Queenie is a risk card, Prince Ted is always wild apar' from on a third run and you never wanna get caught in a flip-off," said Caine, beaming a semi-toothy grin at his companion and taking a healthy swig of Grog from his tankard. Satisfaction writ upon his face, Caine's confidence was unwavering. Yet it often was, right up until someone attempted to pour boiling hot tar over him or sacrifice him at an altar to their favourite deity.

"They are all rules to card games... different card games," replied Korin. And so this went on for the rest of the evening, a vibrant conversation taking place under the Parallelogram's thick cloud of smoke (there were more pipes in the pub than on a cathedral organ).

During the evening word had reached Alcap Noe of the interest shown in participating by both Caine and several wealthy high rollers. Sat in his study surrounded by books he'd never read, Alcap, wearing a debonair pin-striped flannel suit, cigar in mouth, reached for a mug of tea. Alcap Noe was not a risk-taker. You didn't get to maintain the influence and power he had over the years by throwing caution to the wind. You locked caution up and swallowed the key. So, under no circumstances, did he want a loose cannon such as Caine buying into his game. Nothing against him personally. It was simply that Caine had a habit of things just *happening* to him. The last thing Alcap Noe wanted was anything *happening* to his own home. No amount of insurance mattered if the place was nothing but cinders and ash by morning. He needed to prevent Caine taking part. But how?

***

By morning it was settled. Caine was going to play the Big Roller. It's a well-known fact that rumour travels faster than the speed of light. No amount of chalkboards with collections of numbers and letters and brackets and rude doodles could disprove this. So when Caine stumbled out of the Parallelogram and said to Korin before they parted ways: "itss shettled, I'ma playin' it," and toppled over into a puddle, it took the best part of a split-second for everyone in a fifty mile radius to share this knowledge. Alcap Noe sat in his black armchair and pondered. Firstly, he decided he needed a white cat for all future pondering. Secondly, raising the buy-in wouldn't work with Caine: he needed to send one of the boys to have a word with Caine.

***

Later that evening, Alcap Noe's boy returned to him. The boy in question was confident he'd tried to have a word with Caine about the situation but had been politely told to 'shove it up 'is arris'. Once he'd clarified what this in fact meant, he'd attempted to exert further pressure via the means of intimidation he'd been blessed with at birth:

his brutish strength. And then he'd learned why experience is a great deal of use in a fight. Economy of movement, resourcefulness, tactics, all were on show during the scuffle. Waking with this new knowledge about twenty minutes ago, stars flittering before his dazed eyes, the boy had stumbled back to base.

Of course, Alcap Noe's boys weren't renowned for their ability to weave an anecdote. What he actually said was this: "da bugger hit me ova da head with a wheelbarra."

To this, Alcap Noe groaned. There wasn't much more he could do at this late stage. So he sat and waited, gave the orders to set the cards table up, have the refreshments ready and to altogether make the place perfectly presentable for a night of indecency and gambling. Wide bay doors opened out onto Alcap's decking, with his lounge acting as the casino. Everything was spick and span, even the chandelier had been shined.

The action was due to start at eight o'clock sharp. The dealer was ready by the table, waistcoat tight, bow tie straight. It was a pleasant evening, a light breeze whistling as the sun set in a mix of purple and orange, one of Torvacane's rings slowly appearing, glistening silver high above. Eight o'clock sharp came and went until it was blunt. Alcap Noe stood outside his arched front doorway listening to the mildly violent ruckus coming from the Boulevard. Around half past nine Caine strolled into view carrying a small brown pouch containing his buy-in for the Big Roller.

"Eh up Alcap, 'ow ya doin'? Sorry I'm a bit late, ran inta an old chum, you know 'ow t'is. 'ope I'm not too late t'play?" Caine declared, semi-toothy grin fixed in place. Almost, it seemed, too fixed, a degree of falsehood beaming through his beam. However, Alcap Noe didn't detect it.

"No one has turned up, Caine. This is completely unprecedented. I'll be sending the rest of the boys out in the morning to find out what happened. I believe one of them needs a rest day tomorrow," he said through gritted teeth. There was a nagging suspicion in his mind, but he doubted whether he would accrue any evidence to prove his theory. People have loose pockets in Broth Zolust but tight lips.

"T'is a shame that, a shame. So… I guess that means I'm t'winner?" said Caine, with a face so straight you could slice cheese with it.

"Yes, yes it does. There are no winnings, you understand, other than those in your hand?"

"Aye, that's fine tha', fine by me. Believe ya've got some grub and drink on for the victor, by way of an extra prize?"

"Yes. How rude of me, do come in. I'll send for Korin, no doubt he'll enjoy a refreshment with us too."

"Aye, I bet 'e will!" Caine said joyously. He knew Korin would be along soon enough. He was having a nap. They'd had to get up pretty early in the morning in order to threaten every single renowned gambler in Broth Zolust. And in a place like Broth Zolust, the list of high rollers is exceedingly long, so it was exhaustive work. But, for the prestige of winning the Big Roller without knowing anything about the game of cards, Caine considered it worthwhile.

The Running of the Elephants

A Tale from Torvacane

For several years it had been a tradition in Broth Zolust, the filthiest city in Seven Cities, in turn the most degraded continent on Torvacane, in turn the most unexplainable planet in the universe, to set six elephants loose in the city. Not just regular, docile elephants. Large white battle elephants. There was, of course, a story behind this. One Caine and Korin enjoyed regaling the occasional well-wisher with when lounging in the Parallelogram, all while allowing the listener the honour of buying them a drink. Popular drinking haunt of those semi-retired adventurers (adventurers never truly retire, there's always one last job), it was a famous little bar on Broth Zolust's famous little avenue, the Boulevard. The story of the elephants, in short, involves Caine and Korin precipitating city-wide carnage by releasing fifty white battle elephants, elephant-napped from the city's steward, In Seish Abel, with the aid of a bustling bag of sewer rats.

In order to save face, In Seish Abel cleverly contrived a celebration of this disaster and it had quickly become an annual festival that brought in more tourists by the year. And it was that time of year again. The Boulevard, lascivious hub of the city, was festooned with stalls selling elephant stuffed toys, elephant masks and various trinkets for good luck and so on. Anything for a quick buck in Broth Zolust. An amiable looking young man (save for the sword swinging by his waist) and a stern, blonde-haired young woman with a bow and arrow strapped to her back, emerged from between two such trinket stalls, one of them complaining loudly about the festival.

"It's cruel, that's the bottom line," said Amelia indignantly, tying her long blonde hair back into a ponytail. "The elephants haven't done anything to deserve this. They're probably scared when they're running along the streets crashing into things, it's not natural." She had huffed and puffed about the cruelty of the event for the past hour. Drago didn't disagree, but he'd confess to a lack of passion on the subject. Frankly, he'd been more concerned with what had just happened. He felt sweaty and his throat was dry. The event which caused these symptoms was Amelia meeting his mother for the first time. This was the mother who still insisted on calling him Graeme no matter how much he insisted he went by Drago.

He tried to change the subject.

"What did you think of my neighbourhood?" Drago asked.

"What? Oh, yes. Quite nice, a bit claustrophobic though. All those houses in terraces so close together, like a banana in its skin."

"Yes, poor bananas," added Drago absently. He could see Caine beckoning them into the Parallelogram through the grainy window. A drink seemed a great idea, despite his famous inability to handle more than two or three. This did, however, lead to Drago's other famous ability, which was to get a comfortable night's sleep on any surface no matter the rubbish or debris it was covered in.

Stopping outside, the young couple looked towards the end of the Boulevard. The steward's workers were finishing up the temporary pen which would hold the elephants once they reached the end of their run (correction: stampede). The pen, at a glance, was rickety and ramshackle, much like everything else in Broth Zolust. But behind the back wall of the pen was a spider's web of poles and blocks and bags of sand to reassure it. This was a mere precaution. Every year so far, the poor befuddled animals, having been herded in the pen's direction, had lost most of their verve and steam by the home straight.

Amelia tutted and, Drago thought, growled a little. It was a portentous growl. No doubt something was happening in Amelia's head. Gears were grinding, wheels were turning.

They wandered into the pub, Amelia recommencing her tirade against the event's organisers.

There were the usual gruff regulars dotted about the pub. Improvements had been made since Drago's last visit. A brand-new picture of a pony in a field hung over the bar, the stools had circular cushions softening them to the sitter's bottom, additional wooden booths had been constructed, and overall many of the sharper edges had been sanded down. Largo, the owner of the Parallelogram, was pleased to see Drago. Largo's thick short hair had whitened, and the lines of his face had deepened. Drago's hair was down to his shoulders, but his face was still youthful, the worry lines not yet kicking in.

Drago ordered up a round of Grog and joined Caine

and Korin at their table. It was unusually bright, and the air seemed less viscous than often it was. Drago looked up and noticed the beams above had been polished and funnels created to siphon the smoke out. The regulars were chain-smokers and they hated breaking the chain, leading to a peculiar atmosphere and stench that was what polite people would call an 'acquired taste'. But the new filtration system had affected one significant change: you could now see the entire room and everyone in it.

Whether this was an improvement was questionable, thought Drago.

"Aye, got ya bets in?" declared Caine, waving several slips of paper as Drago and Amelia sat down, "I'm expectin' three fires and b'tween ten and fifteen serious injuries. What do ya think?"

Drago noticed Korin shaking his head and keeping unusually quiet.

"I think it's horrible," declared Amelia, crossing her arms, "it's cruelty, pure and simple." She drank from her glass and slammed it back down on the table, spilling a few drops.

"Ahh nonsense, the elephants love it, they rear 'em for it, practically their callin'," added Caine.

Korin finally chimed in, but with a certain reluctance. "You can't argue with the revenue it brings from tourism." What he failed to factor in, what was often overlooked by Zolustians in this equation, was that most of this additional revenue went into repairing the damage caused by releasing six elephants into the city in the first place.

"Well I'm going to go to In Seish Abel and ask for this to be stopped," said Amelia, finishing her drink and standing up. She didn't add anything further, but Drago took this as his moment to do the same. Finishing a drink so quickly went straight to his head, of course, leaving him more liable to agree to any outlandish schemes suggested/forced upon him. With this they said their goodbyes as quickly as they had their hellos and disappeared. Caine and Korin remained seated. They had a good view of the action from the relative safety of the Parallelogram and could rush out after the last elephant had gone past to see them rounded up in the rudimentary pen.

"What's she planning?" wondered Korin aloud. By their time of life Caine and Korin had developed a nose for sniffing out a scheme or seeing one coming and this one stank to high heaven of rashness and danger. These were usually their favourites.

"No idea, anythin' that starts a fire is good by me, just nay more three."

***

The festival cannon fired to signal the start of the run. The stalls had all been dismantled and moved so as to curtail the total amount of destruction the bookmakers needed to calculate. People were stood in the streets, front doors open, ready to dive for cover. Others dangled out of first and second floor windows hoping to catch a glimpse of the rampant white battle elephants. Smoke could be seen emanating from the north side of the city.

"One fire already!" said an excited Caine. They waited and, bit by bit, the noises grew more distinct. Louder and louder it became until the elephants crept into view, emerging from a cloud of dust.

They pounded down the Boulevard at an

unprecedented pace. An overwhelming speed. Korin was first to recognise this and yelled for everyone in the vicinity to take immediate cover. He then had to run back out onto the avenue to drag a jubilant Caine back to safety. The two senior citizens had to dive through the Parallelogram's wonky door, only just evading the thick grey feet crashing down the street. Windows shattered with the weighty reverberations. After the elephants had passed, Caine and Korin ran back out onto the Boulevard.

"They're going' too fast," said Caine, advancing up the street followed by Korin.

"They'll smash into the wall. It's going to be messy," added Korin dejectedly. He'd always thought this was too dangerous an exercise. For amateurs, that is, not expert hustlers such as Caine and himself.

But this wasn't quite what happened. The elephant in the lead hurtled into the back wall of the pen like a cannon ball. However, the flimsy and thin partition collapsed in a collection of splinters and planks as if it were constructed from paper. The elephants advanced right through it, beyond the city limits and, gradually, step by heavy step, out of sight.

In Seish Abel, holding onto the regal hat that made up half of his full height, sprinted up the Boulevard. "Somebody removed the reinforcements. Who tampered with my pen, who tampered with the royal pen?!" This continued for about an hour as he lamented the loss of more battle elephants. The award for information doubled with every piece of rubbish he kicked across the street. Right until he unwisely graduated to kicking a wall and spent several minutes shouting curses and hopping towards the Concordia Plains wondering why bad things happen to terrible people. And they could all wonder as much as they liked, there was no such thing as CCTV on Torvacane, so the criminals would likely go unpunished.

It was only later in the evening that Caine and Korin felt they'd received definitive proof as to what had transpired.

Amelia passed Largo, the owner of the Parallelogram, his heavy and dusty bag of tools back. She then purchased a round of Grog. With all the repairs Largo had been making to his little establishment, it logically followed that he'd have a substantial toolkit. Tools, as well as being useful for putting things together, were also quite useful for pulling things apart.

Drago felt grateful for a drink. Spending part of the afternoon chasing sewer rats with a brown hessian sack he'd freed from ownership caused quite the thirst to develop. Factor in throwing said bag of rats at a small herd of large white elephants and Drago was positively parched. He'd had enough stampedes to last a lifetime.

Caine paid for the round of drinks. His bet that there would be exactly three fires had been successful. That two of them were started by him inside the bookmaker's shop mattered not.

About the author

Stephen Howard is a British novelist and short story writer born and raised in Manchester, England. He was always an avid reader but finally decided that, aged twenty, perhaps he too could write stories people may enjoy. This eventually led to the self-publication of his first novel, *Beyond Misty Mountain* (2013), inspired by an enduring love of Terry Pratchett's *Discworld* series.

Since then Stephen has completed his Bachelor's degree in English Literature and Creative Writing with the Open University, gaining First Class Honours, alongside full-time employment working in marketing, then in elderly care, before settling into local government administration. During this period Stephen has had short stories published on The Flash Fiction Press website, in the Tigershark Publishing ezine and in Scribble. His first collection of short stories, *Condemned To Be*, was self-published in 2019.

Outside of writing, Stephen supports Manchester United and tries to get to Old Trafford when he can, although he does enjoy watching the match in the pub. He is also a fan of pub quizzes — you may even have caught his brief appearance on Mastermind in 2017.

Printed in Great Britain
by Amazon

39155090R00145